REBORN

KALIYA SAHNI BOOK FOUR

K.N. BANET

PROLOGUE

JULY 10TH, 2019

I waited for the call impatiently, tapping my foot in anger about how long it was taking. I had scheduled and rescheduled this phone call at least ten times over the last month and a half. Today, I hadn't received a message with an excuse to reschedule once again, but it was already late. I had even set up a new communication system.

I hissed as the seconds ticked by until I heard the little ring tone from my computer and hit answer.

"Damn it, Adhar. Why have you been avoiding me?" I snapped, looking at the new monitor mounted on my wall with a camera at the top. Standing in his office, probably in his private residence, was Adhar, the male ruler of the nagas, my counterpart, the bane of my existence.

Adhar narrowed his eyes, then grew a deep frown.

"Kaliya. You look as if you haven't slept in a week, and I don't know when you last brushed your hair. As for avoiding you, I haven't been. I do rule our people in India while you are busy running around America, trying to get yourself killed," he retorted. "There are now three babies, and all the parents need constant help with them."

I pushed my white hair out of my face and glared at him. I couldn't exactly be mad at him because he had a point. Beyond Roshni, who had been born earlier in the year, there were now also two boys.

"And I am still living with Nakul. He is making improvements, but it's slow. I must be watchful of him. He's a strong warrior, and he is mentally fragile. I can't leave him unattended for long."

"Did you even collect the information I need?" I asked, rubbing my temples.

"About the rakshasa?" Adhar sighed, shaking his head. "I'm wary of sending it, Kaliya. If you say you think a rakshasa is responsible for the killing of our people, you will invite conflict on us in India. Many of the rakshasas are still here, and they won't take it kindly."

"I don't think anything," I snarled. "Damn it, Adhar, I need you to trust me! I saw him at that lab, and he fucking admitted it. I remember his face from the night my family was butchered, and it's been haunting me while I sleep. I know he was involved, and I need to find him!" I slammed my hand on the desk in frustration. "Don't make me fly back to India, find you, and steal the books I need. I know you keep the old texts about them, and I need that information!"

"I'll send you a set of the reproductions," Adhar conceded. "But, Kaliya, you cannot go public until you have his name and evidence to back it up. You will not go to any other rakshasa with this because they will see it as a threat. You cannot invite conflict on us. We're too vulnerable."

"I know. Fine. I promise not to piss anyone off yet." I just needed something to start with. "Thanks, Adhar."

"Of course." He looked through his camera as if he was staring into my soul. "While I have you...you never did tell me what happened with your mate. I have been nicely ignoring that, but since I am giving you this, you shall give me what I would like to know."

"A story for another time," I whispered, feeling the pain strike through my heart like a bullet. My fangs ached at the loss of his presence. Just thinking about him made me want to run out of the house and find him. He would be in a temporary home now on the new land he bought for the cambions while their home was being built. I didn't know where that was but knew I could find him. Cassius kept me updated on how things were going, and Sorcha sent me pictures, knowing I always wanted to see him.

"Are you certain that's your answer? I could decide not to feed this obsession of yours and keep the old texts safe to teach the next generation instead of sending their replications to you."

I had been so careful about not letting Adhar know anything, but as I looked at him on my screen, I was filled with the foreboding sensation I wasn't the only source of his information. I clenched my teeth as I realized Adhar had been planning this trap.

This is the last time I'm calling for your help, asshole.

"What do you know?" I asked softly.

"I can put two and two together, Kaliya. You and this

new warlord of the cambions have had an...interesting relationship over the last several months. People talk to me, telling me how you helped him free his own kind and establish them as a species of the Tribunal. Your mate also needed your help, if I remember correctly. The timelines match up nicely. You met him, then I learned you had a mate. Now, his identity is public." Adhar raised an eyebrow. "The only thing that doesn't fit is he is not human, nor is he a naga. He is a cambion, a human-demon hybrid of sorts."

"Yeah." I leaned back and sat on my desk, staring at my fellow naga.

"So, he is your mate," Adhar said softly, his eyes narrowing. "How?"

"My business, not yours." I crossed my arms. Not that I had an answer, but even if I did, I wouldn't have shared it with Adhar. He was a man of many faults, but there was one way he was like me—he would do anything to help the nagas. Most of our fights came from the fact we disagreed on what was really necessary. "He's the ruler of another species, so put it out of your head. I'll find another one—"

"Multiple mates were more common when there were more nagas. You could wait thousands of years before another mate comes—"

"Good," I growled. "Fucking perfect. You want to know why? Maybe when I finally have a mate, I won't have to hide him from the world. He'll be able to live a normal fucking life without worrying about whatever enemies we've made trying to kill him. Maybe we can just be a happy fucking couple without wondering who is going to kill us tomorrow and skin me alive!" I turned away from the camera. "Which is exactly what I'm giving Raphael. A chance at a normal life, or as normal as he can get, considering his circumstances. So, why don't you stay the fuck out of it?" I turned back to him. "Send me the intel, Adhar, because I am *never* mating if I think my mate is going to be butchered in front of me."

Adhar disconnected the call. A moment later, my email dinged on my phone. He sent digital versions of what I wanted. I hadn't even known there were digital versions, and he certainly hadn't given me a hint they existed.

I had been played into telling him about me and Raphael, and that pissed me off a little more. I shoved the feeling aside since I knew Adhar couldn't do anything, not to me or Raphael. Besides, I had more important things to think about.

I opened the files on my computer and devoured the secrets of the rakshasa, which the nagas had from years of spying and close proximity. I knew much of the basics but had never run into one in the United States, so the refresher on what they could do was important.

I read through the files for hours, stretching through the night and into the next day. I put my phone on silent when Cassius tried to call me, then went back to it. After I was done reading, I put out feelers to others I knew working for the Tribunal, asking them if they had run into a rakshasa. This was the fourth time I had reached out, trying to get ahold of anything, even an old case everyone had forgotten about.

I messaged Paden with a run-down of what I was

looking for. He returned with a fee to keep him on retainer, to look for intel on the matter. I had the first month paid for in a matter of minutes. If I couldn't find anything on my own or through my own leads, Paden would dig something up. I knew he would.

Knowing it would take time to get any answers, I finally went to sleep and was haunted by nightmares of my parents screaming in pain, their blood covering the floor. I was haunted by flashes of the rakshasa's face as my brothers laid butchered on the floor. They hadn't been murdered quickly.

When I woke up later in the day, I continued my task, ignoring the cold sweat that covered my skin. I'd been having nightmares for over a month, and nothing was going to chase them away until I found the man who killed my family and ended this. I tried to look up known rakshasas, wondering if any of them would be willing to talk to me, but the species was just as reclusive and elusive as my own. This was going to be a long hunt.

That's okay. I can hunt for days if I have to.

The days turned into weeks.

And the weeks turned into months.

1

CHAPTER ONE

OCTOBER 15TH, 2019

It was another average morning, waking up sweaty and terrified as I did every other morning—one where I had little for plans and a permanently frayed mental state. I picked up my phone as I stared at the half-eaten yogurt I couldn't be bothered with. It joined the several other half-eaten yogurts I couldn't be bothered with. I hadn't called Paden in a month, and he hadn't called me. It meant he hadn't found anything, but I had nothing else I could do except try again. I hit his name in my contacts and waited, putting the call on speaker and leaving it on the table next to the yogurt.

"Paden, do you have anything?" I asked wearily as I heard the click of him answering his phone.

"Ah, no, Kaliya, I don't," he answered, sounding a little distracted. "I've got everyone I know out there listening, but nothing has come back. Whoever knew about him at Mygi is either in hiding or dead. You have all the records of that."

"Yeah. He was there to look over the project for his

employer, but they never wrote down who that employer was or why the interest. No one from the prison lab knows anything about him or his employer, and I couldn't interrogate the others before their executions." I leaned over and put my head in my hands. "I need to find him, Paden."

"You need to go back to your normal life," he retorted. "It's been months. If we haven't found a whisper of him yet, we're not going to unless he slips up, and it doesn't look like he slips up often, if ever."

"*Everyone* makes mistakes," I hissed, frustration threatening to drive me up the wall. "I know they do. I know he must have somewhere. We just need to find out when and where. A lead...all I need is a lead."

"Kaliya—"

"I'll try again at the prison." I would try everything again if I had to. I had solved difficult mysteries before, and this one haunted my dreams. This rakshasa had been one of the people who killed my family. He had to lead somewhere.

"Kaliya, no," Paden snapped. "You need to get out of your house and do anything except think about this case. I know I don't normally get on to you, but I like you too much to keep watching this—"

I hissed at the words and hung up the call before he could continue. There was a reason I didn't pick up calls from Cassius, Sorcha, or anyone else. I talked to them through texts and pretended I was enjoying a nice vacation away from the drama. I wasn't going to give up or let anyone take me off this. If I let it go too cold, I would only have another piece to an unsolvable puzzle.

I walked into my private office and glared at the Board, finding the face of the man I despised. I got his picture from the security footage of the lab, but it was all I had. No one had ever seen this man for more than a few moments, and no one knew his name. It was hard to maintain that sort of secrecy in the supernatural world. Everyone knew everyone through someone. A face always had a name, yet he eluded me.

I brought down an entire supernatural pharmaceutical company, and I can't find one fucking rakshasa?

I tapped my foot. I had promised Adhar I wouldn't go to any other rakshasa about this. I had promised him that months ago, but I regretted it by the end of the first week. If I could reach out to the rakshasas, maybe I could get his name. They were hard to find, but they would be easier than this man. Criminals covered their tracks more than the average person, and this rakshasa was a murderer with a death sentence.

I started a new hunt, hoping to track down contacts to any rakshasas who weren't insane murderers who had killed my family. It was bold to assume they would know who I was looking for, but someone could point me in the right direction.

The day turned into evening as I dug through public records and some not-so-public records, things the Tribunal wouldn't appreciate me looking through during my hiatus. I was still, on paper, a Tribunal Executioner, but I wasn't working. They knew I needed a break to focus on myself and other things, so I really shouldn't have been using their databases for anything.

I was startled when my security system told me

someone was coming onto the property. I grabbed a sword hanging on the wall, not caring which one it was.

Shit. Is someone coming for me?

I was at the front door before it registered that my security allowed whoever it was to drive up to the front of my home. Only a few people could do that. I didn't let go of my sword as I pulled open the front door and saw Cassius' SUV.

As the fae couple stepped out, Sorcha kept her expression blank when she saw me, but Cassius had a narrow-eyed, sly expression as he walked around the front of the SUV and came toward me. Finally, Leith got out of the backseat and stood patiently behind them, but I could have sworn he was about to smile or grimace.

Of the three of them, it was Leith's sudden appearance that scared me the most.

"I got a call from Paden," Cassius said in that noble clip that said he was borderline pissed off but was willing to listen. "It made me think it was time for Sorcha and I came to see how you were doing."

"I'm doing fine," I offered quickly, swinging the sword in my hand casually as if it wasn't a big deal I had it. I watched his gaze flick to it and back to my face.

"Are you?" he asked, raising an eyebrow. "Because the security spells I placed on your property would have told you it was Sorcha and me or someone else you trust."

"You certainly aren't sweaty enough to have been in the middle of practice," Sorcha added. "Nor are you wearing the right attire for that."

"Right?" Cassius nodded at his wife's assessment. "I think you were paranoid someone was coming up here and grabbed the first sword you could find. Which means you're into something, and you don't want us to know, not that we needed to figure that out. Paden wouldn't break client privilege with you. He reached out as a friend and said he was...worried. You haven't gone to the Jackalope since you went with Sorcha. It's unlike you unless you're into something and don't want the distractions."

I stopped the sword and stared at them, unable to say anything without making it even more painfully obvious. There were few people in the world who knew me so well. Sorcha didn't have the time or experience that Cassius did, but she was smart. Paden had known me for decades. The only one who was missing was Raphael. He would have figured it out quickly enough.

"What's got you like this, Kaliya?" Cassius asked gently, closing the distance. He stopped only a few feet from me, something either of us could close in a second.

"There was a rakshasa at the lab," I answered. "He was one of the people who murdered my family. I've been trying to hunt him down. I need to know why he was at the lab, why he killed my parents and brothers. He promised to see me again. I want to catch him first, but he's a ghost. I've had Paden on it since July, and I've reached out to other Investigators and Executioners, hoping they would have suspicious rakshasas they've been looking into. Everyone has come back with nothing." I put the sword down, leaning it on the wall. It wasn't a useful short sword—a historic piece more than a capable one. "Today, Paden tried to tell me I needed to try living a normal life again."

"So, he called me," Cassius said, nodding. "I see..." He

looked at his wife, who nodded. When he looked back at me, he seemed resigned but decided.

"Oh, we're going to fix this," she said with an undignified huff. I stared, my eyes going wider and wider as Sorcha breezed past me and entered my home. "Leith! We'll need you."

Leith nodded at his lord, then at me, then entered my home and shut the door, leaving me on the outside of my house with Cassius.

"When was the last time you went outside?" Cassius asked. "Or thought about looking after yourself?"

"Does it matter?" I snapped.

"I think it does. Do you know what I see? Your jewelry isn't in. Your braids aren't done. You haven't taken a bounty to give yourself something to do. I thought you were avoiding Raphael, which I understand, but I also figured you were going about your life. Looks like I was wrong, and I don't care what you're working on, Kaliya. I am not allowing this."

"Allowing it?" I hissed, glaring at him as he tried to reach for my front door to follow his wife and butler. "You don't *allow* me to do anything. I don't answer to you."

"I'm your friend," he snapped. "Whether you want me to be or not, I am one of the few friends you have, and this is unacceptable. You need to find balance, and we're going to make that happen." He pulled my door open and went inside. I heard the soft string of curses as he saw the state of my home. I followed slowly and sighed as I watched him pick something up off the floor and put it on the entryway table.

"Cassius, we can't let this continue," Sorcha said,

coming into view. "She hasn't done dishes in weeks. She has half-eaten food on the counter. Her laundry... I don't know what's clean or dirty."

"We'll send it out to the dry cleaners. All of it," Cassius answered. "I knew we should have checked on her sooner. I didn't think it was at this point yet."

I winced at his words. Oh, yeah, this had happened before.

"I'll make a call to the cleaners," Leith said from a distance. "Don't worry, everything will be treated with care."

Sorcha looked past Cassius at me, her moon-grey eyes pinning me in place.

"Why?" she asked very softly. Cassius stepped out of the way for me to walk forward and take in what I had done to my home.

"I need to find him," I whispered, hearing the pathetic excuse tumble from my mouth.

"Go clean up. We're going to take you to dinner while Leith makes some calls. You can't live like this. I won't allow it." Sorcha waved her hand at me dismissively as she turned away. Cassius gently pushed me toward my bedroom, forcing my feet to keep moving even as I gave a half-hearted attempt to fight him.

The shock of their arrival and the shame of what they saw wore off while I was in the shower. It wasn't like I hadn't bathed. I just hadn't cleaned up after myself or gotten pretty for a few weeks...or months. I was clean, and I was wearing clean clothes. I wasn't unpresentable. I didn't stink.

It's not that big a deal. I'm working on a case. Don't they get that? Cassius knows. Why does he think this is such a problem? I'll clean up when I have time.

When I got out, I did everything I could to make sure they thought I was normal. I dried my hair and braided the sides, pulling back everything from my face. I put my jewelry on and found clean clothes that suited me in the closet. No more holey sweatpants because no one was around. I wedged myself into leather pants and a black top.

Normal.

When I walked out of my bedroom, I had renewed vigor, ready to fight off the fae and get them out of my house.

"Look, I know it's not a big deal to any of you about why the nagas are being murdered, but I saw one of my family's killers at the Mygi lab. That's fucking important to me. So, you don't get to march in here and demand anything of me—"

Power whipped through my house quickly enough to silence me.

"Are you trying to say we don't care?" Sorcha said in a deadly whisper from across the living room. "Because I would like you to rethink that very quickly." Her hair fanned around her head, and her body took on an ethereal glow. Her glamour dropped, and her long, pointed ears revealed themselves. The angles of her face grew sharper, and I could see the very inhuman teeth in her mouth.

"Well..." I hadn't expected Sorcha to remind me she was a predator. The more powerful the fae, the more terrible they could be. Cassius had always kept himself on a short leash, never showing even me that terrible creature he could become, but I had already seen sneak peeks of Sorcha's.

"You can hunt down the killer of your family and take care of yourself," she snapped, suddenly closing the distance between us. I didn't even see her do magic. One moment, she was across the room, then she was directly in front of me. "You can ask for *help*!" She waved a hand over my living room, and from my position, I could see the kitchen and dining room. "Look at it, Kaliya. See what you're living in."

I didn't need help to see anything. I could see it just fine.

"Consider this an intervention," Cassius said mildly from the center of the room. "Leith shall handle all your documents and books to keep them out of the hands of any strangers. He'll also manage any other delicate items you might own. He already knows the full inventory of your home, so nothing will be stolen. We know a brownie who runs a service for other fae. They can clean this up in an hour or two."

Leith was already working on picking up all the papers and books strewn around the living room.

Sorcha stormed out when I refused to say anything. Cassius watched his wife leave, then came over to me.

"This is her first time," he said softly. "And it will be the last time."

I swallowed. "What do you mean by that?"

"I mean, you are going to learn to handle this little problem of yours, Kaliya—even if I have to drag you out of your house kicking and screaming. You will learn how to balance this obsession of yours with taking care of yourself and stop pushing everyone away. You've said it to others. You can't let the work consume you because it does no one any good. Why don't you try to take that advice for once?"

"I say that so people..." *So they don't become like me.* I gritted my teeth. If I finished that, Cassius would strangle me. "This rakshasa killed my family, Cassius. I finally have a lead to something."

"And how have the last four months of searching for him gone for you?" Cassius retorted. "The case is cold, and you know it. Paden knows it. You didn't even bother to ask me for my help. Why?"

"You wouldn't be able to help even if you wanted to," I muttered.

"Why?"

"Because if Paden and I can't figure it out, the case is cold," I whispered, lowering my head.

"Let's go to dinner. You look nice, and we shouldn't let that go to waste." Turning on his heel, he walked away, not sparing another glance at the mess that was my home.

I turned to Leith, who looked up with a glare. It was easy to know what he was thinking.

Cassius and Sorcha care about you, and you are the most self-destructive thing I have ever seen in my life. What is wrong with you?

"Yeah, I'll go," I said, following Cassius out of the house.

2

CHAPTER TWO

It was like breathing fresh air. Getting out of his SUV at the upscale restaurant of his choosing, I felt as though something new was being breathed into me. I had spent months refusing to leave my house unless I absolutely had to, and generally, that was to question something. If something forced me out of the house, I would grab groceries and go back into hiding.

The ride into Phoenix had given me time to clear my head, and by the time Cassius parked, I was looking forward to an evening with friends, good wine, and good food, talking about nothing. It was a dose of medicine I hadn't known I needed.

"You know this place," Cassius said, coming to stand beside me. "The menu changes seasonally, so hopefully you can find something you're willing to eat."

"I'll be fine," I answered with a small smile. I always liked the food here, and he knew it since I only ever came with him. It was one of our favorite places to eat together when we hadn't been really dating, but definitely something. There were a lot of old memories here. Sorcha ignored us both and headed inside. I grabbed Cassius' arm and held him for a minute, letting her disappear. "Look, thanks for getting me out of the house. A trip out is nice."

"Any time." Walking inside with me, we found Sorcha had already claimed a table toward the back of the restaurant. They were pricey clientele, which meant there was always a seat open somewhere for them. Sometimes, it was the patio, sometimes it was inside, but there was always a spot.

I sat across from the couple, and we quickly put in our orders. I picked a salad that looked good and a glass of white wine. I didn't pay attention to their orders. Once the waiter was gone, I could taste the fae magic in the air and knew we were protected and could talk about whatever we wanted to. It was an invisible soundproof bubble, only ever really used in public human spaces, since it was rude to do with other supernaturals. Cassius would never come to a public place like this with so many humans and talk about supernatural things without making sure he was protected.

"So, you're stuck working a cold case with no leads and nothing else to do with your time," Sorcha said, sipping on the water the staff had brought them the moment they sat down. She knew as well, Cassius was protective and had covered for them. "You need something to do to keep your mind off it."

"I'm not going to stop working on it," I said, leaning back in my seat to get more comfortable. "This is important. This is who killed my family. Sure, I go a little off the deep end, but that's better than the alternative of just ignoring it until someone gets killed again."

"She's not saying you can't work on it." Cassius was still looking over the drink menu. "But you can't stay at home and run around in circles. You do need something to do. Normally, you take bounties to keep yourself occupied."

"Yeah, well, the last time I got wrapped up in one of those..." I grimaced. Illegal experiments, my mate, and two new species of supernaturals. "I decided this deserved my focus."

"Well, after Paden called, we thought about what we could do to help you," Sorcha continued. "Which is why this table seats four." She moved her finger slowly around the rim of her glass. "We're going to get you a job. You can keep Paden on retainer to keep an eye on this case and work on something else during the day. You can use your free time to continue working on this case of yours."

I frowned.

"Something new for you to try. Not bounties or working for the Tribunal," Cassius added. He put the drink menu down. "You might even enjoy the job. This particular person has been trying to convince me to offer it to you for weeks, and I kept saying I wasn't going to be a middleman. Considering the circumstances, I've decided to just bite the bullet, as they say, and do it. You need something, Kaliya. I don't like when you have nothing to do, and you're stuck on something."

I perked up after hearing more. "Really? This sounds interesting. Tell me more."

Then I was hit with a chill as the door of the

restaurant opened, and a breeze came in. Or maybe it was a sixth sense, but the hair rose on the back of my neck.

I was hit with his scent, and my fangs ached in a way they hadn't in months.

"Oh, he won't need to," Sorcha said with a purr. She lifted a hand and waved.

I didn't turn. I knew the heat signature of the man coming closer to the table. I knew everything about him.

The chair next to me was pulled out, and he sat down gracefully. The heat poured off him, begging me to lean into him, but I held myself very still, not wanting to act like anything was wrong. Cassius, for a moment, wore an expression of 'you brought this on yourself' before he turned away.

"This is a nice place," Raphael said as Cassius waved over a waiter for the table.

"Isn't it?" Sorcha smiled. "I do enjoy it. Apparently, it's a favorite of Cassius and Kaliya. They've been here together several times. The menu changes every season, so feel free to pick several things to try because they'll be rotated out, eventually."

"Thank you," he said. A waiter came by, blinking in confusion at the new member of our table. Raphael took a menu from him, ordered quickly, then handed it back. The waiter was gone in less than two minutes. There was a confidence in how Raphael ordered that made me pay attention.

He's a different man. He got all his memories back, and ever since, he's been different. I can't forget that.

"So...did they tell you?" he asked me, turning slightly to position his chest in my direction.

"They told me they had someone looking to give me a job," I answered. "They didn't say it was you."

"I knew I would never get you to work with me if I didn't go through them," he said, smirking at me. "Do you want to know what the job is?"

"Sure," I answered, grabbing my water to have a sip, pinning my gaze on Sorcha. That woman looked all too pleased with herself.

"You promised to help me and the cambions," he reminded me. "I'm calling that in. Our home is nearly finished. We should be completely up and running by the end of the year. Totally off the grid, with our own power and water in a small neighborhood situation. The only thing we'll need to do is take stuff to the dump once a week. Now, with all that finished and their general education in supernaturals being handled by Cassius and Sorcha, I need someone tough as nails who can teach them how to fight and defend themselves."

"Cassius and Sorcha know how to do that," I pointed out, kicking myself for offering the comforting words of help when I knew I would be running the moment I had the chance. I should have left the damn state.

"They're not you," he said. "I know how good you are, and while I don't want them to be assassins, I do want them to learn from one of the best."

"Sammy—"

"Sammy is a warrior-caste cambion, sure, but she's rough and unrefined. She charges straight into things and tries to kill them. I need them to learn how to take someone down, interrogate, and all the other small things no one really thinks about. This is about their security if we run into problems down the road."

"Is there a reason you think you'll have problems?" I asked, looking directly at him. Curious, but not unexpected. From the whispers I heard online, people were downright terrified of the idea of cambions. The word was spreading fast, but since there were so few of them, the general consensus was, 'Thank the gods they're in Arizona and not near me.'

"Not yet," he admitted.

"Sammy," Sorcha got out between polite coughs before Raphael could say any more.

"But I think someone once told me better safe than sorry," Raphael finished, rolling his eyes at her.

"I'm certain many people have said that to you," I murmured, reaching for my glass. I remembered Sammy. Vicious and powerful with a gnarly temper, if I could trust my judgment of her. "None of you are going to let me leave this table until I say yes, are you?"

"Well, I wasn't going to hold you hostage, but I can't speak for them," Raphael said, chuckling. "Obviously, there's something I'm missing here."

"It's nothing," Sorcha said with a beaming smile. Raphael took a sip of water while I stared at her.

"Which means it's definitely something," Cassius muttered. His wife elbowed him as Raphael choked on his water. "Kaliya, you don't have to take the job, but I do recommend it. If not for yourself, then for the cambions. They need the training, especially the warrior-caste cambions. Sorcha and I are too busy with the rest of their education. We're hiring from the pack and the nest to make sure the cambions at least understand the big five. Even Monica has offered two of her younger witches to help, as long as they're paid."

"I said no to that offer," Raphael admitted. "The other cambions are a bit wary of witches."

"For good reason," I said, sighing heavily.

"They know you and have seen you in action. I think they would listen to you and learn something. They think of Cassius and Sorcha as rich people who can't relate to them, but you have that... 'I've struggled' thing going on." Raphael leaned over and tapped his fingers on the table. "I think you're the perfect choice to make sure they learn self-defense. We already have a gym where you can teach them."

"How did you already get a gym?" I glanced at him, frowning. That was fast.

"We prioritized. We built three houses, and everyone has to live together for now. Then we made headway on the secondary buildings, security center and gym for recreation to start. We're in phase three, getting the rest of the homes finished, so everyone has their own place. We're not doing much for customization yet. We wouldn't be this far if it weren't for Cassius and his aunt, Alvina, knowing every fae contractor in the world. Or the werewolves. They've offered to do a lot of the heavy lifting. Alpha Wagner is a good man. Helpful."

"I hope you made sure none of this help came with strings attached," I commented, annoyed he would take so much help. People would come back one day to ask for favors.

"I wrote the contracts," Sorcha said primly. "The

cambions have nothing to worry about for now. They are paying customers at a reduced rate, nothing more."

"If I remember correctly, your home is last," Cassius said.

"Yeah. I want to make sure everyone is on their own first, but I get the biggest house, which will take the most time. As the leader, I'll probably have people visiting all the time or staying over. We're basing it on the werewolves. Essentially, I'll have a mansion, which will be the center of the community."

I nodded. It was smart. The nagas did similarly. Adhar, as a ruler, had the biggest property in case others needed to stay with him. Everyone else had smaller homes, more suited to raising a family and easier to keep clean.

"So, we have a gym," he said, leaning toward me again. "Which means you can have a large space to train them."

I clenched my jaw as I considered it. Cassius said I could say no, but I knew if I did, I would hear about it. Sorcha, however, acted as if she wouldn't let me say no at all. And Raphael...

I gave him a sideways glance, taking in his scarred but handsome face. I remembered nights in bed with him and how easy he was to talk to. Only four months without him, and it felt like I hadn't seen him in centuries. I was dying for a drink of water, and he looked like an oasis. His warm chocolate eyes were just how I remembered them, and I was certain they would consume me if I gave them a chance.

I needed to stay away from Raphael, but I couldn't

find a way out of this without being a petty ex-girlfriend. It had been hard walking away from him the first time, and I didn't have that strength today. It helped that he hadn't brought up how I walked out on him. He acted as if we had never slept together. He kept himself at a good distance, our legs not brushing together, no arm over the back of my chair. He was treating me the same way he was treating Cassius and Sorcha.

Maybe we can make this work.

"Fine, I'll take the job," I decided.

Everyone smiled around me as if I had just made their day. There was something stiff about Cassius, though. Maybe others missed it, but I didn't.

"We'll start tomorrow?" he asked.

"Sure."

3

CHAPTER THREE

The dinner had gone surprisingly well. Raphael had offered to drive me home, but I had firmly rejected that offer, and he had given me no problems. Instead, Leith drove to the restaurant with my car, promised everything was once again in order, and I went home alone.

A good thing, since I knew I would need a lot of sleep before I faced the cambions on their home turf.

As I got into my car to head there, I was hit with a wave of anxiety. I had disappeared from their lives the moment we got them to Arizona from that lab. Many of them had seen me break it off with Raphael. They didn't know I was being hunted and haunted. They had no idea why I did what I did, but they knew I hurt their leader. There was no doubt Raphael and I had been in a relationship. They only knew I ended it the moment I got the chance.

Will they hold a grudge? Raphael better have considered that before I drive in and kick a fucking hornet's nest.

Raphael and his cambions were closer than I had expected. Only thirty minutes, heading farther into the desert and I saw a sign for private property.

Someone had taken black spray paint and wrote **DEMONS LIVE HERE** underneath it, and I wondered if Raphael knew. It was pretty ballsy to announce it to the world. Humans would mostly laugh, but some would be stupid enough to try their little paranormal investigations. And other supernaturals? They would take it seriously. It was a giant red bullseye on the property.

I turned down the gravel road, gritting my teeth as I heard the rocks kick up and hit my BMW. This was one of the reasons I had finally paved my own drive.

I'll tell him to get around to it.

The buildings came into view, and everything was very Tucson in style, blending in with the desert around them. Construction workers were wandering around, working on three different structures I could see. I could also see the security building before I ever reached the houses. Some idiot put up a gate, thinking that was helpful.

I rolled my eyes, left the gravel road, and drove around it.

Lesson one: Secure everything if you're going to secure anything.

Checking my mirror, one of the cambions ran out of the building, chasing after me, waving me down. I kept driving and went around the construction. Raphael had told me to look for the biggest building, and it wasn't hard to find. I pulled up at a door, parked, then jumped out as if nothing was wrong. Before anyone could approach me, I entered the gym and grumbled at how cold they were running the a/c. It was already October, and things were beginning to cool down, much to my dismay. They didn't need to make the gym so cold; I couldn't think straight. I hunted down the thermostat, glad I was alone to fiddle with it, and turned it off completely. It was ninety-eight outside, which was perfectly pleasant. The cambions would survive.

Then I waited, finding a bench to sit on. Kicking my feet out, I checked the time and realized I was twenty minutes early. Well, it gave me time to get used to the space.

I looked around, impressed by the amount of equipment already set up for strength training and cardio. Knowing Raphael as I did, I had a feeling he spent at least two hours a day in the space. I could taste him on the air, but I could also taste several people, from cambions to humans to werewolves and fae. The humans I wrote off as other cambions, but the werewolves and fae were probably people who had built and set up the gym.

I heard the click of the door nearest me but didn't turn to see who it was. The warm breeze told me everything I needed to know. I continued to look over the gym, pretending as if I didn't notice him.

"Do you like it?" Raphael asked. "I based it a bit on yours but had to expand. This needs to serve more people. I'm thinking about putting everyone on a workout schedule."

"Don't run their lives," I said softly. "They just got out of that."

"I can't help it, and they can't help but listen to me." He came closer, and the bench creaked as he sat down on the other end, putting the maximum distance between us. "I have the urge to make sure they're taken care of and under my control. I try not to order them to do anything they wouldn't want to do, but they have the inclination to listen to me, which makes it hard. It's a rigid system."

"Easy to abuse if you're not careful," I pointed out and could see his nod of agreement out of the corner of my eye. "But yes, I like the gym. You set up a good area for hand-to-hand practice. We can do blade work over there as well. I'll find a place outside to set up a shooting range. I'll just need to put a table somewhere and get some bottles. It's an effective practice."

"You don't want me to build one?" Raphael chuckled. "Thank God. Everyone wants me to build more and more every day. That's how we ended up with everyone getting their own homes, instead of an apartment-style building, which would have been completed faster."

"It's coming together pretty quickly. You don't get to complain. Everyone has been locked in a building without being able to see the sun for several years, decades for a couple of them. They're going to want space to stretch out. Trust me."

"I do."

We sat in silence until he rubbed his hands together.

"So, blades, guns, and hand-to-hand."

"Yeah. You want them educated, so I'm going to give them the education of their lives. By the time I'm done with them, they'll be proficient in all three. Everyone will have their strengths and weaknesses, but if you stick close during training, you'll start to see who is best with what." I took a deep breath. "While I have you, I need to know more. What I'm working with and who. You're a warlord. Sammy is a warrior. These are important distinctions. What are the others, and where do they fall in the ranks? I'm assuming some might be better or worse at this sort of thing, and I don't want to put someone at the bottom against someone like Sammy."

"Sammy is one of our two warrior-caste cambions. I'll make sure she and Mateo stay paired," Raphael said as it was the most important promise he could give me. "They're violent by nature, good at killing. The demon magic they have makes it easier for them. Saleem was a warrior-class cambion, too." He leaned back and put his arms across the back of the bench. "We also have a slightly lower rank in the mage-caste cambions. They're still experimenting with what they can do, but it's certainly magical. They don't have the same physical strength as Sammy, Mateo, or me, but what they lack, they make up for in pure oomph with magic. One blasted me across this gym once."

I hissed in annoyance. I wasn't a magic user. I was going to get a witch or a fae in to help with that, but I didn't know which of those would be more helpful or more trustworthy.

"Yeah," he said, chuckling again. "Then we have...I guess they would be civilian class. They're like grunts in an army or..." He grimaced. "Servants of a powerful house. They're stronger than most supernatural species, definitely stronger than humans, but they don't have anything special with magic or abilities. They have the three typical forms, and that's it. From what I know, their demon and cambion forms are smaller than mine or a warrior. Mage class demons are also fairly small."

"So, we have four classes. Rulers, fighters, magic users, and the rest," I said, nodding slowly.

"As far as we know, yes."

"I can work with that. It'll be hard, but I can work with it. I can't help them learn their magic, but everything else? I'll teach the weaker ones how to use their body weight. I'll teach the stronger cambions better control. You don't want accidental deaths on your hands. That will quickly make you a nuisance around the supernatural community."

"You mean if they get into a scuffle, it doesn't have to be fatal? That would be nice," Raphael muttered.

"Oh, no. Sounds like you already have experience."

"A werewolf hit on Sammy, and when he realized it was her who smelled bad to him, insulted her. Sammy..." Raphael made a noise of annoyance. "Sammy doesn't do well with attention. Positive, negative, doesn't matter. He catcalled her, then insulted her so..."

"What did she do to the werewolf?" I wasn't surprised. With the limited experience I had with her, Sammy seemed hostile and temperamental.

"She broke both his arms and threw him off the scaffolding. She went into what we call 'warrior mode.' That full black, very fast and dangerous thing she can do," he explained. "He didn't stand a chance. Wagner was pretty pissed off, but his werewolf healed fine. No one talks to Sammy anymore, or any of the other cambions, because they think everyone can do what she did."

"That's useful and problematic at the same time. Don't want everyone to be terrified all the time."

There was a whole list of other problems with the situation. The ways it could have gone wrong for Raphael because Sammy had a temper.

Yeah, that's a problem. I'll need to talk to Sammy. She's the one who did it and needs to understand why it can't be done.

"Exactly. Gabrielle is so..." Raphael groaned, rubbing his face. "She's naïve. She thinks everyone wants to be her friend. She healed the werewolf, and now they all want to talk to her. It's been a bit overwhelming for everyone."

"She's going to be here for training, right?" I couldn't imagine Raphael would let the soft-hearted nephilim get out of learning to protect herself.

"She will be," he confirmed. "How well she'll do...I don't know. She's never been forced to do anything too physical, straining, or intense. She wasn't required to fight like the rest of us to figure out what her powers were. They were all just enamored with her wings and treated her a little better than the rest of us. I'm glad someone in the lab wasn't treated terribly, but it's left her at a minor disadvantage."

"I'll be her partner if we have odd numbers," I offered. "I'll be able to keep a special eye on her. She's probably going to need more work than anyone else."

"That would be nice. I'm going to have to stick close to Sammy and Mateo. They're going to put holes in the building."

"Like you wouldn't?" I raised my eyebrows. "Aren't you the strongest out of all of them?"

"I..." He chuckled. "I'll do my best. If I put holes in the

walls, it will because I threw one of them into it. I'm the strongest, but Sammy and Mateo can give me a run for my money if it's both of them."

The conversation died, and I secretly enjoyed his company. His new confident energy was a welcome change from the man who had no idea what was going on or how to deal with it. He seemed self-assured as if he knew he ruled and how to do it.

"So, what have you been up to?" he asked softly.

"Nothing in particular." I knew he would ask, eventually. He hadn't the night before at dinner, and Cassius and Sorcha hadn't mentioned to him what I had been up to. We had talked about useless stuff, like our favorite places in Arizona. Now that he was able to walk around a bit more freely, he was able to see the sights. Banal conversation that had saved me from shoving my foot in my mouth.

"You've spent four months doing *nothing in particular*?" He shook his head, not believing me. "Come on. I know you better than that. You don't know how to relax. I remember you getting caught up doing your own thing during our break-in at the lab to free the other cambions. Have you done anything with that?"

"I've done a little," I admitted. "But it's not a big deal."

"You know I would help if you need me, right?"

I glanced at him. Before I could reply, I was saved by a door swinging open and hitting the wall. Sammy, with a long blonde ponytail and generally pissed-off expression, came storming in. Behind her, there was one other. He was big but not the size of Raphael. I recognized his face from that night but had never caught his name. His dark eyes took in the gym before coming to me. He was expressionless, but I had a strong feeling he didn't like me.

"I don't need some fucking boring-ass training from her," Sammy snapped, pointing at me as she stopped in front of Raphael. "Mateo and I are warrior-caste. We don't need someone to tell us how to fight. We can do it pretty well ourselves."

"Well, that covers it. No guns or sharp objects for Sammy or Mateo," I said to Raphael, smiling a little.

"Shut the fuck up," Sammy growled. "You left us out to dry the moment you had the chance. You think we wouldn't notice? You probably aren't even as good as Raphael thinks you are."

That pricked my temper. I had very few things I was proud of—only a handful of things I could hold to my name and have confidence in. One of them was my skills as an assassin, a fighter who could take on the bigger, meaner things of our world.

"Oh, excuse me. I'm the ruler of the nagas, and I work for the Tribunal. I'm sorry I couldn't cater to your whims," I retorted, standing. "I'll work on that as soon as I finish kicking your ass across *my* desert." I hissed, my fangs down and ready. "If I didn't want you in Arizona, you wouldn't be in Arizona."

"Whoa," Raphael said, getting to his feet and sliding between us. "Let's not get into this. There's no reason to pick fights. Sammy, you're going to train with everyone else. You can't kill everyone you meet, and that's what Kaliya is going to teach you—"

"Fuck yes, I can," she snapped.

"No, you really can't," I said around him. *Guess we're doing this now.* "It's stupid and short-sighted. If you attack any more werewolves, the pack will descend on you. Raphael will be forced to give you up for execution or fight back. You don't want to be the cause of that."

"Like a few werewolves—"

"The Phoenix werewolf pack is over two hundred werewolves strong." I watched her take that in, and her eyes went a little wider. "And they hunt as a pack. You're lucky the one you hurt was healed because if he had died, you probably would have answered to murder, and guess who would have had to take you out?"

I waited as she figured that one out. Taking on a cambion would be hard, but I had nearly a century of experience, and she was a temperamental, emotional fighter. I knew cambions could be killed, but it wouldn't be a fatal fight for *me*.

Sammy glared at me, her blonde hair falling into her face as she fought her temper. I knew the cambions were temperamental and was beginning to think it was a class thing. The more powerful they were, the stronger that temper could be. With a born warrior, it was a fierce thing, but it didn't scare me. Her eyes were red and black, but the black veins were already retreating, and I saw her real eyes. They were light brown or something like a scotch, with a touch of reds and golds in them.

"She's a bitch," Sammy said, looking at Raphael. "I don't know why you want her here."

"She's blunt, honest, and knows the political landscape we're dealing with. She can give you the lessons you seem to think I can't teach any of you. You don't listen to Cassius and Sorcha, both of whom are good friends of mine. You need to learn. All of you do. We're not the top of the food chain. We're not even close to it."

"Maybe in a one-on-one fight, but as a community?" I shook my head. "There's nothing wrong with being the toughest bitch in the city, but there's always going to be a way for your enemies to take you out. You're just getting on your feet. You're vulnerable. You don't want to be making enemies with your neighbors."

Sammy growled, but her shoulders relaxed, and her face smoothed out just a little. The tension gripping the room relaxed with her.

"We start today?" she asked.

"Yes. Go find everyone," Raphael ordered, nodding to the door she and the other cambion had come through. Sammy turned on her heel and walked out, leaving me to look at Raphael and Mateo.

"You've been quiet," I pointed out, looking at the one who had smartly stayed silent. "Hi, I'm Kaliya." I extended my hand to him.

He looked at it, then at me.

"Yeah, I know who you are," he said, then walked farther into the gym.

I turned to Raphael with my eyebrows up again, wondering if he was going to say anything.

"The warriors are temperamental in their own ways," he said with a grimace. "Don't worry. They'll listen because they know I want them to."

"Okay..."

I'll believe it when I see it.

4

CHAPTER FOUR

I didn't know what I was doing, standing on the center mat of the gym. I had agreed to this, and until Sammy and Mateo's arrival, I had figured it would be an easy thing to pass the time.

Now, I was facing down more cambions than I could shake a stick at. It was easy teaching one person the basics. This was a group of annoyed human-demon hybrids, who were going to have different needs—eleven of them, in fact, not including Raphael. Then there was Gabrielle, at the back of the group, with her white wings shining, almost too bright to look at, illuminating the room more than it needed.

Thirteen to train, if I include Raphael. I'll have him pair with a weaker one, and I'll go with Gabrielle.

"Hi, I'm Kaliya Sahni. We've met before," I said, putting my hands on my hips. "Raphael asked me to make sure everyone here was trained in hand-to-hand combat, blades, and guns. This is for your protection. Everything we'll focus on as a group will be self-defense.

If you want more specialized training, you can let your warlord know, and he'll extend the request to me."

"Why you?" one asked. I remembered the youthful face. He'd been excited about my cellphone. "Cassius and Sorcha probably know how to fight. I've seen them carrying around swords."

"What's your name?" I asked, moving to stand in front of him but keeping ten feet between us. I wanted to see the entire group at all times, especially with Sammy's dark mood and Mateo's brooding stare focused on me.

"Cole," he answered.

"Well, Cole, I'm what's called a Tribunal Executioner. My whole job is about killing people and trying not to get killed in the process. I think we've talked about that before. Cassius and Sorcha are fae. Most of their combat tactics are magical or old-fashioned. A good sword will take you a long way in the supernatural community, but it's not the only thing you may need. You can't all do magic, so it wouldn't be fair to those who can't if that's the focus. I have a wider range of training than they do. I can't help with magic, that's my weakness, but I've made up for it in other ways. I want all of you to learn everything you can in case you don't have magic or can't use it for whatever reason."

"Where did you learn?" Sammy asked, her overbearing confidence refusing to diminish. She was trying to make me seem as though I wasn't good enough.

"A werecat called the Assassin taught me," I answered. "He's a few thousand years old and considered the best assassin in the world. If you want to know more about his reputation, feel free to ask the werewolves about him. They're normally the ones who end up dying when he gets involved."

"A really dumb nickname," Sammy said with a huff.

"It's a werewolf and werecat thing," I explained. "He's from the ruling family of werecats. His eldest siblings are lovingly called the General and the Politician. He has a younger brother the werewolves call the Traitor. They don't like calling him or his family by their names. Some werewolves consider it bad luck. They're that powerful. But I call him Hisao." I continued walking. "He taught me both how to stay alive and to kill. I'm not here to turn all of you into assassins, though. I'm only here to tell you how to survive in case someone takes it upon themselves to try to kill you."

Sammy snorted. Her derision, I knew, was coming from her belief she was powerful. She was, but it was foolhardy. She was running into a world she knew nothing about, and it was going to get someone hurt.

"Sammy...if you keep acting up, someone is going to try. The stupid ones will try to kill you, but the smart ones will only kill everyone around you until you find yourself alone and desperate, eaten away by the guilt that your actions have brought the deaths of everyone you love. But keep snorting. We'll see how well that plays out for you." I shook my head in annoyance, dismissing her grumpy expression.

"Everyone here is powerful, but fighting isn't just about strength. It's about understanding. You need to quickly judge the strengths and weaknesses of those you come across." I waved a hand at all of them. "When Raphael and I trained, I knew he was stronger, but I'm faster. I have, quite literally, a snake's reflexes. When he tried to shoot me once, I was able to dodge, and it was practically point-blank. A werewolf will always have its pack waiting for its call. A werecat could take you on in brute strength, and they'll always know where you are in their territory. It makes them an outstanding ambush predator if you go into their territory. Vampires have shadow magic and can also heal through nearly everything, just like you, though not as fast. They can reattach a limb and keep fighting. If they drink your blood, specifically a cambion's, they'll turn into monsters, and those are..."

"A pain," Raphael finished.

"Yes. These are all things you need to think about the moment you find yourself in a fight. Beyond that, you need to think about what's going to happen when you win. As I reminded Sammy earlier, she hurt a werewolf. If she had killed him, the pack could have taken action against her. They hunt in a pack and would have killed her or anyone protecting her. Or they would have gone to the Tribunal, had her tried for murder, and an Executioner like me could have been called in. You're lucky Gabrielle healed him, or you would have hurt your community before it even had a chance to find its feet."

"And that's why I called in Kaliya," Raphael interjected again. "She's going to make sure everyone knows how to defend themselves and hold themselves back if needed. We don't need a pile of bodies at our feet. It's not a good look. Kaliya?"

"I'll teach both lethal and non-lethal," I confirmed. "Now, pair up with someone close to your own strength to learn the basics of hand-to-hand, then we'll switch it up once everyone is comfortable. Gabrielle, I'm going to pair with you. Raphael, pair with whoever is left. You know how to control yourself."

He nodded. I went to the nephilim and pulled her through the group as they walked around, grabbing each other for pairs. Sammy and Mateo moved away from the group, Sammy grinning at Mateo, who kept his blank, dangerous expression. I had seen a face like that before. It was Hisao's go-to expression, which made me more scared of Mateo than Sammy's blustering. They were an effective pair. Sammy kept someone interested in her and the boisterous danger she presented, while Mateo probably silently plotted how to kill the idiot who ignored him.

Yeah, I can't make any mistakes with those two. They'll take advantage the first chance they get.

"Why me?" Gabrielle asked as I brought her to my spot, away from the others.

"You don't seem good with violence, so I need to pay attention to you. We're going to go slow, and I'm going to make sure you get comfortable," I answered, not looking at her yet. "Okay, everyone, face your partners."

So, it began. I kept it simple to start—how to throw a punch and multiple ways to deflect, dodge, or stop a punch. I corrected hands and posture, making sure Gabrielle was putting power behind hers. She wasn't okay, which I had expected.

"What if I hurt you?" she demanded, pushing her dark wild curls out of her face. "I don't want to hurt people."

"People may want to hurt you," I reminded her. "Or kidnap you to use your powers or keep you from healing someone. The cambions want to protect you, but you'll need to learn to protect yourself."

She frowned, and her lips had a cute little pout I knew would break some boy's heart one day. It was pitiful and adorable.

"Throw another punch," I ordered. "With all your strength. Come on."

She threw it, and her thin arm seemed like it was going to break when I caught her fist and realized how pitiful it really was. She wasn't even going to hit my face based on her trajectory.

Oh, man, she's going to need private lessons...and strength training.

"When do we get to the fun stuff?" Sammy asked.

"When I decide you get to do the fun stuff," I answered, looking over my shoulder as I released Gabrielle's hand. Sammy had Mateo on the ground in a hold, and I sighed.

Those two are going to need private lessons, too.

I had a distinct feeling Cassius and Sorcha had known what this job would be like and decided not to tell me.

I'm never going to get off this compound if this is what I'm working with. Vastly different levels of skill, some who need me to keep them in check, while others need me to force them to work a little harder. Fine. I'll do a morning and afternoon schedule after today. At least I can judge them all at once.

I went back to Gabrielle, keeping everyone else in my

view as she continued to work against herself, trying to punch me.

Finally, I just let one go through and clip my jaw, letting it connect because it would give me the chance to see just how bad she was with violence. It was enough to push my head back, but it wouldn't bruise. I might have a red mark, but nothing more.

"I'm so sorry!" she wailed. I grabbed her hands before she could touch me and try to heal it.

This isn't going to work—time for a new game plan.

"You need to get over it," I said softly, making my words only for her ears. "Gabrielle, you remember that man who was dragging you down the hall? When I found you?"

She nodded.

"Think about him. Would you apologize to him for a good punch to the face? Or a swift kick to the balls? Would you?"

She shook her head.

"Then think of me like him. All right?" I released her hand and stepped back before she could try to heal me again. It also gave her a moment to breathe before I tried something new.

"I'm going to drag you off this compound and take you away forever."

I grabbed her wrist again and twisted it behind her back. She yelped. The cambions turned on us and glared, everyone freezing as the most vulnerable member of their community showed a sign of pain. Raphael moved the fastest, putting himself between me and his people. I knew he would trust me and had probably been paying attention to us the entire time.

I started walking, forcing Gabrielle to come with me, yanking her a little hard, like I was someone she shouldn't be friends with.

"What is she doing?" Sammy snarled.

"Teaching Gabrielle a lesson," Raphael answered, loud enough for me to hear as I took the struggling nephilim toward a door.

It was harsh, but I needed this to sink in for all of them. I wasn't physically powerful, but I could easily grab Gabrielle and drag her off. Gabrielle, most of all, needed to realize how easy it was. She was the one who would lose everything if she didn't get over her mental hurdle and do it now.

I was five feet from the door when she realized I was absolutely serious about dragging her out of the building and out of the sight of the cambions.

She kicked at my feet, and I felt an elbow skim my ribs. Then a knee came up. I released her and grabbed it before she dropped me with it. I wasn't a man, but a knee to the crotch was still a knee to the crotch.

"Better," I said, smiling. "Remember that feeling, Gabrielle. Use it. Every time I ask you to hit me, think of that moment."

She glared at me, and I knew I was in for it now. She swung, and I ducked faster, then headed back for the group, leaving her standing there. When I glanced back at her, she was staring at her fist in shock, then turned to me, her mouth gaping open like I'd done some sort of magic she'd never seen.

"All right, let's talk about the schedule. In the mornings, I want you all." I pointed to the largest group of them. The "grunts" and the "mages," as Raphael had called them, including Cole. "In the afternoons, I want Sammy and Mateo. In the evenings, I'll take Gabrielle aside for her own training. She's not a cambion, so I'm not going to train her like the rest of you."

They all nodded.

"How many times a week?" Raphael asked, coming closer, his arms crossed.

"Five?" I shrugged. "How much do you want them working on this?"

"Monday through Friday sounds great. Makes them keep a regular schedule and gives them the weekends to practice on their own time." He turned to them. "And they *will* practice on their own time."

"Then it's decided," I declared, clapping my hands together. "Sammy, Mateo, stay here. Everyone else can go for the rest of the day. Think about what I've said and remember how important this will be. Also, whoever wrote on the private property sign should clean it off...before I leave. You shouldn't give that sort of stuff away. Humans get curious, and someone could get hurt."

I watched a head duck down. Raphael growled, and the head ducked further.

"He's a bit of a prankster," I was told as he stopped at my side. Sammy and Mateo drew closer.

"You two. Look, we don't need to be friends, but I can't be watching my back with you. During training, you'll listen, and you'll learn. We'll try to find ways to incorporate your abilities and strengths into the things I can teach you."

"You're not worried we'll get better than you?" Sammy asked, grinning.

"No," I answered honestly. "I've beaten people who were probably better than me before. Everyone has a bad day. Everyone has a weakness to exploit or a strength they rely on too much. Really, I just want you two to be the best warriors Raphael can have, and you need discipline. So, we're going to start by focusing on that."

"We don't need discipline," Sammy growled.

Wow, she's feisty.

"I asked you to punch your opponent. I asked you to work on deflections and dodges. You grappled him to the ground. You couldn't follow simple instructions. You need discipline. Now, you can go." They walked out, Sammy storming out like a tornado while Mateo moved quietly just behind her, a stalking predator. I looked at Raphael, waving at the door they had left through. "How do you deal with this?"

"They can't tell me no," he answered. "They'll argue, but they'll do what I tell them." He sighed. "But Sammy was extra mean today. She's normally better for me. I'll talk to her."

"No..." That wasn't going to work. "She has a lot of pride. She won't like a practical stranger coming in and asking you to get her into trouble. Maybe she'll get over it once she realizes I can teach her something. If it gets out of hand, I'll teach her a lesson."

"Should I be concerned?" He stepped between me and the door.

"Can she heal as well as you?"

"A little slower, but it's negligible."

"Then no, you have nothing to worry about," I promised. "I just need to know their limits. The last thing I want is to send her to the infirmary, if you have one of those."

"I knew I forgot to mention something. Yeah, we have one. It's about the size of the security building. Speaking of the security building..." He side-eyed me. "Any reason you drove completely around it?"

"If you feed me, I'll tell you," I said with a small smile as my stomach growled. "I ran out of the house too quickly to put anything in my stomach." And I had no food left in my house. Leith had cleaned me out of everything that was past its expiration date. That was seventy-five percent of my food and nothing left seemed worth the time or energy.

"Come on. I'll give you a tour of the property, too." He jerked his head and started walking.

5

CHAPTER FIVE

The "compound" was sparse, with only a handful of buildings standing in the harsh, barren landscape of the desert. This wasn't the Sahara, where literally nothing lived, but it was still a profound change for most people. There was something harsh about its beauty, like a blade. It could and would hurt you if you made a mistake with it, but it was also beautiful if you knew how to appreciate it.

To my surprise, Raphael had built in a way that blended in instead of standing out. They didn't detract from the desert or try to make it into something else. They embraced it—the sandy color of the walls, the maroon of the roofs, the gravel pathways that meant not laying permanent concrete. Maybe in time they would do more, but I liked what they had so far, just from a simple glance.

"You seem lost in thought," Raphael said as we stood outside the gym.

"You picked a nice piece of desert," I said softly. "What's the water situation out here?" Water was a commodity in the desert. Arizona was running out, and farmers were having trouble in the more rural areas. I knew there were magical solutions, but those were complicated and expensive.

"It was bad, but the fae tapped for a couple of wells." He pointed to the east, and I turned to see a small water tower. "That holds enough to give everyone the water they need for a week if there are any problems."

"Magic wells or real ones?"

"Magic. We talked to the pack about it and decided we didn't want to be a drain on the natural water for the humans in the area."

I nodded. It was easy for one supernatural to get away with living on the humans' system. My impact was fairly inconsequential. There was a chance Raphael could build an entire town.

"Where do the wells pull from?" I was curious, and it kept him talking about this amazing thing he was working to build.

"Lake Superior."

I whistled. That was a complicated and pricy bit of magic, but it was a good source.

"I bet that's cold," I mumbled. "And expensive. Over that sort of distance? That had to be millions." He had those millions now, but I was worried if he drained them too quickly, there could be problems. Eventually, the cambions were going to need to figure out an income source. Every supernatural did. We had centuries ahead of us. Money needed to be invested wisely, and budgets strictly maintained if they didn't want to work full time or open businesses.

"Freezing, which, you can imagine in the middle of July, was really nice." He chuckled. "Thanks to Cassius and Sorcha, the initial setup was the only cost we had for each well. And they have safety precautions, so no one ends up going to Lake Superior if they fall in. If the magic begins to falter, I have the contact information to fae who can fix it for a minimal charge. It also gives us enough water to try farming if any of the cambions get bored enough to want to. They can have gardens and grass, something they haven't had for a long time. We're not there yet, and it was expensive to set up, but it's a good investment for the future."

"I get it." It was complicated and expensive magic but getting water from one place to another wasn't impossible, and it was useful in the long run.

"Now, for the houses..." He took us down a gravel path through open desert. There were werewolves and fae all over, hauling and building as fast as they could. They were doing a job for the new warlord of the cambions, so they were on their best behavior. Some threw wary glances at me, but I didn't react. Both groups had to know I had a connection to the cambions.

"There's the first few there," he said, pointing to the three single-story homes. "Each has three bedrooms and twenty-five hundred square feet, which leaves space for an office or whatever they want to use it for. Right now, everyone is bunking up and sharing space, but eventually, everyone will have pretty much the same thing. We went with single-story homes for ease. We have the land, so we're not forced to build up."

"They looked spaced out enough for additions if anyone is really interested," I agreed. "Where are they going to put your mansion?"

"Farther back, with a wall around it," he answered, sighing heavily as if he didn't like the idea. "In case of attack, we'll be able to bunker down, not that they can't at home. Each home also has a room-sized, sealed concrete basement in case of emergency."

"Are you going to fence the whole property? You should. Or at least part of it. It's pretty stupid to have a security checkpoint entrance that someone can just drive around."

"Yes, I heard about that. You proved your point without needing to say anything. I was hoping we wouldn't have to go over it." His smile was both endearing and annoyed with me. "We're going to fence the immediate town we're building, then leave the rest of the land empty. I don't want to disturb the local wildlife too much."

"Good. Even a fence is better than nothing. Magic?"

"Cassius and I already talked about it. We're going with the same mix of magic and technology you have. It's not as secure as his place, but he's a fae prince who did his own security."

"Yeah, he has that advantage," I agreed.

We walked past the homes being built. As we went farther into the small community, I saw the broken land where they were going to build his home.

His home. Not mine, not his room. Just his.

A part of me felt a pang of heartbreak as I reminded myself. A larger part of me was happy to see him stepping up so much, building the life he wanted with his cambions. This was what I wanted for him, but it was a life for cambions, not a life for me. I had long gotten over my need to live with a community and share things. I enjoyed my solitary existence.

Maybe if he wasn't their ruler, we could make it work, but I can't exactly mate him and force him to live away from them.

I huffed as I stared at the little world around me. The cambions I had been working with were milling about, some talking, others laughing and goofing off with a water hose. Gabrielle was talking to a werewolf, but when she saw me, her eyes went wide. The werewolf's frown was visible from nearly thirty feet, and he turned in the direction she was looking. Seeing both Raphael and me made the werewolf blanch.

"Are they trying to poach her?" I asked softly, keeping my eyes on them.

"There's...been some, trying to suggest to her she should open up a healing home in Phoenix," he answered. "I'm willing to let her go out and do that but not until she's ready. I need to know she can defend herself before I let her go off on her own. She knows that and has already talked to me about not wanting to leave. All her friends are here, and she likes knowing someone is watching out for her."

"You could send her with a roommate or two," I said, shrugging. "I just don't want to see her get caught working for a pack. She'll end up becoming a commodity they fight over. At least with you cambions, her healing isn't needed as much. You can reattach limbs if you need to."

"Exactly." He waved for me to keep following him. "I'm staying with Sammy and Mateo right now, but they'll ignore us while we get something to eat."

We went to the closest house and walked through the front door, not needing to knock. We found Sammy and Mateo standing in the kitchen. Mateo ignored us, but Sammy glared at me. I could feel those daggers on my back as I leaned on the center island as Raphael grabbed two plastic cups of yogurt from the fridge and slid them to me. Then he grabbed a spoon and slid that as well.

"Eat both of them," he ordered. "You look thinner than you used to."

"Don't get bossy with me," I countered, peeling open the top of the first one. "I'll eat as much or as little as I want to."

Sammy's low growl annoyed me, but I didn't spare her a glance. Raphael started making a sandwich, also ignoring her.

"You've probably dropped ten pounds since we last saw each other. That can't be healthy for someone with your type of metabolism." He didn't look at me as he spoke.

"I probably gained those ten pounds while living with you," I muttered, shaking my head. When he had lived with me, I had eaten way more than I had before. I hadn't noticed the weight gain or weight loss, but if he did, I knew it had to be real. He was too observant when it came to me.

"Yes, you did," he answered, a small smile forming. "It was never fat. You just bulked up a little."

"Yeah, well, I've taken care of myself for several decades. I'll eat as much or as little as I please." I wasn't going to get into this with him more than once. I wasn't going to let him try to take care of me as though I was one of his cambions.

Sammy's low growl continued as I ate the first yogurt and felt full enough to slide the second back to Raphael. Without even thinking about it, he slid it back to me.

"Raphael—"

"He takes care of people," Sammy snapped. "Let him."

"No," I hissed, turning my head to her and crushing the yogurt in my hand. With a curse, I let it go and reached for a roll of paper towels. I wiped it off while I glared at her, wondering what I was going to do with her. Her eyes were cambion again. She seemed to spend most of her time riding that edge, showing people what she was.

"Sammy, stay out of it," Raphael ordered, his words so patient and calm, I wondered if he was doing it purposefully to hide his anger. I turned back to him and saw his red and black eyes, the black veins growing slowly. "Kaliya doesn't answer to me. She doesn't answer to anyone."

"But—"

"No," he growled. "Go take a run and figure out your temper. Don't come back until you have it under control."

Sammy snarled and stormed out. Mateo looked at her, then at Raphael. With a single nod from the warlord, Mateo followed Sammy out.

"Mateo listens better," I pointed out once they were both done.

"My relationship with Sammy is complicated where it's not with Mateo. He doesn't feel the need to do anything except follow my orders and live his own life," he said softly, looking at his sandwich. I tried to study him and realized he was purposefully not looking at me as he took a bite of the finished sandwich.

I waited for him to continue that explanation, but I never got one as he ate and refused to look at me.

"If I'm going to train them, I really need to know everything," I said simply. "I won't walk into a field of landmines waiting to take my leg off."

"Sammy protected the cambions, and she's killed them," he said quietly. "She's vicious, protective, and dangerous. Once I showed up, she finally had someone she could lean on. For a long time, the other cambions were scared of her and Mateo. Very scared of them. I finally brought them together. Mateo is younger, and they didn't use him to kill other cambions as much."

"So now, Sammy will burn down the world for you or destroy anyone she thinks is offending you." *Or left you in the driveway after breaking up with you.*

"Yes." When his eyes finally met mine, I saw understanding there. We were both talking about the same thing. "I told her it wasn't her problem. She's going to need some time to come around to that. Doesn't help that you insult her pride every time you open your mouth."

"She has to prove to me she deserves that ego," I retorted. "The rest of the world is going to make her do it. Reputations come at a cost. She needs to be willing to pay it and put her money where her mouth is. I have to remind the world all the time my reputation is well earned."

"This isn't just a tough girl who is threatened by another tough girl thing, is it?" He gave a teasing smile, one I knew well.

"No," I hissed. "If Mateo had given me lip, I'd treat him the same way. However, maybe you should ask Sammy that offensive question and see what sort of answer you get."

He had the dignity to wince, knowing he'd been out of line.

"I'm leaving," I declared as I cleaned up the rest of my mess. "I'll see you tomorrow."

"Wait—"

"Goodbye, Raphael," I said as I marched out of the house and headed for my car.

I'd had enough of cambions for the day—enough of the small reminders of the past. As I grabbed my door, ready to yank it open, Gabrielle came running up.

"Where are you going?" she asked, blinking her wide, dark eyes. She was genuinely curious, not maliciously nosy, which kept my temper in check for a moment. It was hard to be mad at her.

"Home," I answered with a sigh. "I'll be back tomorrow for us to start the official training schedule."

"Oh. Okay. I was hoping you would stay for dinner tonight."

"With you?" I raised an eyebrow. I knew Gabrielle better than most of the cambions but not by much. I got her out of the lab, and we had a front-row seat to Maude's death. She had spoken up for me with Sammy outside the lab, but we hadn't talked since.

"With all of us? We like to have barbecues. I figured since you were here, that meant you...you would be back with us."

"Oh." I sighed. "I'm sorry, Gabrielle. I have my own home and my own work. I can't stay for longer than I plan." I watched her face go sad and relented just a little. "Maybe later in the week. I'll see what my schedule looks like." It was completely empty. I already knew that, but I didn't want her to think I could just come by whenever. I didn't want to be that available for Raphael, which meant I couldn't be available for any of them.

"That's perfect!" Her grin was like the sun, and her eyes twinkled like stars. I was normally not so poetic with other women, but Gabrielle was like a fucking diamond in the rough. Literally. She was an angel living among demons—couldn't get more on the nose metaphorically.

"I'm going to leave now," I said, slowly opening my door. She backed away, nodding.

"Okay. I hope you have a safe drive home."

I smiled, trying to keep a happy expression while I got in my BMW, turned on the engine, and slowly backed away from the waving nephilim.

Once I was out of there, I texted Sorcha.

Kaliya: Meet me at the Jackalope.
Sorcha: Right now?
Kaliya: No, in four months. Yes, right now.
Sorcha: On my way!

6

CHAPTER SIX

I pulled into the parking lot faster than I should have and slammed the brakes to miss someone walking into the bar. The guy flipped me off, not seeing who was in the car, thanks to my dark-tinted windows. I rolled down my window and flipped him off in return, watched him pale, then kept driving to find a parking spot.

I was in a mood, and it shouldn't have felt good scaring the shit out of a stranger. Sorcha pulled up only five minutes later and parked beside me, getting out of a hot little red coupe with its top down. Her silver hair was shining in the sun, reflecting it as metal would. It was too early to be drinking, but that wasn't going to stop me.

"What's wrong?" she asked as I met her in the parking lot.

"Today was..." I sighed, rolling my eyes. "Exactly what I should have expected, which tells me I shouldn't have taken the job."

"You're not going to quit after one day," she informed me as if she was a teacher, and I was the student. Or a parent and a child. “Normally, when you have a shit day, you just go home and stew about it. Why are we at the Jackalope?”

“If I’m going to start showing my face to keep all of you off my case, I need to actually show my face,” I muttered. “So, we’re here to drink, talk about my problems, and make sure Paden doesn’t send out another search and rescue mission to my own house.” I gave her a small smile. “Plus, I missed you.”

“Aw, you’re so sweet,” she declared, patting my cheek. I rolled my eyes again as we started walking. She was bringing in her clutch, and I was going with my typical equipment—a sword at my waist, a dagger on my thigh, and a gun in the holster.

We didn’t need to ask to go downstairs. As I made my way into the basement of the bar, the better bar, I saw Paden behind the counter, watching me and Sorcha.

“We’re not going to have any funny business tonight, are we?” he asked, eyeing both of us. “I see neither of you brought your better halves. Fantastic.” His sarcasm didn’t go unnoticed by either of us, but I didn’t say anything, and neither did Sorcha as we found seats in front of him at the bar.

“I got a new job.” I stared at him blankly. “And he’s not my better half. He’s not half of anything.”

“Kaliya broke up with him right after the trial,” Sorcha explained further.

Paden’s eyes went wide. While he had been helping me with finding that rakshasa, I hadn’t told him about the state of my personal life. Apparently, no one had given him a heads up. It wasn’t like it was international news or anything. He had no reason to know, and I knew the people involved in my personal life wouldn't tell him unless I did.

"I see," he murmured, pouring us our favorites, a glass of his best wine available for Sorcha and a whiskey for me. "And the other thing?"

"I'm keeping you on retainer, but it was made clear to me I needed something to do with my time. Hence the new job." I was a touch bitter as I sipped on the whiskey while Sorcha winked at him.

"I'm glad you have something to occupy your time. I thought you at least had Raphael with you the last few months, and he was just too busy to see what was going on."

"We can stop talking about it now," I hissed. "I'm beginning to think my fae friends are starting to meddle a little too much."

"Well, we can't have that, can we?" Paden chuckled. "You'll just ignore us for a few more months and come crawling back. We all know it." This time he winked at Sorcha, who laughed.

"I'm glad you both find me so comical. Does wonders for my reputation."

"Your reputation doesn't need any help," Sorcha said with a glance over her shoulder. "Neither does mine."

She had a very good point as I looked behind us to see the quiet bar patrons. It was a bit empty, but it was early yet. Paden's clientele worked on the line of legality. Most weren't trouble enough for Cassius or me to do anything about. They were just bounty hunters looking for their next paycheck, fixers who solved problems for wealthy clients and needed a place to find the newest intel and pool their resources. On occasion, I found someone I needed to deal with, but that was growing less and less common.

Even though no one in the bar was a criminal worthy of my time, they were quiet, watching me carefully. They all knew if they toed the line too hard or crossed it, I would be the one waiting for them. Maybe. I wasn't active anymore and had no idea if I wanted to be active again. The situation with Raphael had given me a strange feeling about continuing my job as an Executioner.

"So, what's this new job?" Paden asked, curious, but the gleaming look in his eye told me he could probably find someone to sell the intel to. He was my friend, but he had bills to pay, and it was good intel. That was another reason I'd needed to break it off with Raphael. Eventually, he would find someone willing to buy or kill for information about who I was dating, and that wouldn't end well—for Paden or me. It would be a last resort thing. Paden had been tortured to give up my house location, but I wasn't taking any more chances.

"I'm training the cambions," I said with a smile. "Self-defense, asset protection. That sort of thing." I continued to smile as someone hissed behind me, a vampire. It probably didn't bode well for anyone looking for an easy target to steal from. Thieving was big money in the supernatural world, and most of the time, it was completely ignored by the Tribunal. If someone couldn't protect their own shit, they didn't deserve to keep it.

"Well, that should keep you busy all right," Paden said

with a smile in return. "Any of them good enough to get real training?"

I didn't reply. If I was going to train anyone to be an assassin, I wasn't going to publicize it. The world could try to guess.

"Do you have a private booth where we can talk and enjoy some drinks without listening ears?" Sorcha asked, leaning in to keep her voice down.

"He does," I answered.

Paden sighed and snapped his fingers. A door shimmered on the blank wall at the end of the bar.

"Why didn't we ever use that before?" Sorcha demanded, turning to me.

"Keeping you in public with Cassius kept our conversations lighthearted and not serious," I explained. "Plus, I've never used it. It takes a lot for Paden to let anyone use it."

"All you ever had to do was ask," Paden said as I got up. "Usually, you're normally in here alone, and we use my office when we need to talk. If you two ladies want a quiet place, feel free to use it."

"Who do you normally keep it for?" Sorcha asked, frowning at him, then me.

"He won't answer that," I said, heading toward the door. "Because I can't know the answer."

"I see," Sorcha mumbled, nodding respectfully to Paden.

The private room was for those who wanted to broker deals in a neutral location. I was certain Paden had high-profile criminals in here while I was around. My own abilities couldn't see through the door, so I would never know.

What I meant by high profile criminals were people like Sorcha, or rather, Sorcha before I met her. She had been a fae arms dealer, apparently, notorious among her own kind. I never looked up more on her because it wasn't my problem, and she was pretty respectable now.

We took seats in the circular booth inside the room. I sipped on my whiskey as the door closed again.

"I've been in rooms like this one," Sorcha said softly. "Paden has his hands in more than I thought."

"He probably gets a cut of whatever deal is done here. He's not a part of the crime, though. Technically, he's only renting out a private meeting space. What happens once the doors close, he doesn't know, and he'll never ask. He just keeps the drinks going."

"Yes, I know. He's an information broker, and his neutrality is his power," Sorcha said softly. "I never used him because I never came to this part of the country, but I've met his type. They're good people who have found an interesting grey area of the law."

"So, we wanted to talk about my first day with Raphael and the cambions," I said, sipping my drink again as she grew interested, leaning in.

"Yes. You wanted to bitch about your problems. How bad could it have been?"

"It could have gone worse. I could have gotten into an actual fight with Sammy. Instead, she was just bitchy to me the entire time. I have limited experience with all of them, so I'm going to need a crash course. She made it clear I needed to quickly figure out who I was dealing with."

"With her charming attitude and sweet smile?" Sorcha laughed. "Yeah, she gives me and Cassius a bit of a hard time, too. I have a feeling, though, she gave you a much harder time."

"She was a fucking nightmare from the moment she walked into the gym. A lot of hot air and bad attitude."

"Hm." Sorcha frowned. "She's a tough one, but she's never given us more than a hard look or two. She's normally well behaved when we're around. Sticks close to Raphael..." Sorcha inhaled sharply. "She growls whenever you come up."

"Ah, so this is a *me* thing," I mumbled. "Perfect. It wasn't just in the gym either. Raphael offered a bite to eat, and my dumbass accepted. That's another problem. He's my ex—"

"He's more than your ex," Sorcha reminded me.

"I know," I snapped. She raised an eyebrow but didn't seem too bothered. I, on the other hand, felt guilty. Sorcha wasn't the problem. I was. "Sorry."

"How bad was it, really?" she asked gently. "Seeing him, not Sammy. I can tell she bugs the hell out of you, but I don't think that is what's bothering you."

I looked down at my drink. "He's pretending like we never happened most of the time, and that's good. It's easier for me to ignore everything about it."

"But?"

"He's building a life, and I don't have a place in it," I whispered, admitting the pain that had hit me when I saw where his mansion would be built. "And it's really hard to keep boundaries. He wanted to feed me, take care of me like it didn't mean anything."

"But it does mean something." Sorcha reached out and grabbed my hand. "You could have a place in the life he's building, Kaliya. You just need to want it."

Want it? I wanted *Raphael*. I wanted his body stretched out beside mine for eternity. I knew it was a combination of my feelings and my biology. There was no escaping the want. It was everything else.

I pulled my hand away. "No, Sorcha, I can't. I can't take their warlord from them, and that's what I would do to keep him out of danger if I mated him. The other option is to let him be both, and eventually, my enemies would come knocking for him. I can't put his life in danger like that. I won't." I sighed. "I...I gave up on community a long time ago. I like living alone in the peace and quiet of my own property. It was nice having a roommate, but that's not having nearly a dozen people running around all the time, asking me for things. It's all me, though. I can do this job and ignore the personal shit. I just need a place to vent it out." I spun the glass in my hand in circles slowly. "I promised to help them, and I'm going to."

"You're such bullshit," Sorcha finally said.

"Excuse me?" I looked up at her, shocked. I stopped spinning my glass and blinked several times as I tried to process what she meant by that.

"You're full of shit," she said decidedly. "Cassius and I both have enemies, and those enemies have put us both in danger. You stormed a lab and nearly got killed by him to help him, but suddenly, you can't be bothered to let him return the favor—and he *would* in *a heartbeat*—even if it was just to return the favor you did for him. Your self-sacrificing bullshit about protecting him has nothing to do with *him*. It has everything to do with *you*."

I was speechless as she polished off her glass of wine, then glared at me.

"As for Sammy. Well, she's easy to figure out, and I bet you already figured it out as well and don't want to admit it to me. You broke up with her friend and hurt him, leaving him cold in a driveway while she watched. She's not going to forgive easily for that. You're going to have to work through it because you made your bed, and now you have to lie in it." Sorcha huffed indignantly.

"How is protecting him all about me?" I asked, finally going back to that point. Yes, I figured out Sammy's problem with me, so there was no reason to discuss that.

She raised an eyebrow. "You slept with Cassius on and off for years. It was messy and broken in terms of relationships, but it was something you both needed. It was self-destructive and argumentative, fueled by alcohol and bad decisions. You never tried to break it off, Cassius had to, but suddenly, you have a guy who is just around. He's nice, and you aren't drinking to get into bed with him, you just want to be there. You're not scared for his safety. There's no reason for anyone to think he's nothing more than a hot guy, willing and able to warm your bed, just as Cassius was. No, what you're scared of is stability that relies on someone else."

I hissed at her, finished my drink, and glared.

"That's not the problem. There are people out there killing off my people. They target mated couples more than anyone else. And…" I clenched my jaw as my fangs ached at the thought I was about to voice. "I don't have the control to keep him in my life as a lover without biting him, eventually, which would change everything. He would be tied to me for eternity. Do you really think anyone deserves to be tied to someone with as much baggage as I have? That *Raphael* deserves to have someone as broken as me? He deserves so much more than I can give him."

"You think you're broken?" Sorcha's moon-grey eyes searched my face, and I could see the heartbreak there.

I stood up and stared at her for a moment—thinking about my nightmares, how I woke up screaming and reaching for the sword Hisao gave me, thinking about how I couldn't breathe until it was in my hand. The old memories were too close to the surface, and I was dangerous.

"I *am* broken," I said before walking out.

"Kaliya—"

I closed the door on whatever she was going to say.

Going to my car, I got in and headed home as fast as I could.

7

CHAPTER SEVEN

I went to the compound the next day, just as I promised. Sorcha hadn't tried to reach out to me after the Jackalope, and I was grateful. Hopefully, it would be the last time she tried to bring up the topic. I didn't want to talk to her about nightmares, obsession, and trauma. I didn't want to talk about how I would probably spend my life searching for answers I would probably die for in the end. I had set myself on this path at fourteen and had stumbled off at seventeen, compounding my problems. I trained under an assassin to become a weapon instead of a victim.

What was there to say?

I know what I am and who I am.

I walked into the gym, trying to shake off the feelings. I found the cambions waiting on me, but Raphael was nowhere in sight.

"Today, we're going to work on grabs and disabling grabs," I announced. "Simple, effective, and lifesaving. You never want to let someone have you pinned or prone.

In turn, you do want to have them in those positions. We'll start with a simple warm-up, a little stretching, then get to it."

I threw myself into the work. Cassius and Sorcha wanted me to have a life. I couldn't promise that, but I could focus on the job while I was at it.

Four hours later and I had several panting and sweaty cambions on the mat.

"Well…you all did good," I said, nodding as they tried to peel themselves up. "Practice in your free time. Remember the corrections I made so you don't fall into easy mistakes."

"Can't I just be the IT guy and play with computers all day?" Cole muttered as he pushed himself to his feet.

"You can take that up with Raphael."

The other cambions snickered and laughed as if they knew something I didn't. I shrugged and went to find my water bottle. Searching through my bag, I wasn't looking when he entered the room.

But I knew the moment he did.

His scent filled my nose and took over my brain. I stilled, forgetting about the water bottle when my mouth went dry as his heat walked through the room, asking the cambions how their mornings went. I listened carefully, too interested in the conversations he was striking up with each and every one of them. When one complained about how sore she was, Raphael chuckled and promised she would get over it in an hour because they healed so quickly. Once they got used to the burn, they would know it didn't last long.

I listened as the gym doors opened and closed as the

cambions left. I listened for his footsteps to come closer to me, but he never did.

Finally, I remembered what I was doing, grabbed my water bottle, and stood. I didn't turn toward him as I took a long drink. It wasn't too hot in October, but water was always good when one was training.

When I turned to him, he was standing quietly, his hands in his pockets as he waited for me.

"What do you need?" I asked, closing up my water bottle as I stared at him.

"Just wanted to see how it went. Did any of them give you a hard time?" He took the first step closer, and once he made that concession, I started walking to him.

I stopped before I was within arm's reach but close enough to feel his natural heat pour off his body, tempting me. He was a sun rock, and I wanted to curl up on him and never leave. The other cambions were just as warm, but they weren't him. No one could ever be him.

"They were fine. I didn't notice anything," I answered, pulling my towel off my shoulders to wipe the sweat off my face. "I worked them a bit hard, but I don't really know how to do it any other way. They'll work hard until they do it right."

"That's why I wanted to hire you," he said with that easy-going smile. "That's how you learned, isn't it?"

"Yup, except when I got it wrong, I needed a bandage because I was probably bleeding. Hisao started with the sword once he realized I already knew how to use one." I looked at one of the doors, thinking about the cambions. "I won't do that to them. Well, them and Gabrielle. Sammy and Mateo, on the other hand, will be learning quickly with sharp objects. I'm going to need to keep them engaged."

"Of course, and they'll heal faster than you can get a bandage," Raphael commented, his tone strangely light and casual. I had no right, but I was a little frustrated I was standing right in front of him, totally fucked up, thanks to not having him anymore, and he seemed totally okay with it. Like I had been a fun but passing fling.

This is what I wanted.

"Can we order lunch out here?" I asked, hoping to eat before I dealt with the two warriors.

"No. We're too far out for that. Let me make you something."

I turned back to him, eyeing him carefully.

"I can figure something out. Maybe I'll drive out and get something from the nearest town."

"Don't be like this," he said, stepping closer. "I know we had a thing, and you've ended it, but that doesn't mean I can't be a good host. I still consider you a friend. Let me feed you. I feed Cassius and Sorcha while they're here."

"Wow, just cut straight to that, huh?" I didn't really know where to go from there. "And here I thought we were just going to ignore..."

His face made me realize that had come out the wrong way. I had a sneaking suspicion he thought it was easy for me to ignore it, or maybe he was ignorable. Whatever his impression, I didn't want him to have it.

"I'm feeding you," he said, turning to walk out, his face a little redder than normal.

"Wait," I called before he made it through the door. "I

didn't mean it the way it came out. I wasn't expecting you to say anything. It seemed like you were comfortable ignoring it, so it surprised me. You're not ignorable. Or..." I faltered as he turned around and eyed me.

"I didn't want to make you uncomfortable," he said. "But it needed to be said. I'm not going to treat you as anything but an honored guest while you're here, the same as Cassius and Sorcha, no matter our history."

I kicked at nothing, staring at my shoes when meeting his eyes grew too uncomfortable.

"Thanks," I whispered.

He's too good for me. I did the right thing.

"No problem. Come on, let's get you something to eat."

He walked out, leaving me to catch up. Once again, I was walking with him through the compound, heading for the home he shared with Sammy and Mateo.

"Who gets to keep the house when the others are done?"

"Mateo. I would never live in a place Sammy considered hers." Raphael growled softly. "She's already possessive over a bedroom I can't convince her to keep clean. And food? She's violent over food."

"Ah. Should you be telling me all your cambions' dirty laundry?" Not that I minded, but I didn't want them to think they couldn't trust him with their secrets. I understood that fine line, not that I needed to walk it. The nagas didn't tell me their secrets.

"Probably not, but it's easy to talk to you," he said with a small smile over his shoulder.

"Is it?" I stopped, frowning deeply in confusion.

"Why does that surprise you?" He stopped as well, chuckling as he turned to me.

"I don't know."

"Well, Sammy won't care that I told you. She would be more than willing to give you a live demonstration if you gave her a chance." Raphael started walking again. For a moment, I just watched him, thinking about how attractive it was to see him walk with so much confidence yet seem totally relaxed. He truly didn't fear anything or anyone on his little compound, which was sexy.

I took a deep breath and followed him again. I didn't complain this time as he made lunch. He didn't mention my weight or anything else, just prepared the food and put it in front of me. I munched on the salad without complaint, grateful it would be light on my stomach for later. A big meal would kill me when I was training with Sammy and Mateo.

Neither of the warrior-caste cambions showed their faces this time, leaving me to eat with Raphael in silence as we had so many times together at my home and my condo. It was peaceful and easy, and I fucking missed it.

"What's on your mind?" he finally asked, forcing me to realize I had stopped eating as I lost myself in my thoughts.

"Nothing important," I mumbled before shoving another bite into my mouth.

"Don't lie to me," he said just as quietly.

I put the fork down and sighed.

"Nothing you need to worry about," I rephrased, hoping he would accept that.

His soft curse and the way he turned away told me he didn't accept it at all.

"Raph?" I wanted to know what he was thinking. I knew it was unfair because I wouldn't tell him what I was thinking either.

"Nothing," he replied, putting his empty plate in the sink. Turnabout was apparently fair game. "What time does your training with Sammy and Mateo start?"

I checked the time and groaned. "Soon. I should probably head over there." I moved to put my plate in the sink with his and found myself too close to him. He went to grab the plate from my hand, and we touched. For a moment, I wondered if I had put my hand on a hot stove. I jerked away and hissed as the plate didn't make it into the sink. It crashed between us, and I groaned. Raphael stared down at it, sighing heavily. When I started to kneel, he grabbed my elbow and moved me.

"I got it. You go. I can clean this up. If I cut myself, it'll heal in less than an hour. Go."

He gently pushed me away from the shattered plate, and I finally gave in, walking out of the kitchen.

The fuck is wrong with me?

Everything.

I hurried back to the gym, which was quickly becoming the safest place on the compound. At least there, I was in some sort of control. Once I was inside, I could finally breathe again. I had never been a lovesick puppy kind of woman, then I met Raphael. Now, I was dropping plates over an accidental touch. Worse, I knew Raphael would probably take the interaction in a totally different way.

I broke up with him, and he probably thinks I can't bear to touch him, which couldn't be further from the truth.

I was good at so many things, but people were never one of them.

As I collected myself, they walked in. Sammy and Mateo, side by side, as if they were ready to go to war.

"Enjoy flirting with Raphael?" Sammy asked, stopping to stand on the mat.

"I wasn't flirting with him," I snapped.

"Good," she growled softly. "Keep it that way. We're not going to let you hurt him again."

"Oh, we're doing this already?" I rubbed my face. "Day one, air out all the dirty laundry?"

"Might as well if we're going to be forced to spend time with you," Sammy said, crossing her arms and taking on a fucking power stance. "You walked out. You told us you would help us, then broke off whatever you had with Raphael and disappeared for months."

"I'm practically down the road. Raphael always knew where to find me," I countered, guilt stabbing me since she had a solid point. I promised, then promptly walked away. "I don't live more than thirty minutes from here."

"Sure. Whatever helps you sleep at night," Sammy snarled. "People like you—"

"Nothing helps me sleep at night," I whispered, looking down at the sword sitting on my bag. I had brought it, knowing I would probably need it with these two. Plus, it just made me feel safer, and I needed that. "So, don't think you know me. I make mistakes. Big ones. All the time. But don't stand there and pretend to know me. You don't know people like me." I looked up and glared at her. “You have no idea how I think. You certainly don’t know how I feel. Don’t stand there and presume.”

“Raphael is a good man, and you hurt him. I don’t need to know more than that.”

“You don’t need to remind me of how good a man Raphael is,” I hissed. “I know how dedicated he was to helping all of you.”

“Did it make you jealous? Knowing he had all these people who wanted him back and for him to lead? Is that what your problem was?”

“No.” It rubbed the truth, but it wasn’t correct. I wasn’t jealous of the cambions. I was happy for them. I wanted them to keep him as their leader, keep him safe from me and my problems. He deserved that. “I don’t see any reason why I should tell you any more than that. My reasons aren’t your business, Sammy. Let’s just get on with this, so we can both make him happy and move on with our lives.”

“No, I want—”

“I don’t *care* what you want,” I snarled, stomping over to her, staring her down. “I was hired to do a job, and I’m going to do it. My personal life isn’t your business. We’re going to train. I’m going to teach you, and we’re going to try to be fucking civil.”

“I’m not going to be civil with someone I consider the enemy,” Sammy growled, meeting me chest to chest.

8

CHAPTER EIGHT

"Enemy?" I laughed in her face. "You think I'm the *enemy*? Because I broke up with Raphael and told him we couldn't *sleep together* anymore? You need to get your priorities straight." I turned away from her, shaking my head at her logic. "I mean, come on. There are people out there who would cut out your eyes for a keepsake. There are people who would look at your demon forms and slaughter all of you because they think you're monsters. There are people who would look at you and just see big game, another warrior to defeat to maintain their dominance. There are people who would kidnap Gabrielle and keep her for their own uses, put her in another cage without a single care for what she wants. And you consider *me* the enemy? Sammy, you need a fucking reality check. If you're not careful, people are going to think you're in love with him because me breaking up a purely sexual relationship doesn't make me the enemy. Unless..." I waved at her as I turned back around, having put some distance between us. Once it came out of my mouth, I wanted it to be true. "Are you?"

Say yes.

Sammy's face flushed, but she kept her mouth shut. While many would consider that a yes, I didn't. There was a firm chance I had just embarrassed her, making her seem like a little girl who couldn't control herself.

"No. He's...he's more than that. He's the only leader we've ever had. I won't see him get hurt." She was flushed, but her words held conviction. "You hurt him."

"Ah, well..." I shrugged and kept walking.

"I hate you," the cambion said softly as I reached my bag again. "You have no idea how important you are to him."

"How could I be that important? I helped him find his people, free all of you, but we had only been together for a few months," I retorted as I reached down to grab my sword. I wanted it in my hands. I didn't like the sound of Sammy's voice. I was probably not helping, trying to brush off her words about Raphael's feelings, but I didn't owe *Sammy* anything. If Raphael walked in here and said the same thing, I would have a much different response.

"You..." she snarled, and I turned to find her coming for me, her eyes red and black, the veins growing on her face at a rapid pace. I stood my ground, as stupid as that was since she was certainly stronger than me. She got in my face this time.

"Use your words," I ordered, keeping her gaze, refusing to be scared as her skin didn't turn marbled grey but inky black. She was going into that uniquely warrior-caste thing I had seen and heard about.

"You don't care at all, do you? About him," she growled and tried to grab my collar. I jumped back faster than she could.

"The next time you try to put your hands on me, you'll regret it," I warned softly. "And I'll repeat myself, but my personal life and feelings aren't your business."

"You can't make me regret anything. We both know I could break you in half." She dragged her eyes over me. "You're fragile and arrogant."

"Don't, Sammy," Mateo said softly, walking over. "Raphael won't like it if someone gets hurt." His eyes fell on me.

"What? You think we need to tolerate her?" Sammy snarled again as her powers continued to change her form, and horns started to curl from her forehead. "I don't need this bitch's training, and I'm going to prove it." Her scent filled my nose and mouth, overwhelming and strange. It wasn't Raphael, but it was close. In the strange combinations of scents that made up the cambions, she had a little more of B, while Raphael had a little more of A, whatever those scents were. I still didn't have a real reference to compare them to.

"You can try," I said lightly, ready to draw my sword in a relaxed position. To anyone who didn't know me, I was just holding it, but to those who knew me, they would know I was ready to strike if I needed to. "I warned you. If you try to touch me again, you'll regret it."

She lunged for me with a roar.

I moved fast. She had no finesse, only raw power. While she was quick, I was clearly faster. While she just wanted to barrel into me to hurt me, I wanted to send a message.

I could have taken her head from her shoulders, but that wasn't what I wanted. Instead, as she flew past me while I dodged, I sliced one of her outreached hands. Her scream echoed around the gym, the ear-splitting screech making me wince as I whipped my katana and knocked her black tar blood from it. Mateo snarled, but he ran to her, not to me.

I looked down to see what I had just done, and guilt ran through me just as quickly as satisfaction.

I had cut her hand off.

I sheathed my sword and gently picked up the hand, careful not to damage it more. I went to her, where she sat on the ground, holding her stump, and placed it next to her and Mateo, who was pulling his shirt off to stop the bleeding.

"Bandage it on," I ordered. I had aimed for her hand for a reason. "It'll heal back on. It might take a few days before everything is good again, but—"

Sammy looked up at me, her eyes wild with rage. I reacted a second too slow, still registering that look, not prepared to be assaulted. The fist landed on my jaw as I reeled back, and it felt slow as bones cracked under her knuckles. She lunged for me again, but Mateo threw her to the wall. I heard the impact, and dust from the new building began to drift down, but pain and dizziness kept me from focusing on anything. I went to my knees.

I didn't know how long I knelt there, but it was long enough for me to know something was terribly wrong. I heard roaring and yelling and doors being slammed.

"What the fuck is going on in here?" Raphael's voice cut through the ringing in my ears.

"That bitch cut off my hand!" Sammy screamed from across the room.

Hands touched my shoulders, and I hissed, jerking away, only to stumble and crawl away. Hissing made my jaw hurt worse as I realized it was probably broken and not cleanly. Sammy's fist had done a number on my face. That much was certain.

"Fuck," Raphael growled. A hand grabbed the back of my shirt and pulled me up to my feet. His face swam in my vision, making multiple copies of him so terrible, I had no idea which one was actually him. "Gabi!" he roared, and I whimpered as the words made my head pound. He didn't hold me gently, but he did pull me toward his chest, and I sighed as the heat of his body tried to ease the pain of my face. "Mateo, bandage that hand back on Sammy. It'll heal without any help. It just needs something to stabilize it while everything reattaches."

"Yes, sir!" Mateo called.

His large hand touched the back of my head.

"Good job, getting the hand and not her head," he whispered into my hair. "Remembered that from me, huh?"

I couldn't speak, but I tried to look up, wobbling on my feet. I would have fallen again if it wasn't for him holding me. Sammy had hit me like a truck.

"Holy shit," he said, sighing, but I wondered if I really caught panic in his expression. "Gabi, over here. She needs you."

He turned me, keeping my back to his chest. Gabrielle was in front of me now, her wings visible and too bright. They made light spots in my vision, and I groaned as I realized I was going to lose my lunch but couldn't open my mouth anymore to deal with that.

"Whoa," she whispered, reaching out to touch my face as if I was a horse that needed to be calmed. "I have you. I can fix this. It's a lot of bone, which makes everything harder, but I can fix it."

I whimpered as her fingers brushed over my jaw, then a pleasant heat washed into me. As I felt the pieces of my jaw move, it was uncomfortable but not painful, which it would be if I used any other kind of healing. Fae and witches couldn't dampen the pain from magical healing or not very well. It was retribution for the magic. Someone had to feel it, even if it wasn't the one being healed.

From the look on her face, Gabrielle didn't have that problem. She concentrated, her eyes focused on mine, but there was no sign of pain.

"She should still ice it," Gabrielle said softly, pulling her hands away when the uncomfortable sensation was over. "Swelling can still happen because the body might remember the trauma and have already started to try to fix it. Bones are like that. Soft tissue isn't nearly as problematic, but bones..."

"I've got it from here," Raphael promised behind me. "If you're up for it, check on Sammy."

"I'll see what I can do, but at least she can put it back on," Gabrielle said, disappearing from my view.

I was still dazed. Nothing hurt anymore, but my brain was still pretty rattled.

"Let's sit down," Raphael whispered into my head, his hands on my hips as he guided me to a bench along the wall.

I fell to a seat and groaned, clutching my head. I didn't try to speak, scared of testing the newly healed jaw, and my head was throbbing. Gabi healed the worst parts but left me with the aftermath, or maybe she wasn't experienced enough to stop a headache. It didn't matter.

"Can you tell me what happened? I have a feeling Sammy is going to say this was your fault," Raphael said, his arm outstretched behind me on the bench. "Mateo would tell me the truth, but Sammy would talk over him. I'll need to split them up before trying. Considering you just cut off her hand and that needs to heal, she's not going to let Mateo go far, and he won't leave her alone."

"Sounds like they're fucking," I mumbled, my words thick and slurred. Talking wasn't painful, a good thing to learn. I could work through whatever thing was causing me to slur.

"They are," he answered. "It's not serious, but they look out for each other."

I looked up at him, narrowing my eyes as best I could. He chuckled, telling me he got the message.

"Yeah, I didn't think that was important to tell you. Thought you would figure it out."

"Nope. Sammy was acting like..." I hissed as I sat up, deciding not to elaborate further. "We were arguing...sort of. She doesn't trust me because of us, because I broke our thing off, then did my own thing for a few months. She's also insulted you think she needs the training. Essentially, she was trying to scare me off. I warned her if she tried to touch me again, she would regret it. I made her regret it."

"Ah..." Raphael moved his arm from around me and rubbed his hands together. "Was that before or after she broke your face and left you staring off like you had brain damage?"

"Before," I muttered, pissed off more at myself for getting hit than I was at Sammy. "I was giving them her fucking hand and telling them they needed to get it bandaged on. She took a potshot with her remaining hand." I gritted my teeth, the action making a small pain shoot through my jaw. I rubbed it and sighed. "This is going to take a few days to get normal, isn't it?"

"It's your jaw. Lots of moving parts, teeth, which I'm amazed you didn't lose, muscles, nerve endings. Gabi is good, but that's a lot. She probably did everything she could afford to do and got you to a place where it doesn't need a doctor."

"But I still have a bit of healing to do. Got it. She still doesn't have much stamina, huh?"

"We've made some rules. She's not allowed to heal anyone to the point where she can't walk away or run if needed. While helping others is fine, when she helped that werewolf, she passed out. We would rather leave people hurting a little than see her defenseless."

"Good rule," I agreed. "So...am I fired? I cut off Sammy's hand—"

"No," Raphael answered, looking across the gym where Sammy was being tended to by Mateo and

Gabrielle. The nephilim didn't try to heal Sammy from what I could see but helped Mateo secure the hand back to Sammy's arm. The tissue would reattach, along with the blood vessels. The nerve endings would heal last, or so Raphael had once said. Sammy would be without a working hand for a day, maybe two.

"Why not?" I crossed my arms. "It'll make her mad that you won't."

"If it worries you so much, then quit," he fired back. When I didn't reply, he chuckled dryly. "See? You aren't. I probably should be madder, but you did something to her that can be fixed. It'll leave her with a scar, but I expected a few of those when you told everyone they would be trained in blades. She tried to kill you."

9

CHAPTER NINE

I started to shake my head. "No, she didn't."

"Yes," Raphael growled, leaning closer, "she did. Maybe it was rash, maybe she wasn't thinking, but she knows what she can do to someone as fragile as a human. You are. You freely admit it. While you're deadly, you're fragile, and she aimed to put you in the ground."

I swallowed, trying to scoot away from him.

"Raphael, she's not a murderer." I knew those types.

"No, she's not, but she'll make herself one if she keeps this up. It's day one, and we've already had serious injuries. So, I'm changing this up. I'm going to be at every training session you have with her. I'm even going to join in. I'm not going to let her temper get the better of her, and I'm not going to put you in the position to defend yourself again."

"She'll be furious," I pointed out.

"She'll survive. Sammy is well-meaning but aggressive and dangerous. She's not fit for society until I can get her to move past her issues. Maybe between my constant attention and your training, we might make her somewhat suitable for living with other supernaturals. As it is, she's never left here since we came, and I never let her out of Cassius' place. I sure as fuck can't send her to the Market when the time comes, which leaves Mateo as a guard for every cambion who needs to run an errand. That's not fair to him."

"No, it's not," I agreed. Raphael had put a lot of thought into this, and I was helpless to convince him of another option. I couldn't even think of one. Sammy definitely needed training so she didn't accidentally kill anyone, and she needed constant supervision from Raphael because she hated me. "Were you planning for this sort of thing?"

"No, but it's easy enough to solve." Raphael reached out and motioned for Sammy and Mateo to head in our direction. As they walked over, he looked at me again. "Take the rest of the day off. Gabi is going to need a nap after healing, so there's nothing left for you to do today." He flicked his gaze at the two cambions as they stopped in front of us, then focused on me once again. "I don't think you should drive. I'll drive you home and have someone follow us to give me a ride back."

"That's fine." I wasn't going to argue with his stony expression. Satisfied with me, he turned on Sammy and Mateo.

"If this happens again, you'll answer to me," he warned them as he stood. I took his offered hand and got to my feet but quickly pulled away once I was certain I wouldn't wobble. "I'll be coming to every training from here on out. Sammy, consider yourself lucky you didn't kill her."

I started walking to my car, not wanting to stand there while he berated them. It was a mess, and I felt guilty. I hadn't been the one to start the fight or the one pressing the issue, but none of that eased my guilt.

"Raph—"

"You know what I would do if you killed her," Raphael snarled. "You *know*. Don't *ever* make me cross that line."

I tried to ignore those words, but they hit me just as effectively as Sammy's fist had.

"Yes, sir," Sammy mumbled, almost too quiet for me to hear as I kept walking. Almost. If there had been any other noise in the gym for me to focus on, I would have been grateful. Pushing open a door, I went for the sun, catching a ray of light and letting it warm my skin.

Raphael stormed out only a moment later, his eyes on me as if I was about to get yelled at, too. After a moment, the stony expression disappeared, and he softened into the Raphael I knew. The good-natured man who had shared my home with me for months was the one who stopped beside me and closed his eyes as the sun hit his face.

"We keep the gym a bit cold, don't we?"

"Yeah. It's fine. I would say something if it was too cold."

"I noticed you changed the thermostat the last time you were here. You didn't today, so I guess I picked a good new temperature."

I eyed him. "You can't help but notice everything, can you?"

"When it comes to you?" He looked down at me, his expression honest and open. "No, I can't."

I swallowed. There were a number of ways I could approach this particular situation, but I decided avoidance was the best.

"I left all my stuff..." I pointed to the gym door.

"Anything you need tonight?" he asked, putting his hands in his pockets.

"No, it can all stay until tomorrow."

"I'll have someone put it in a locker for you," he promised, pulling out his cellphone. He typed quickly with one hand and held out his free hand. "Keys, please. I'll drive your car, so you don't have a stranger behind the wheel."

I handed them over and quickly turned to my car, regretting it as a wave of dizziness hit me. His hand touched my back, warm and stable as I tried to steady myself.

"She hit you too hard, and I'm still debating if I should kill her, so please don't fall over right in front of me. I won't be able to handle that," he murmured in my ear, helping me walk to my car. "If you're going to pass out, please do it once you're in your home and behind a closed door."

I kept my mouth firmly shut. I remembered the last time he watched someone die who he liked. There would be no forgetting that night at the lab and Maude's body on the ground. Or the demon he had shifted into and terrorized everyone. He'd nearly broken Sammy in half that night, and he'd gotten close to killing me. If he was riding that sort of temper, the only thing I could do was keep my mouth shut. It was the safest option.

I slid into the passenger's seat without his help. It took less than a minute for him to get us out of his little compound.

"I'm not completely helpless, you know," I finally said, staring out my window.

"I know you're not, which is why I hate this." His words were tight, as if he was trying to keep from growling at me. "You could have killed her, and you know it. I know it. Sammy should know it if she knows what's good for her. You're the one who decided to give her a warning instead. Even after she ignored it, you did the right thing. I bet it takes more skill to carefully cut off a hand than it does to kill someone. I bet you could have walked over to her and cut her head off before she thought to stand up and protect herself. She was in shock from losing her hand when I ran in. Instead, you were trusting enough to drop your guard and try to help her heal from the damage you did."

Raphael snarled as his cambion scent, slightly different from Sammy's, filled the car. Now that I had multiple cambions to compare, it was easy to pick out the small distinctions, or maybe it was just Raphael. I would always know him from anyone else.

"She attacked you, anyway, hit hard enough to put you on the ground. If we didn't have Gabrielle, you would be in a hospital right now as they tried to rearrange your face. You would be on a liquid diet for months."

I rubbed my jaw. Since I had no mirror, there was no

way for me to guess what I looked like when he ran in and had no idea what Gabrielle saw. From the way he was describing it, my jaw had probably been completely out of place. He was right. I had been lucky not to lose any teeth.

"So, forgive me if I'm a little pissed off and want to make sure you get home okay," he ended, the growled words sending shivers down my spine. He snarled again, and I turned to see his eyes were not their warm chocolate brown. They were red and black as he glared out the front window, his knuckles white as he held onto the steering wheel. Some tiny part of me worried he was going to bend it.

"Raph?" I frowned at him.

"Please don't quit. You're the only one I trust to teach them."

"I won't," I promised softly. I should quit, but I wouldn't, even though it was only the second day, and blood had been drawn between me and one of his most powerful cambions.

When we parked in front of my house, he got out and walked me to the door.

"I thought this would be easier," he admitted as we stopped at my front door. Someone was already there with a pickup truck, waiting to take him back.

"I didn't," I admitted in turn. "I knew this would suck, but we'll get better. It'll be fine."

"Yeah." He stepped back and looked at the truck. "I'm going to go. Don't sleep for a few hours. Take something if—"

"I know," I said, trying to smile. He waved awkwardly

then walked to the truck, jumping in the back instead of getting in like a normal person. He hit the roof, and the driver hit the gas.

Walking into my house alone, the silence bothered me, but I ignored it. I went to turn on some music and tried to shake the feeling from Raphael's words. What he said to Sammy shook me to my core. My imagination was pretty good at filling in the pieces.

The idea Raphael would kill one of his cambions over me wasn't something I was comfortable with.

I walked to my bedroom, slowly stripping as I went. With a clean house, I had new floor space to throw clothing that I could get in the wash later. My eyesight was still a little blurry, so I resigned myself to stay awake until that annoying blurriness was gone. By the time I made it past my bed into my bathroom, I was completely naked. I hadn't realized I had Sammy's blood on me until I had felt it on my pants.

Turning on blistering hot water, I got under the water and sighed as steam rose up around me. As I watched the steam curl around, I thought about Sammy, replaying what had happened in the gym. I had moved when I realized Sammy was going to attack. I had started pulling out of the way. She had been aiming for a much more dangerous spot. If she had nailed me in the temple, I would have dropped dead right there.

Putting my hand over my chest, I finally realized exactly what Raphael was pissed about. This hadn't been a cheap shot. She had tried to kill me. In the heat of the moment, pissed off, it didn't matter. She had gone for a killing hit, which would have blown my fucking skull open all over the gym mat. Gabrielle probably wouldn't have been able to heal that.

As I soaked in the shower, my security's alarm went off, and this time, I recognized it for the simple alarm, telling me someone authorized was coming in.

I left the shower slowly and looked at myself in the mirror before getting dressed to meet whoever walked straight into my house. Only three people did that, and one of them had just dropped me off. That meant I was dealing with Cassius or Sorcha, possibly both.

"Kaliya!" Cassius yelled into my room, muffled thanks to the bathroom door. "Raphael called and said you got hurt today. I wanted to check on you."

"You could have called," I replied, pulling on sweats and a tank top. When I walked out, my wet hair wrapped up, he was standing in the doorway, his hand still on the doorknob. His eyes were filled with concern I knew was genuine.

"I could have," he agreed. "But Raphael said you took a hard hit to the head. No sleeping and all that."

I groaned, wiping my face with my towel as I kicked away the bra I had dumped on the floor.

"It was an interesting day," I admitted.

"Yeah, you've had a few of those, haven't you? Just two days ago, we came in and cleaned your whole house. Are you sure you want to do this? I can always call him and tell him you won't be going back. Near-death experiences aren't what you signed up for."

I snorted. Cassius and I had a complicated relationship or post-relationship. We were quick to give each other a hard time and call each other out on our problems, but we were just as quick to kill someone for each other.

"It's fine. He's going to stand by for future training sessions." I threw the towel into the bathroom. "Sorcha here with you?"

"No. She's a little upset with you over yesterday," he answered, leaning on the frame, his hair falling over his eyes as he got this boyish, "you know what you did" smile. "Plus, she figured it was best if only one of us bothered you after you took one to the head. Raphael made it seem worse. What happened?"

"Sammy tried to kill me," I answered, shrugging. "I mean, I cut off her hand, so it was fair." I walked by him as he sputtered.

"What?"

I quickly explained as I went into the kitchen, letting him try to keep up with me. It was a short story, nothing too complicated—overprotective feelings, rash tempers, and me not trying hard enough to deescalate the situation. I could have tried harder, but I hadn't, and it got violent. In my favor, I hadn't started the violence, only tried to put an end to it. As I finished, I waved over my face.

"Everything still feels a bit weird, but Gabrielle did a good job putting me back together. I already checked in the mirror."

"Yeah..." Cassius sighed, shaking his head. "Are you sure you want to keep doing this? If this is day two..."

I thought about Raphael, what he had said, and how his temper had threatened to break over my being hurt on his turf. From here on out, he would make sure I was completely safe in the cambion compound. And I had promised him I wouldn't quit.

"Yeah, I'm going back tomorrow," I said softly.

"Okay." Cassius sat down and pulled out a pack of cards from his pocket, shuffling like an expert dealer in Vegas. "When was the last time we played cards? It'll give you something to do until we know it's safe for you to sleep."

"Ages ago," I answered. "Remember when we were staking out Nakul? I think I was the one who busted out the cards that time."

"I do." He chuckled as I sat across from him with a glass of water and two pills to help with my looming headache. As I took the pills, he began dealing. Once I put the water down, he met my gaze. "If anything else happens there, you'll let me know, right? You should have called me this time, but I'll forgive you. But next time, you *will* call me."

"Sure." I wasn't up to arguing with the former prince.

"I'll get you out of there, and no one will be able to stop me," he continued. "Just let me know."

"Cassius..."

"I don't care if he's your mate. You don't want him, and you shouldn't have to put up with bullies who follow him. There was a reason I put off telling you he had a job offer, Kaliya. I will always be more loyal to you than I am to him."

"I'll be fine," I promised softly, swallowing my shock. "It's not like he sent Sammy after me. I think he's having a hard time controlling her. She's all pride and power with no off switch. That's what we need to teach her."

"You better be fine," he said gently, leaning forward. "Or I'm going to remind Raphael's cambions, he might be a warlord, but I'm a prince of the fae, and I have all the power that goes along with it."

I checked my cards, trying to keep my poker face. It wasn't often Cassius swore to use all his power. Even in our most dangerous situations, he actively avoided doing that, knowing the risks he would present himself. He was easily drained in our world, thanks to his nature as a pure fae, meant to remain in the fae realms. Cassius wasn't a risk-taker, not like that. He would rather do something with more physical effort than rely on his powers.

Well, I'll need to try harder to make this work. The last thing we need is a diplomatic incident between the cambions and the fae.

10

CHAPTER TEN

I did my best to keep my head down after that. The incident with Sammy made Gabrielle stay close since she realized I was the one most likely to need her when I was on the compound. She was at every training, asking me if I needed anything, like a personal assistant I couldn't shake. She only left me alone when Raphael showed up. He didn't hover as much, but his presence was like a weight, which kept everyone from losing their tempers again.

Sammy was quiet when he was around. Her hand was fine in only four days. Once it was cleared for use again, I put a sword in it and taught her how to hack things up the same way I did to her hand. Mateo was better with guns, preferring the long-range kill. Working on their strengths gave them more confidence right off the bat and showed them I wanted to make them better, not worse, or show off.

Raphael and I sparred when they didn't need me. He was getting better, too, and I wondered how much he practiced in his off time. It didn't help that I was constantly distracted by him, covered in sweat. His shirts clung to him like he was in a wet t-shirt contest, which did bad things to me. But that was life. My heart wasn't palpitating because of the physical exertion. It was purely him.

"That's everything for today!" I called out to Sammy and Mateo as they grappled on the mat. I gave them a free thirty minutes at the end of every training to do what they wanted while I commented. "Sammy, good job using your speed on Mateo. He's bigger, bulkier, and I like that you use that to your advantage. Mateo, I want you to start trying to anticipate her more. She has speed, but you can overcome that by changing up your own moves or realizing what her favorite things are. Every fighter has a tick, something they like doing or a tell that gives away their next move. If you're fighting someone repeatedly, you'll start to catch those things."

"Okay." Mateo got off the mat, nodding. "Do you think we could sit down and pick out what sort of equipment we should keep for emergencies?"

"Well, it's Friday..." I crossed my arms, thinking about it. "We can set aside time on Monday. I know you want to look at sniper rifles. I don't own any, but I know where we can look at some, where you can get your hands on them and see what feels the best." I looked at the blonde. "Do you want to come? I know where you can find some sharp objects. I want you both trained in everything, but it's always nice to pick a favorite weapon to focus on in your free time. Mateo can practice his aim in the desert, and we can find you something."

"Yeah, that sounds cool," Sammy mumbled, looking at her shoes.

"Hey, Sammy, she's offering to spend her money on you. Look up and answer her," Raphael said with a growl. I elbowed him in the gut before sending him a glare. I didn't need him getting on to her for everything. That was the only problem with this situation. Every time Sammy wasn't on her best behavior, he was there to snap at her. It wasn't like him.

Or maybe it is. He's not exactly the man I knew anymore.

She looked up, sighing heavily.

"Yeah, I'll go. Thank you," she said, meeting my gaze.

"Awesome. Raphael, the others won't have training on Monday. I'll take these two to the Market and give everyone else a three-day weekend. They were great this week, so they've earned it."

"I'll let everyone know," he promised, rubbing his stomach where I nailed him. "You two can go. Good work today."

"Thanks, boss," Sammy said, turning on her heel and walking out.

Once she and Mateo were gone, I turned to him.

"You can't do that to her," I hissed, glaring at Raphael.

"What I do and don't do with Sammy isn't really your business," he retorted, turning away. "She nearly killed you. She's going to respect you. Mateo got with the program, so she can too."

"Raph, you can't talk to her like that," I said with as much strength as I could muster, trying to make him realize it was inappropriate. "You'll undermine her and hurt what I'm trying to build. I'm asking them to learn to effectively kill people and have mercy when they can, to think when they fight instead of relying on their emotions. If you're messing with her, I'm going to kick you out of these trainings. I can't have her always questioning herself."

He sighed, shaking his head slowly as he walked to a bench and fell onto it. We were waiting on Gabrielle, who wouldn't show up for an hour. It gave me time to take a break and drink some water after training with the two warriors.

"I'll watch my words," he said, not looking at me.

"Really?" I wasn't sure if I believed him, but something was bugging him. There was no way he spoke to her like normal.

"Yeah."

"What's going on?"

"She nearly killed you," he answered simply, offering nothing else. The words left the same sinking feeling in my gut as when I heard him talking to Sammy the day we fought. I sat down beside him but kept as much space as I could between us.

I wasn't inept. It didn't take a rocket scientist to realize he still had feelings for me. Most days, he pretended as though nothing was between us, but sometimes, he acted as if we were still at my house. I knew habits were hard to break, and four months wasn't long enough for those things to disappear. There was a reason Cassius had stayed away for so long after we broke it off.

Since I didn't know how to respond, I went for silence, accepting he wasn't going to leave. I needed him for Gabrielle's training, so there was no point leaving and coming back unless something was going on with the construction.

The nephilim walked in, wearing simple yoga pants, tennis shoes, and a white tank. Her dark skin practically shone with her power, and her white wings radiated light. Her light brown eyes flicked between us as she came closer. I didn't move as she stopped and crossed her arms.

"Is everything okay?" she asked.

"Perfectly fine," I promised. "We're just tired from the Sammy and Mateo training session, as usual. Raphael, want to start off the training?"

He turned and grinned, our previous talk forgotten for a moment. He rushed the nephilim and grabbed her.

Gabrielle's training was easy and effective. I had Raphael pick her up and try to drag her off, always pretending she was in the same situation. She wasn't very good at anything, and it always took her a few attempts to get the courage to fight back, but it was better than nothing. I rooted for her, throwing out tips and tricks every time we ran through the scenario, hoping she would remember them in the heat of the moment.

Here we go for another day of wondering whether this will stick.

Two hours in, I wiped the sweat off my face and sighed. Gabrielle was hitting Raphael on the face, and he was pretending as though it wasn't even happening. Mind you, she was just open palm slapping him as if it was going to do anything.

"Use a fist and punch him, Gabi!" I yelled from across the gym. "Fuck," I mumbled under my breath, jogging over as she gave the most half-hearted punch I had ever seen. "Let her go," I ordered, waving Raphael off.

Raphael released her, rolling his eyes. "Sorry, Kaliya. Should I act—"

"Sorry about this," I said quickly, throwing my best right hook at his face. With surprise on my side and the fact my right hook was well-practiced, I sent Raphael back into the wall. Before he had the chance to say anything, I pointed at him as I turned on the nephilim. "Like that. Hit him. He'll be fine. This is why we're using him. He knows how to take a hit, and he'll heal. There's no way you can hit him as hard as I can, but do your worst, Gabi."

Her eyes were wide as she stared at me, then her eyes moved to Raphael.

Before I noticed what he was doing, too exasperated with her, he grabbed me from behind and threw me over his shoulder with a snarl.

"Give her a real demonstration," he taunted, holding my thighs as I dangled over his shoulder. His warm hands didn't drive terror into my heart, though. My first inclination was to let him drag me off like a caveman to his cave, which would hopefully have a bed.

"And no snake," he snapped, hitting my ass. That shocked me, and lust ran through me as I realized no one had touched me there on purpose in months, and it was *him*. "She can't do that. Fight back and show her how it's really done." He pinched me, which shoved through the unintentional lust and forced me into action.

I made a fist, then covered it with my other hand. I brought both down on his lower back as hard as I could, earning me a grunt as he arched, trying to handle the pain. When it didn't take him down, I squirmed, kicking my legs and trying to go further over his shoulder. If I had to land on my head, that's what I had to do. I scratched my nails over his back then grew frustrated as I watched those claw marks heal.

"Cheater," I hissed.

"I'll pretend they're still there," he answered over his shoulder. He gave a fake stumble and the most unenthusiastic "ouch" I had ever heard. I squirmed harder, but his grip was tight. Unbreakably tight. He was giving this his full power, something he wasn't supposed to do for Gabi. For her, he needed to build her confidence.

He was making me work for it.

When I hit him again, I aimed for his kidneys. This time, I got a groan of real pain, and he tilted. I swung one of my feet down, hopefully shoving my toe in his balls, full steel-toed boot and all. He was forced to move to catch it, which was enough space for me to swing my weight and slide over his shoulder. I rolled as he cursed and turned to grab me again. When he finally reached me, I was able to fight back.

"Try me," I taunted, bouncing on the balls of my feet. "Cheater."

He lifted his hands in mock defeat and looked over my head.

"Like that, Gabi. Don't be afraid to hurt someone. We can't keep working past this every time we train. You need to fight, and you have to start doing it the moment someone puts their hands on you."

I smiled at him as I listened to Gabi's soft, mumbling reply about not wanting to hurt people.

"You can go," he said, waving. I listened to her run out and the soft click of the gym door as she retreated.

"I wonder how much of it is because she's a nephilim and how much conditioning she had in the lab," I pondered as I walked to my bag. "Angels aren't non-violent like she is. They're beings of divine power and retribution. One of the reasons they appeal to humans so much is they're an intelligent species with strict guidelines of morality, and they make sure people follow those guidelines with power and destruction."

"I know. I've been doing some research. After everything that happened, I was able to get back into the archives, and the librarian gave me all they had on demons and angels. From what I know, thanks to Mygi, that one guy was right. Angels and demons are like fae, with complete civilizations on another plane. The fae have permanently open portals, but the others don't. We need to let them in, or they find a way in. From what some believe, there could be hundreds of side worlds with other beings. It's all a bit much for me." He ran a hand through his hair as he stopped next to me. "To answer your question, I think it's conditioning. I think they realized she could heal and raised her to be soft, so they could use her."

"It would make sense. Make her feel like she's too weak to do anything more. I bet she has some offensive powers we haven't seen yet, but..." I groaned. "I don't ever want to put her in the situation that would call those out. Someone could get killed."

"Yeah, and we wouldn't want that to happen again."

"Sammy has been behaving," I pointed out, a response to the guilt in his voice. I grabbed my bag and started walking, knowing he was going to follow me to my car. "She's been fine, regardless if you think she's rude. You made the right call, deciding to stand by for the training. Just don't overstep and undermine her. It's helped me with Gabrielle as well. She can beat you up, and you won't feel it the next day. That will hopefully keep easing her guilt about hurting someone."

"I'm glad I've been helpful." He stopped me from opening the gym door, and I turned to him, patiently waiting for what else he wanted to say. "It's Friday, and I've been debating asking you this all week. Do you want to come for our weekend cookout? Wagner is coming by, so are Cassius and Sorcha. It's a big get-together, fun for everyone."

"What's the special occasion?" I tilted my head, curious. I would say yes to good food, and it would let me talk to the cambions outside of training. I needed a better rapport with them to make training even more effective, and a barbecue was a great idea.

"There isn't one. We do this every couple of weeks to feed the werewolves and fae who have been building. They've only been getting one day off a week, and there're rotating teams. We're just giving back to them for working so hard." Raphael leaned on the door over me, his broad chest most of what I could see. To him, it probably seemed natural, but to me, a man was trying to look good, even if it was a subconscious effort. And he looked *good*. "I'd like you to come. Consider it an apology meal for what happened last week with Sammy."

"I'll come," I answered, stepping back until I hit the door and leaned against it. My fangs ached brutally at the sight and smell of him, too close for comfort and without the adrenaline of training to help me focus on something else. "I don't need an apology. Shit happens, and we're both as good as new."

"Are we?" he asked, leaning down a little, taking a half step closer.

"I think we're talking about different things," I said, moving out of his space and stepping to the side. As I moved, his eyes tracked me with a gaze I was used to.

"No, we're not," he replied, moving to grab the door handle and pushed it open for me. I went out first, trying to get to the fresh air. He followed me to my car, now parked in the official parking lot instead of haphazardly next to the gym. He'd gotten onto me a few days into the job, and I had agreed to park in the correct place and stop speeding past the security building to annoy the cambion stationed there. Poor David was always hitting the emergency button when he didn't need to, thanks to me, and only four days in, it had annoyed Raphael.

"Drive safely," Raphael said gently, leaning on my car as I threw my bag into the back.

"I always do," I mumbled, closing the trunk. "Go on. I'm sure there's a meal waiting on you, and you love your food. I'll be here tomorrow at..."

"Noon works," he said with the smile I liked so much.

"Noon it is," I agreed. "Be nice to Sammy. Forgive her.

We all make mistakes, Raphael. Trust me. I'm a master at them."

I'm staring at one of them right now.

He slowly nodded, then backed away from my car, letting me open the driver's side door.

"See you tomorrow," he said, closing me in my car once I was in the seat. Then he was gone, walking off to talk to the werewolves as they finished their day.

I took my chance to get out of there, trying not to think about the strange hot-and-cold relationship we had now.

11

CHAPTRER ELEVEN

I woke up screaming, as I did most mornings in recent days. My katana was already in my hand, ready to cut open an attacker and protect me. My hands were shaking, and I was covered in sweat as I came out of the night terror.

When my family had been killed, I had been weaponless, a child who was told to run, and run I did, but not fast enough. I had lingered too long. Not long enough to get caught, but long enough to give me the visceral nightmares that refused to stop plaguing me. I had been over them for years, but one face stood out over the rest. I always remembered him now, how he shoved a sword into my mother's chest.

Fuck. I need to get moving. At least when I'm at the compound, I'm not thinking about this.

I scrambled out of my bed, which felt too large and too empty now. I didn't let go of the katana until I was at my shower and the water was on. I didn't bother looking at the time until I was ready to go and saw it was just past eleven. If I drove slowly, I could get there on time without looking like I was trying too hard to get there early. I realized I was early when there were no other cars parked at the compound. I checked the clock on my dash before I looked around. I was right on time.

He'd said noon. Where is everyone?

I got out slowly, frowning as I saw no one else around. It was a little disconcerting, to say the least, as I locked up my BMW and walked toward the gym, wondering if I could find anyone working out on their days off. I didn't care who I found as long as said person had answers.

"Kaliya!" Gabrielle called. "Raphael said you would be coming soon. I was supposed to meet you. Sorry, I'm late." She ran up, stopping right beside me, looping her arm in mine. For a young woman who hated violence, she enjoyed touching others; the simple, friendly touch I wasn't used to and didn't like all that much. It was too personal, too friendly, and I barely knew her or anyone else at the compound outside of training.

"Where is everyone? He said there would be lots of people here." I gently tried to take my arm away, but she didn't realize it.

"Oh, we actually start in an hour. That's why I'm late to get you."

"He said noon," I grumbled, letting her drag me once I knew there was no escape. I was going where she wanted, and that was that. I was going to be a good guest —even if it killed me.

Apparently, I had missed part of Raphael's tour. Gabrielle took me behind the houses to a makeshift park. Tables were set out under a pavilion, and two grills were already on, Raphael manning one and another cambion, Stephan, manning the other. I didn't know Stephan all that well. He came to training, did as I asked, worked hard, then left. Aside from those two, there weren't many there yet. Mateo was setting up another foldout table with Sammy while Cole carried paper plates and disposable silverware from one of the houses. My eyes went back to Raphael, enjoying the view of his shirtless chest as he concentrated on whatever was cooking in front of him.

"Kaliya is here!" Gabi announced, pulling me into everyone's view and proverbially pointing a spotlight at me.

"Don't drag her around," Raphael said, looking up from the grill. "She doesn't like to be touched that much."

She let go of me quickly, looking aghast as she turned. I wrenched my eyes off the shirtless Raphael and met her gaze.

"I'm so sorry," she said softly.

"It's fine. I would have said something if it was really bothering me. If I wanted to make it stop, it would have," I said with a tight smile. "No harm, no foul."

She didn't believe me. She walked away to sit with Jessie and Laura, two more cambions. I went to Raphael, keeping my eyes on his face and avoiding the expansive, defined chest that made my mouth water and my fangs ache.

"Noon?" I said innocently as I waved around.

"I wanted you to have time with just us. Go sit and get to know them," he answered, not looking up from what he was doing. "They've wanted to get to know you."

I looked at the cambions meandering about, then back at Raphael, arching an eyebrow.

"Oh?" I said sweetly. "Do they?"

He looked over my head and narrowed his eyes. "They better."

I left him, putting the pieces together quickly. He wanted me to feel *welcomed*, to feel like I was part of the *community*. I didn't want to think about his purpose for this apparent ploy. It was just a piece of a puzzle that meant I would need to have a long conversation with him soon.

As I sat down at a random empty table, Cole sat down across from me, a cautious smile on his face.

"He's not lying," Cole said, leaning in. "You helped save us, and most of us haven't forgotten that. You just aren't...easy to approach."

"Yeah, I get that a lot," I mumbled, looking down at my hands on the table for a moment before smiling up at him. "I'm a busy woman."

"Yeah, I bet. So, uh, how ya been?"

"Good," I lied. *Terrible. Missing your leader. Going insane, though that's getting better. Having something else to do was what I needed to keep from losing my mind.*

"Um..."

"Why don't I ask the questions?" I offered, laughing and hoping it didn't sound fake. "From the sound of things, you've really become attached to modern technology. Have you gotten a computer yet?"

"I've already built one," he said, his expression turning bright and excited. "And I'm working with the werewolves to set up the camera security system around our new home."

"That's awesome. I'm glad you've found something to be passionate about. Let me know if you want a second opinion. I know my way around some security systems." I had become too practical to get excited about new tech, but it was nice to see someone who could still appreciate it. "How do you like my desert?"

"You know, when Raphael said we were moving to Arizona and the desert, I was really confused, but I get why he likes it out here. It doesn't feel so cold." His eyes grew distant for a moment.

"The lab was cold, wasn't it?"

"Yeah, they kept it really cold." He nodded before ducking his head, his eyes flashing red and black. His cambion scent filled the air for a moment before the breeze took it away. "We're really warm compared to humans, so when they were comfortable, we wanted to bundle up in blankets."

They weren't given enough blankets.

"Well, it'll get a little chilly over the winter if you like it hot like me, but don't worry. Most of the year, we're over eighty during the day, and you'll have everything you could want to bundle up at night."

"Yeah, Raphael promised that, too," he said with a small smile, the peek at his cambion nature gone. "So... you've been training us, and we both know I like computers and stuff. Do you like fighting? Is it your hobby?"

"No," I answered softly, this time hit with the hard

question. "It's not about liking it or not liking it. It's about necessity."

"Oh..." Cole slumped. "Do you have any hobbies?"

"Not really," I admitted. "I do what I have to because my survival depends on it. The survival of people I care about depends on it. Like the cambions, we nagas aren't that many. While you're a new species, we used to be several hundred strong. Now, there's a handful of us left. I'm the only one who lives a public life, and I needed to be strong if I wanted to live freely instead of stuck on a compound."

"Like us," he said, putting his elbows on the table. "Raphael said there was some stuff going on with you, but...I guess I didn't realize. You seem so strong as if you could take on the world and come out on top."

"Ha, I wish. It's the reality of things. Sometimes, we do things we don't like because we have to. If it's better for everyone, I put my own wants to the side and keep moving. Protecting my people is more important to me than anything, including my own happiness." The last year, something shifted in me, and it was all because of Raphael. Now, it wasn't that I didn't want a mate; I couldn't risk it. I wanted him, sometimes more than I could breathe. I could see him over Cole's shoulder, watching us. Our eyes met for a moment, then I looked back at Cole, hoping Raphael got the message. "So, no hobbies for me, barely a social life. Some friends that are willing to deal with me."

"I...I thought you were so cool, but you sound kind of sad," Cole admitted, his face showing me everything. He pitied me, felt bad for my life, was now awkwardly trying to find a way to change the subject. "I'm sorry, that was rude. Um..."

"It's fine," I promised. "It's just the reality of my life. I'm over a hundred years old, Cole. You don't need to feel bad for me. I accepted the state of my life a long time ago. I made some mistakes I couldn't afford to make more than once and got with the program."

"Why are there so few...nagas left?" He stumbled over the word 'nagas,' as if he was still unsure about it, hoping he got it right.

"Someone is trying to drive us to extinction. You don't need to know more than that. Let's just say, there are a few people and different species around the world who completely understand what you cambions are going through, kind of. We know what it means to be the only holdout for a species, hoping no one comes after us and wins. That's why I took this job and offered to help."

He nodded, then looked around. "I'm... uh...going to..."

I waved him away and enjoyed the silence when he left. I had been more open with him than I should have been, but they wanted to know me. I could see other cambions hovering around, tilting their heads as if they were trying to catch the conversation, and one of them was just plain staring. I looked at Raphael again, giving him an annoyed look.

Really? You couldn't tell them more? I know I explained all of this to you, and it's not like it's a secret. Everyone in the supernatural world who knows my name knows why I'm like this.

I rubbed my temples, and Gabrielle was at my side again.

"Do you have a headache? I can—"

"I'm fine," I said quickly. "Experiencing some oversharing regret."

She plopped down in the seat next to me. "You know you can tell us anything, right? I know most of us would die for you after you helped free us."

I was concerned I couldn't tell if she was exaggerating.

"She's kidding," Sammy growled, taking Cole's seat across from me. "I wouldn't die for you."

"I said *most*," Gabi retorted.

"I wouldn't let anyone else die for her, either," Sammy retorted, then a growl filled the space, louder than any of the quiet conversations going on. Sammy rolled her eyes. "Sorry. I..."

"You know what?" I crossed my arms and put them on the table, leaning forward. In a whisper, I offered an idea. "Why don't you and I pretend to like each other? It's easier than dealing with him."

Sammy snorted. "You mean pretend as though we're buddy-buddies until he gets off my back?"

"Yes." I nodded. "I asked him yesterday to stop giving you a hard time, but I can always make that message a little clearer. Or...we just give him what he wants, and he'll eventually move on. Then neither of us needs to deal with that, and I won't have to defend you after you try to kill me again."

Sammy's lips twitched, then a small smile formed.

"You know, it would stop if you gave him what he

wanted," the warrior said mysteriously, but again, I could put two and two together.

"Sometimes, people need to give up what makes them happy to protect the ones they care about."

Her eyes narrowed, and I could see she was beginning to put the pieces together.

"Monday?" she asked softly.

"Yeah, I'll explain on Monday." *And maybe you and I might finally find some common ground.*

She nodded and settled in, ready to be my constant companion for the cookout. As we enjoyed the companionable silence, Gabrielle grew more and more confused.

"What did I miss?" she asked, frowning between us.

"Two women learning to understand each other," Sammy answered.

12

CHAPTER TWELVE

Cassius and Sorcha showed up fifteen minutes early for the cookout, and behind them, the other fae arrived as if they had been waiting on the two nobles. Right after them, nearly fifty werewolves arrived, and I realized why Raphael and Stephan had started cooking so early.

Right as the werewolves were arriving, I watched as Raphael disappeared into his home, then came back out with a shirt. As I stood up to make space and greet Cassius and Sorcha, the people I didn't know flooded the pavilion.

"Hey," I greeted. I hadn't seen either of them since Cassius had come by my place. We texted infrequently, but I hadn't asked Sorcha to go out for drinks with me since I had stormed out on her. When she took my hand, I met her moon-grey eyes and gave a tentative smile. "Are we going to be good?" I asked softly. "I'm sorry—"

She lifted a hand, all class and dignity, in one simple gesture. "I don't know what you're talking about. You're my best friend. There's never anything wrong between us."

"Okay."

She wrapped her arm with mine, and we walked away from the growing crowd, Cassius following us quietly.

"How have things been here?" she asked as we got some space.

"Good. Everyone has behaved, and I just had an interesting conversation with Sammy. Why the show? I know you're mad at me."

"Wagner is here, and we don't want him to think we are anything except a united front," Cassius explained. "He's been posturing to make the cambions his allies, but we have the better claim since we actually helped the cambions and know Raphael. I think his real goal is Gabrielle on his speed dial."

"No one uses speed dial anymore," I commented. "But I get it. We need to be Raphael's best friends, so Wagner doesn't think he can slide in and become his *only* friend."

"Exactly. So, we can't have any problems between us," Sorcha said with a tight smile. "And I'm not mad at you. I'm mad at how you think, the way your mind works. It annoys me sometimes. Sometimes, Cassius annoys me, too, yet I married him less than a year ago. That doesn't mean I don't like you anymore."

"Of course," I agreed, nodding as I let her explain away the way we had left each other. "Are you annoyed with my mind and Cassius right now?"

"Yes," she snapped. "But they don't need to know that, so we're going to keep smiling and pretending like we're the best of friends, and we'll do anything for Raphael, so we don't need Wagner hanging around. Because all of those things are true."

"Let me guess, you're only here to stake your claim and chase off the dog before he pees on your fire hydrant."

Her hand on my forearm grew tighter, and her nails threatened to sink into my skin. Sorcha was still smiling, but I watched as her glamour slipped and her human teeth became those of a predator. There was something feral and dangerous in Sorcha, thanks to how she became a fae, I had to do my best never to forget about.

"I like barbecues," she said, her false voice telling me this was not her scene.

"Of course, you do," I said mildly, not completely terrified. Fear was a healthy response to whatever Sorcha was.

"I really do like barbecues," Cassius said. "I offered to come alone, but Sorcha wanted to make sure she attended and got what she wanted."

"Oh, politics," I mumbled. "Fun."

"You're going to help me get what I want," she said, her smile returning to sweet and human.

"Actually, I'm here to get to know the cambions better. I want to build a relationship with them because our training will only get more dangerous, and they need to know me a bit better before they trust me to take them to those limits." I gently pulled my arm away from Sorcha. "I am not getting into politics between werewolves, fae, and cambions. You'll notice, nagas are not part of that equation."

She kept a single clawed hand wrapped around my arm.

"You'll help because you don't want Wagner poaching everything we've already built for these cambions, and you know we would never abuse them. Werewolves are a violent species, always fighting over pack structure and power. Wagner could use them to help him bring other packs in line. We're not going to allow that."

"And you wouldn't use them like that to keep power among the fae?" I retorted, being brutally honest with her. "You and Cassius are two of the most politically powerful fae around. He's the son of a prior king, and you…" I waved at her with my free hand. "I'll remind you, I broke things off with Raphael to keep him *out* of my problems."

"No, we wouldn't, and you know us better than that," Cassius said, reaching out to detach his wife from my arm. "He's a good friend, and they're vulnerable to people like Wagner. He will smile to their faces and use them the first chance he can. We were here when Gabrielle healed that werewolf. You didn't see the hunger on his face."

"Fine," I relented. "What do you want me to do?"

"Keep Raphael away from him, keep him busy. If Wagner tries anything, remind him Raphael has plenty of allies. Why would he align with the werewolves when he doesn't need the witches and vampires? He already has the fae and you." Sorcha took my hand and patted it. "Thank you."

"It's not for you," I mumbled. The idea of Gabrielle becoming a political pawn was why I wanted to train her to protect herself. Raphael being stuck in fights he had no business being in was exactly why I left him. If I had to protect him from everyone else, I was willing to do that. I would do it for all of them. "But you're welcome, I guess."

She laughed and threaded our arms again, leading me back to the pavilion. I noticed Wagner was trying to talk to Raphael, but my mate was only looking at me across the crowd. He was probably wondering why I wandered off with the fae, but Cassius and Sorcha were my two best friends, so it wasn't much of a mystery.

"Raphael!" Sorcha called. "You didn't tell us that you invited Kaliya this weekend!"

"Well, this was the first chance I had, and I only asked her yesterday," Raphael replied, smiling and turned, ignoring Wagner without considering how that would work out. "I'm glad she came."

"Ah, Kaliya," Wagner said softly, turning to see me. He was a big man, the werewolf Alpha of Phoenix. "Good to see you again."

"Good to see you too." *Not.* "How's Wes?"

"He's...the same, but we have him comfortable, and now he has a few others who survived the lab to keep him company. I'm glad you ask about him. Good to see you still care about the job you don't do."

I gave him a brittle smile. "So, you know I'm on hiatus."

"Everyone in Phoenix does. It's important to know the Executioner, who is supposed to keep our streets clean of criminals, is not active," he replied, leaning on the table behind him. "Heard you're training the cambions in self-defense now. You're a bit overqualified for the job, aren't you?"

"They're friends of mine," I reminded him. Kind of, but he didn't need to know about how tense it was between Raphael and me. "And I like the busy work."

"I'm sensing some hostility here," Sorcha interjected. "Is something the matter, Alpha? Kaliya is a prominent member of the Phoenix supernatural community, works directly for the Tribunal, *and* is a leader of her species. Of course, she would be willing to help the new arrivals. She did, in fact, help free them and bring them here, which I'm sure you already know."

"Oh, yes, I know," he said with a toothy smile. "I was just in the middle of a conversation with Raphael that was interrupted."

"Raphael, do you want us to go and let you finish this?" She pointed between them.

"Wagner, you can talk in front of them. It's fine," Raphael said easily, a small smile playing on his lips. I had to work to keep my eyes off them. "We were talking about security measures. Wagner was offering a few wolves to stay here full time to manage my security."

"That would break Cole's heart," I said softly, shaking my head. "You can manage with what you have."

"That's what I was saying," Raphael agreed. "I mean, you manage on your own, and Cassius manages with a skeleton staff and Sorcha. I think my cambions can manage here."

"Yes, but none of them are protecting the world's only nephilim who can work miracles," Wagner retorted, eyeing Raphael as if he was sizing up the cambion warlord.

Oh no, you don't, Wagner. Don't get greedy now.

"Good point, but Gabrielle has the choice to leave. They're not going to hold her hostage, or let anyone else do it," I fired back. "She deserves a normal life. That doesn't mean locking her away. They'll be fine. I've seen the cambions fight. Anyone stupid enough to try to abduct Gabrielle better be ready to die."

"And you're teaching them self-defense," Wagner growled. "If they needed those lessons, then they're vulnerable right now."

"I'm not only teaching them self-defense," I whispered, stepping closer to him to keep my voice down. I didn't want to scare people. This was between the rulers in the circle, no one else. "Mostly, I'm teaching them how not to kill people when they get into a fight. Consider that the next time you try to make a judgment on their abilities. I've watched them roll through a lab like a wave of death, killing everything in their wake. I saw witches dropped and torn to pieces, unable to defend themselves from the onslaught. They don't need your werewolves. And while you might not respect me personally, you do respect my professional opinion. There it is."

"Thanks, Kaliya," Raphael said gently, reaching out to pull me away from the Alpha. "For sticking up for us. We've got it, Wagner. I trust my cambions."

"Certainly," the Alpha said, nodding briskly. "I'm going to go enjoy the food, then. We'll talk about the next phase of construction on Monday."

"Of course," Raphael agreed.

We let the werewolf Alpha wander off. While he disappeared, Sorcha also pulled a disappearing act, leaving me with my exes.

"Well, this isn't awkward at all," I muttered, stepping away from them. "I'm going to find something to eat."

"I'll come with you to make sure you get the good stuff before it's all taken," Raphael declared, moving quickly to guide me through the crowd. I cast a desperate glance back at Cassius and watched him sigh. He started to follow but only made it a single step before his wife reappeared and grabbed him. Her smile told me I was where she wanted, while Cassius looked a little upset about the situation.

"Right here," Raphael said, leading me to a table and forcing me to pull my eyes off the fae, who were now engaged in a very hushed conversation I couldn't begin to discern. "We have turkey burgers, pulled pork, chicken. You name a meat, we've probably cooked it. And sides. Potato salad and other general fixings." He paused. "I mean, there's beef, too, but...I figured I've never seen you eat it, and I know..." He was stumbling now, something I never really saw until recently. He was normally pretty easygoing, but now he was stumbling over his words.

I looked over the table and saw Stephan standing proudly behind it. No one else came for anything while Raphael stood next to me. I looked back at Raphael and chuckled.

"I am not classically Hindu like a human would be..." I said carefully. "But thank you for thinking about my possible dietary needs. I avoid beef. If it's the only option, I'll eat it, but thank you." His smile was everything I ever wanted it to be. I turned back to Stephan. "I'll take a chicken sandwich."

He made it for me, then handed it over, letting me

deal with my own sides. Raphael stuck to my side, making his own plate. This wasn't the only food table, which meant Wagner was getting something to eat somewhere else. It was a smart move and kept the crowd from rushing one table and spread everyone out a bit more. There had to be seventy-five people. I looked around as I carried my full plate, wondering where to sit. The fae were sticking together, and so were the werewolves. The cambions were in the middle, talking to each side, mingling a little more. This was their home, and they had to put on a good show and make friends. From the looks of it, they already had relationships with several people in attendance.

Raphael pointed to an empty table outside the pavilion in the sun. It was empty because no one wanted to sit in the sun and so far from the food. It wasn't the only table, but it was empty, and I would take it.

13

CHAPTER THIRTEEN

I went first and took a seat that let me see the get-together Raphael had planned.

"You've been acting strange," I accused the moment we were out of earshot from everyone watching the party. Raphael sat next to me, always keeping his eyes on the crowd, but as the host of this event, I knew it was important for him to keep an eye on everything.

"Have I?"

"Yeah, you have," I snapped. "I don't know the Raphael you are now. This..." I waved at the cookout. "This isn't what I thought you would be doing or how you would act when it was all over with Mygi."

"I'm still the Raphael you know. I'm also the Raphael I became in the lab," he answered, sounding a bit lame at the end. "I don't know what to tell you. I rule here. I learned how to maneuver people like Wagner, thanks to you, Cassius, and Sorcha. I'm not that different, Kaliya."

"Yes, you are. I see it in the way you move. You have this straight-backed confidence you never had. It's not a bad thing, I just wasn't expecting it. I should have. I caught how you acted the night you got your memories back. I knew something was different, changed, but I didn't realize how much."

"How little I've changed, you mean," he retorted. "With you, I'm the same I always was." He grumbled and used a plastic fork to push around his food. "The only reason we're different is because of you."

"Touché," I said, looking down at my own food. "It's just weird. I haven't been here for four months like everyone else, watching this happen. It's not like Sammy cares how you treat her. She doesn't want me speaking up for her. Though, I really didn't like that growl you gave her earlier."

"You really aren't in the position to talk to me about how I lead my cambions," he growled softly. "And it's not for everyone. You helped free them. They need to respect you. Beyond that, you're the ruler of another supernatural species. I won't have them saying shit like that to Wagner...or Cassius and Sorcha. I don't care if they verbally spar with some no-name werewolf, but they'll have manners. The only reason you think it's just Sammy is you only see when she's acting that way, and I need to step in and remind her of the rules."

I lifted my hands in mock defeat. "Fine."

We both started eating until he sighed.

"You know I'm right and just don't want to admit it," he whispered in my ear, sending shivers down my spine. Suddenly, the conversation had turned playful. Apparently, Raphael didn't want to argue and was making it clear he didn't want heavy conversation.

"Do I?" I arched a brow, turning to him, trying to ignore how close his face was to mine. "If I remember right, I had to teach you everything you know."

"That's how you know I'm right," he said with a wink.

He's flirting.

Oh fuck, he's flirting, and we're alone, away from the party.

"Well…I've been known to get it wrong sometimes," I retorted, slowly moving away from him, taking my plate with me. "Maybe you should think about all the times I've been wrong."

"I can think of one time in particular." He watched me, a small smile beginning to form, and the smolder in those chocolate brown eyes threatened to melt me.

"I got you a gift," he said quickly, reaching into his pocket. "Just something small to say thank you for taking the job."

"You already pay me. Gift enough," I said quickly. I didn't get gifts. No one offered, and I never wanted any. I didn't know how to accept them. All this could be awkward, and I wasn't going to make a fool of myself.

He put down the little box on the table. "I went to the Market without you. I saw Devika and asked her what I could get for a *friend* doing me a favor and getting paid less than she was worth."

I winced. I could have asked for double what he was paying and gotten it, but I hadn't thought he would figure that out. Someone had to have told him.

I took the box slowly and opened it. Inside was a snake-shaped bangle made of oxidized silver, making it look black. Set for its eyes were red rubies, bright and catching the sunlight.

"This is custom," I whispered.

"Yeah, and it's not just for you helping now. It's for everything. All of it. Helping me from the beginning. I needed help, and you gave it to me without ever asking for something in return. You educated me, even though it took time out of your day. You fought for me and for them, even though it almost killed you. You deserved something to show for it." His words were so surprisingly genuine, I pulled the bangle out and couldn't stop the gasp as he touched my heart with the gesture.

"It's *me*," I murmured, leaning down to look at it.

"Yes, and I was glad to see it came out as beautiful as you. I was worried she wouldn't be able to do your snake form justice when I told her my thoughts on what to give you."

The scales on the bangle were intricately carved and so well done, running a finger over it felt like I was touching a snake. I pulled it to my chest and looked up at him again, overwhelmed. I had never received a gift, certainly never one like this, and it hit me where it hurt—my heart.

He was so different, yet the same thoughtful and observant man he always was. He'd been right. He hadn't changed much at all.

"Thank you" were the only words I could get out. He had disarmed me so perfectly with this surprise.

"I've been trying to find the right time to give it to you. During training never seemed right, and that night at dinner with Cassius and Sorcha didn't feel right, either. I have you over here now, and you can finally see what you helped give me and my people—a home. So, it felt right."

"It's wonderful," I said, unable to resist the urge to lean forward and kiss his cheek. I was suddenly hyperaware of everything, including the sudden pulse of need running through me. My fangs ached, demanding I take the chance to claim him. If I wanted, I could make this problem of wanting him but not having him go away.

Except I would have a thousand new problems to deal with.

"I'm glad you like it," he said softly, reaching up to touch my cheek. I turned away before his lips could find mine, letting him kiss my cheek. "I'll let you sit here and eat. I need to make the rounds and see how my guests are doing."

"Have fun," I whispered, unable to put the bangle away. He gently took it from my hands and slid it over my left hand.

"There. Perfect."

I was left alone with the gift, my food, and my view of the cookout. It didn't take long for Cassius and Sorcha to arrive, realizing I was alone.

"What's that?" Sorcha asked, sitting next to me. Cassius took the seat in front of us, his back to the party. She reached out, pointing at the new jewelry.

"Raphael had it made for me," I explained. "He just gave it to me..." I lifted it and let her examine it. A fae with power over silver and other metals, she probably knew what it was, if there was any magic on it, and how it was made.

"This is fine work," she said softly, running her finger

over the scales as I had. "Very beautiful work. Did you say thank you?"

"I did," I promised. Sorcha frowned, still staring at the bangle. "What's wrong with it?"

"Nothing," she said, but she seemed a little more upset than nothing.

"She didn't make it, and it's beautiful work," Cassius explained, chuckling. "She's jealous he went to someone else when she can also make jewelry out of silver."

"And here I thought you only made weapons," I commented with a teasing smile as Sorcha rolled her eyes and released my wrist.

"Jewelry is easy," she said, drumming her perfect nails on the table, then looking them over. "Weapons are harder. I haven't done jewelry in a long time."

"He said it was for helping him with everything," I explained. "He got it from a witch I introduced him to. She's from home." I didn't elaborate where or what home was. Cassius told Sorcha everything, so they both knew I meant India. "She works in the Market."

"Ah," Sorcha deflated. "Then I have no reason to be jealous. He wanted something from the witch I can't offer."

Before we could continue the conversation, music started, and fae began to dance. One jumped on a table and started to sing. I smiled at the fun while Cassius and Sorcha began to clap in time with the music. The fae noticed them and held his drink up to them as he continued, his feet moving faster than I could see.

"Did he bring tap dancing shoes?" I asked, laughing.

"Seems like it," Sorcha replied, grinning.

After a moment, Cassius stood and held a hand out to his wife, which she took gracefully.

"I think this is where you and I show the others how it's done," he said with an amused smile.

"Oh, I do like that idea."

I watched them join the dancing fray as cambions tried to keep up, and the werewolves started to howl, adding their own music to the fun. Once I was done eating, I threw away my disposable silverware and paper plate, which required me to make my way around the crowd. As I threw it out, I was cornered by Wagner.

"Is there a reason why you're putting your nose in business that has nothing to do with you?" His tone was mild, and he didn't look at me, keeping his eyes on the crowd as he spoke.

I turned to the crowd as well, watching the rare sight of Cassius dancing with other fae. I didn't know if Sorcha was big on revelry, but in all the time I had known Cassius, he had never been one for fun, not public dancing sort of fun. He was more uptight than other fae, probably some combination of his position and the responsibilities that came with it.

"Nothing to do with me?" I asked in turn, chuckling. "I'm closer to the cambions than you will ever be, Wagner. I won't have them drawn into your politics."

"You think a fae prince and his wife are better options? Are you so blinded by your connection to them?"

"No, I'm not blind." I shook my head slowly. "That's not it at all. I trust them. Cassius isn't his father, his uncle, or anyone else in that crazy fucking family, and they're connected to ruling fae. Cassius could have been king, and there's not a fae in the world who doesn't know it. You, on the other hand, are just a werewolf Alpha of a single city."

"I'm a member of the North American Werewolf Council," he retorted.

"Ah yes, which is constantly under the scrutiny of the human government—because we should let actual demon people rub elbows with humans. Great idea." I snorted in derision. "Are you blind or just power-hungry?" I turned to him. "Or is this not about the cambions at all?"

"Don't ever imply I would do something dishonorable," he growled, glaring at me. "Plus, it's not like the cambions are numerous enough to protect themselves or *her*. Anyone could walk in here and grab her if they really wanted. That's the point I'm trying to make."

"If anyone touches Gabrielle, they won't need to worry about the cambions coming to get her," I whispered softly. "They'll have to worry about me. Pass that around. I helped get them out of that lab, and I'll take on anyone who wants to shove them back in cages. Cambion, nephilim, it doesn't matter. I don't care if it's a physical cage or a political cage. I'll fucking end whoever tries. Are we clear?"

"And what are you doing to protect him from you? You have enough political entanglements to drive most people mad. You have the Tribunal whenever you want them, you are required to uphold the law, and you are also the ruler—"

"I ended a perfectly nice relationship over it," I snapped, getting in his face. "Not that it's any of your business. You've had four months to convince him to ally himself with the werewolves, and he hasn't. Now I'm back, so you've run out of time." I walked past him. "Have a nice day."

I headed for my car. The cookout was fun, but it wasn't for me, and the politics were pissing me off. Sammy came up beside me, looking between me and the party.

"Heading out already? He's going to be upset you aren't stopping to say goodbye or just staying longer."

"I'm annoyed, I'm not in the mood for politics, and..." I turned back to the party. "Maybe saying goodbye isn't the best idea."

"You really don't want him back, do you?" Sammy frowned, tilting her head to the side as she studied me.

"We'll talk about this on Monday," I reminded her.

"Yeah, we will, because you're right. Maybe saying goodbye to him isn't the best idea." Sammy walked back, and I got into my car, sighing as I put my head on the steering wheel.

Well, the entire day couldn't have gone worse.

14

CHAPTER FOURTEEN

No. Not him.

I stood alone in the desert, watching, my feet pinned to the ground as the rakshasa lifted his ancient sword.

For weeks, I had watched him butcher my parents, over and over again. Never escaping, never able to help, just as weak as I had been as a child.

Tonight, it wasn't my parents' blood that would turn my colorless world into a red haze.

It was Raphael's, and he wasn't moving. He was lying there, vulnerable, and wouldn't move an inch as the rakshasa took his aim.

"RUN!" I screamed, but no sound came out of my mouth.

The sword came down.

I WOKE UP SCREAMING, but my hand didn't go for my sword. It was stretched in front of me, reaching for someone who wasn't there. A weight sat on my wrist, the black snake bangle with ruby eyes haunting me, a reminder of what I was toying with.

I'm going mad. That's what this is. I'm losing my mind.

I checked my phone, trying to ignore how my sweat stuck to the sheets and the frigid air chilled my skin. It was Monday morning, and I had to get moving. My alarm wouldn't go off for another twenty minutes, but I was already up. As long as my feet were moving, I could pretend nothing was wrong. I knew how to put on a mask. As I waited for my water to heat up in the shower, I stared at myself in the mirror, noting my wild eyes full of fear, my messy hair, and glossy damp skin. I could make it all go away, and no one would know I could barely sleep at night.

It didn't take me long. It was a skill I had mastered ages ago because appearances were important. No one outside of my closest friends could know I was barely hanging onto my sanity. Even Cassius, who could see the signs and wanted to help me, didn't know just how bad it was, and he never would. I intended never to give him the chance to see it again—one glimpse was enough.

I got into my car, checking for my bag of gold coins. Today was the day I finally got the chance to talk to Sammy. We needed to put our shit behind us so Raphael would get off our backs—for her sanity and my own. I just hope she realized we had to be allies.

I didn't talk to anyone at the compound, so I stopped where they were waiting on me, waved at Raphael as they got in, then drove off before he thought of small talk.

"Wow, you in a rush?" Sammy asked, looking back at Raphael.

"Yes and no," I admitted. "Just want to get this trip started, so we can get finished in a reasonable time. It's going to be a long day if we hang around talking to people."

"He was cranky when you left without saying goodbye, just like I warned you," Sammy said as we got onto the freeway. "I figured you have a reasonable idea why that is."

"We'll talk about it later." I very subtly jerked my head at Mateo. I didn't know how much he would report to Raphael later.

"Oh, he's fine," Sammy said with a shrug. "Mateo doesn't care. Do you, Mateo?"

A growl filled the car. Mateo had taken the back seat, but his growl felt as though it was right next to my ear.

"Sammy, you know he doesn't want you to say anything," Mateo warned. "He doesn't want any of us to say anything."

Oh, that sounds mysterious, but at least it's confirmation the cambions know what's going on. That there is *something going on.*

"Oh, please. I think we're all owed an explanation why this mess even exists," Sammy snapped.

"Mateo, just plug your ears if you have a problem with it. I think I know what's going on, and I want confirmation of it." His words were important, though. He was loyal to Raphael by following orders. Sammy was loyal through protecting Raphael, even if he didn't know he needed it.

"Fine," Mateo grumbled. "You women talk, and I'll pretend like I didn't hear anything. I don't like being a pawn, anyway. Not my problem if the big man can't get laid."

"Turn off your phone," I ordered, ignoring his sudden teenager persona. It was a side of him I hadn't seen yet, but part of me didn't find it surprising. One thing I was learning about the cambions was they all had a piece of them that didn't grow up all the way because they didn't have the chance to.

He made the effort to put it in the cupholder where I could see it. Once it was there, Sammy turned it off and put her own with it.

"So, what do you think is going on?" Sammy asked, leaning closer.

"He's trying to win me back, isn't he?" I turned to her, not too concerned about the road since the morning rush was over. I had my suspicions about Raphael. The pieces were falling into place, the only reasonable explanation.

"You're right. He wants to *woo* you," Sammy said with a snort. "He wants us all to be on our best behavior, be your friend, and give you a place among us, so you feel welcome. That way, he can play good boyfriend and make you want him again. Why do you think he went through so much effort to get you *that*?" She pointed at the bangle on my wrist. It suddenly burned on my skin and felt heavy, reminding me of its presence. I hadn't taken it off since he gave it to me. I couldn't bring myself to. "And he'd have noticed you wore it today. Even if you didn't stop to talk to him, he'd think it's a sign his shit is working."

"He's good at catching the little things," I muttered,

knowing she was right. "You don't want us to get back together."

"I think he's crazy. You left him. Why should he be wasting his time with this? Why should we all play house for you? It's fucking annoying, and you're only going to break his heart again," she scoffed.

"I had to," I said softly. "I don't want to get tangled up with Raphael again. I don't want to be in a relationship with him."

Which fucking sucks because he's amazing, and I want a piece of him. I want all of him with me, all the time. Every time he does something or touches me, he becomes my entire world again.

"Liar," she said, glaring at me. "You want him. We can all see how you look at him when his back is turned. You're just playing hard to get. I can see it on your face right now, the longing. I recognize that look because I saw it on every cambion face in the lab when we thought about going home and being free. You can't fool us."

"I *can't* be with him," I said, rephrasing the situation. "My enemies will go after him, which could get him killed."

That made her eyes go wide.

"What?"

"I'm a naga, and our enemies often target our mates to stop us from having children. They'll kill him for being with me if they even assumed he might be my mate. I had to stop things while I could to keep that from happening."

"Wait. Did you just say they'll target your mates?

Raphael said nagas mate for life. It's like a thing, a specific person."

Wow, Raphael, just tell them everything about me while you're at it.

"Yeah." I nodded, turning back on the road. "Raphael isn't my mate, and I'm not willing to let others think he might be. I won't risk his life just to have a good time. He's a great man, but I ended our relationship to protect him. Not because I didn't care, Sammy. He's one of the best I've met in decades. That's why I refuse to risk him."

"Oh…" Sammy slumped back in her seat. "Well, shit. I thought you were just stringing him along."

I laughed. "No, Sammy. I'm trying to stay in the friend lane. Fuck. You tried to kill me for that?"

"I mean…" Sammy winced. "I don't know how to control my temper sometimes. Sorry. Raphael was right to be pissed off."

"It was cool how you cut off her hand," Mateo commented benignly from the back. "Are you going to teach us that?"

"In time. It takes a lot of practice and experience, but we're all immortal. You'll get there with enough practice." I ran my hands over the steering wheel. "So…is there anything coming up I need to watch out for? With Raphael? It's easier to keep the boundaries if I know what's coming."

"He's going to ask you out to dinner sometime this week," Sammy said, sighing. "He's mad for you. You were right to say I sound like a jealous ex or something. I looked back on it later and realized I was acting a bit awful. I'm not, I promise, but I see where you got that impression. But he's...he's so into you. The last four months have been fucking miserable. You walked away from him, and he's either been obsessing over getting you back or working. None of us are free from it. It's frustrating because there's so much other stuff we could be working on. He could get any girl in the city if he wanted to, but he only wants you."

"Yeah..." Mateo's confirmation was sad and drawn out. "He's done a good job hiding it recently."

"That's only because she's around, and he thinks his plan is working," Sammy replied, looking back at her partner. "She's wearing the bangle."

"It is very pretty," I pointed out, aimlessly touching it. "Thanks for the heads up about his plans. Look, we got off on the wrong foot, and I want to change that. I knew you didn't understand why I did what I did, but I wasn't sure of how much I could tell you."

And I still won't tell you all of it or the truth.

"I think if we're on the same page, we'll be fine." She looked away from me and sighed. "But you do like him a lot, don't you?"

I opened and closed my mouth. I needed to say the right thing.

"I care for him enough to give up a chance of happiness," I said softly. "He's worth dying for, but I'm not. My parents died for me, friends have died for me and *because* of me. I'm trying to turn over a new leaf and keep the people I care about safe from my problems. I don't want to drag them down with me."

"That's more noble than I thought you were capable

of," she said, crossing her arms. "But it makes a lot of sense."

"Thanks for understanding. So, we can play nice for him, and he'll eventually leave us both alone?"

"Yeah, we can definitely do that, and that starts today. I didn't get to go to the Market with Raphael. Mateo did, but he's really not all that talkative. What's it like?"

I smiled, remembering the joy of showing Raphael the Market for the first time, and I was genuinely looking forward to that experience again. Then I realized something.

"Who gave him the coins to go?" I asked, trying to look over my shoulder at Mateo.

"Um, one of the fae. The woman, Sorcha."

Another piece of the puzzle fell into place, and I gritted my teeth. I was going to need to talk to her. The picture was getting clearer, and my friend needed to explain what the hell she was doing, trying to set me up with Raphael.

When we got to the Market, I parked close to the broken elevator and led my two cambion followers to it. Already, there were a handful of werewolves and witches waiting to take a ride. More interesting, there was a native man standing far from the group, looking annoyed and uncomfortable. I wasn't well versed in Native American culture, but I always tried to be respectful when I saw them or just stayed out of their way.

"How long have you been waiting?" I asked the closest, trying to aim the question at one of the werewolves or witches.

They all looked over, eyeing me, then the cambions

flanking me. I licked my lips, trying to judge what the Native American might be as a supernatural, and caught he wasn't one of the werewolves. He was a *werecat*.

Well, that is a strange find. Don't catch them in the city that often. Or ever. I don't know this one. Maybe he's why Wagner is so cranky. I wonder how long he's been in the city or if he's just making a day trip to get something.

Either way, it's really not my problem.

"Only about ten minutes," a witch finally answered, then swallowed, a clear sign of nerves. Either she was uncomfortable with the cambions or the tension between the moon cursed. Werewolves and werecats didn't play well together. "So...um...you're Kaliya Sahni, and these must be..."

"Sammy and Mateo. We're two of the new cambions in the area," Sammy answered with a sharp smile I caught out of the corner of my eye. "And you are?"

"Oh, uh, nobody," the witch answered quickly, turning around. I cleared my throat. It was rude to take a name and not give one. "I'm just a low-ranking witch from Monica's coven. Clarice."

"Nice to meet you, Clarice. Tell Monica I said hello. It's been a while since I've seen her," I said with an easier smile than Sammy gave her.

"I'll pass it along when I'm done with this errand for her," the witch promised.

After another five minutes of silence, I was growing impatient. The stares from everyone waiting were beginning to annoy me.

"I don't have time for this." I stepped around the crowd and knocked on the elevator door a few times, listening to the echo behind it. A moment later, the "broken" elevator started to move, and the door opened.

The old fae yawned as the door opened.

"Come on," he said, waving us in.

"Let's go," I ordered my charges for the day. Sammy and Mateo were allowed onto the elevator next, then it was crowded with werewolves and witches. Before the door closed, a fae I didn't know snuck on and tried to make himself small. As the doors closed, I chuckled at the sight of another running to catch up, but she would have to wait for the next trip.

When the elevator stopped, I threw three gold coins at the fae and walked out with my cambions.

"They fucking stink," the werecat softly growled as he walked past us.

"Yeah, they get that a lot from your kind," I said, shrugging. He hissed and kept walking, leaving me with Sammy and Mateo. Once we were alone and the elevator was gone again, I looked at them sympathetically. "All the moon cursed have sensitive noses, and for some reason, they don't like the scent of cambions."

"Yeah, we get it from the werewolves working at home, too," Sammy said with an equally nonchalant shrug.

"Ah, yeah, that's right." I was so used to explaining things, thanks to Raphael. "Well, let's get on with this."

15

CHAPTER FIFTEEN

I led them into the Market. Mateo's reaction didn't give me any sort of satisfaction, but Sammy's did. I watched her eyes go wide and her mouth drop open.

"So, this is what it's like to be supernatural," she said, taking it all in.

"This place is special, but yeah," I said with a smile. I would never tire of seeing this. I hadn't expected to love it so much when Raphael first saw the Market, but now I knew. I was going to chase this feeling forever.

People were stopping to stare at us. When I came with Raphael, it hadn't been so extreme. Everyone mostly went along with their business unless they cared about the rumors that had been floating around at the time.

This time, people were stopping to *stare,* in some cases, outright gawking.

The cambions were out, and everyone knew about them. There were so few, and they were so new, it was quickly becoming a circus.

"One of you...power up or whatever it is you do and give the crowd a scare," I whispered.

"Got it," Mateo said with a growl, also looking around at everyone. His eyes turned red, the sclera going black. The veins spread quickly, and his skin turned grey, getting a marble effect no other supernatural species I knew could do. He grinned as his horns began to form, rising out of his skull yet not drawing blood. He grew, reaching over six feet, yet his clothing still fit him. Their transition from human to this form, which I believed was unique to them, was seamless.

Raphael and Cassius must have taken them to the fae to get their clothing spelled to fit them no matter what form they're in. Good thinking, guys.

Sammy chuckled as people started walking again and began her own transition, but I put my hand on her arm.

"One is enough to warn them, two is a threat," I said quickly. "Mateo, you can switch back whenever you want."

"I'll stay like this," he said, his words a little different, more a lisp. I frowned at him, and he revealed his canines had grown into animal-like fangs, bigger than most vampires.

I headed for the weapons shop I wanted to show them. It wasn't on the main street with all the other wares. It was tucked into a medieval building, out of view and where the goods could be protected. I was once a regular customer, but I took good care of what I owned, so I didn't need to come by nearly as often as others did.

It was run by an old rogue werewolf, Cromwell. He saw me and who I was with and growled softly.

"Something I can do for you?" he asked, eyeing Mateo.

"We're looking to pick up some items. They need to see what you have. We're not sure what we're looking for yet."

"I have a client right now. Give me thirty minutes, and you can come in next."

"Wait! I've been waiting for an hour!" someone snapped.

"Yeah, well, Tribunal Executioners come first," he snarled. "You're just a punk. Make a name for yourself and get a reputation, and I might give a shit about you. Until you do that, you'll wait for everyone else."

"Cool," Sammy mumbled. "So, you really are well known."

"I've been in the business for a long time," I replied, trying to keep my voice down.

We waited patiently. Rather, Mateo and I waited patiently. Sammy was bouncing her foot, pacing to look at everything in the room, groaning and mumbling about being bored. Finally, he called us to the back room. The previous client had used a separate exit, wanting to keep their visit a secret.

"So, based on your previous complaints about my lack of weapons from outside of Europe...well, it wasn't just you. I heard it a lot." The werewolf growled. "I expanded my wares, made some partners, and we now offer a wider selection."

"Fantastic, thanks." He'd never offered weapons from outside his homeland before. Since I was from the subcontinent of India, it had always been disappointing. I didn't think it really mattered for Mateo and Sammy, which was why I had brought them, but it was nice hearing he wanted to cater to more of us from around the world. He was finally getting over his "only Europe matters" mindset. I knew he would come around, eventually. He had started supplying firearms fifty years ago. He was open to change, just slow.

He only grunted, closing the door behind us and leaving us with the vampire who protected his wares.

"What are you looking for today?" Dorset, Cromwell's vampire assistant, politely asked as I let Sammy and Mateo wander.

"They're looking for the right thing for them. They'll know when they see it." I shrugged. "You know how it is. First time picking out that thing you want to learn first."

"Ah, yes. I can offer some recommendations."

"No, let them touch things, get a feel for everything." I never really had this experience. The talwar my parents gave me was my weapon from home. The katana from Hisao was a treasured gift I knew I would keep at my side until the day I died. Beyond that, my decisions were always practical or for show. I had a weapon collection that rivaled museums, partly because I never wanted to be caught without a weapon, even in my own home.

Mateo went straight to the back wall. They didn't keep every firearm on the market available, but the ones they did have were the best—and spelled. Accuracy help, weight changes, so they felt lighter than they were, small touches that turned a good gun into a great gun. He picked them up, took aim, judging how they felt against his shoulder and in his hands. He played with different scopes, attaching them to look down the sights with some of his clear favorites. I let him do his own thing since he had a clear idea of what he was looking for. The cambions already had a supply of guns, but I had no idea of their origin. If I had to guess, probably a purchase from the werewolves. Mateo liked playing with them.

Sammy was different, slower. She let her fingers trail over different blades, looking at everything—swords from all over the world, daggers, and spears.

"Anything interest you?" I asked as she moved from the classic Japanese wall toward my area of the world. It was pretty neat seeing a talwar hanging there.

"Not yet..." she sighed. "I like using my hands. I don't want to have to carry something. Something I could throw..." I watched what she picked up, and my stomach did a couple of flips.

It felt like fate, and I wanted to scream in frustration.

Oh, please, not those. You're going to cut my head off while I'm trying to train you. We're going to need Gabrielle on hand full time.

"What is this?" She seemed so excited as she looked over the beautiful circular blade.

"A chakram. You would have a few of these on your arm, some had up to eight, and they come in different sizes as well. They *are* throwing weapons, which have been known to cut off limbs. If you got good with them, you could be a really dangerous opponent."

"Do you know how to use them?"

"Yes, but I don't. I stopped formally training in techniques from home when I left. My parents gave me the basic lessons when I was young, so I could get a feel for them, but real training wouldn't have started until I was in my twenties or thirties. It's muscle memory, though. I bet I could send one of these off and do just fine with it."

"Could you tell me more?" she asked, holding it close to her chest. I reached out and gingerly took it away from her.

"Well, first is how you hold it. It's dull on the inside and sharp on the outside. You'll see..." I spun it to show her the sharp blade, formed into a perfect circle until I got to one section different from the rest. "There's a safe place where it's completely dull, which is pretty standard nowadays. A long time ago, they were fully sharp, but this section is your handhold and should help you keep from cutting yourself. Some people have started to put real handles here instead of just using the steel. Some put handles through the middle, but you lose the chance to do one of the most advanced techniques. If you want a handled version, let me know. I won't get you middle handle versions, but I can tolerate a handle here." I ran my finger over the dull section.

"What do you mean? Wouldn't a middle handle help you throw it?" She was more interested than I wanted her to be.

"True masters spun the entire blade on a finger," I said softly. My father could do it. "At high speed, they launched it. Rumor was some people could get a hundred meters and remain accurate and deadly. I could probably hit something at thirty meters with a different type of throw. I could teach you the basics, but it would be riskier than throwing daggers. These things, when you misaim, you can decapitate someone, and none of your friends would come back from that. They can heal from a gunshot or a dagger, but this…this can go very wrong." I handed it back to her, a little proud she listened to know where to hold it.

"I want to try. I mean, I probably shouldn't pick a weapon because it looks cool, but…" She held it up, and her eyes lit up with excitement.

"I'll teach you. I have some family I could ask for advice if I need it," I said with a sigh and nod, resigning myself to my fate. This was part of why I wanted this trip. To give them something they were interested in and help them accomplish it. I just hadn't expected her to wander to chakrams and pick them.

"Can you imagine how many people I could take down if I hit them with these before I even got into the fight? Just…" She mocked a throw and made the vampire jump. I lifted a hand, trying to stop it from escalating. "It would be cool. If I don't take them down with these, I'll just jump into the fight."

"Fine, we'll get you a set, and we'll work on them with your hand-to-hand." I took it away from her again and put it down, then waved the vampire over. He pulled out a notepad, ready to write down what I wanted. "I'll take the full set you have here, all six of them." To explain, I looked back at Sammy. "Four just to use as needed. Those are standard. The smaller ones you would wear on your wrist. We'll hold off using those, to begin with, but since you heal so well, there's no reason not to try, eventually."

I knew right then Sammy would kill for me if I asked her to in the next twenty minutes.

"Mateo, have you found something you like?" I asked, turning back to him, and blanched.

He was standing at a table, and there were not two or three guns in front of him. He had six.

"Yeah, all of these," he said, nodding happily at his pick.

"Mateo, we can't carry out all of those." It would be a nightmare.

"We have someone who can walk with you to your exit of the Market," the vampire said quickly. "We don't often have people buy off the wall so quickly. Normally, we take custom orders to fulfill within a time period, so we have delivery people for drop-offs."

Damn it.

"Uh..." I looked at the vampire, wondering what my bill was going to be. He looked at Mateo's table and nodded slowly, making notes on his little pad of paper, then tore it off and held it out to me.

I wanted to die, but I handed it back to him and sighed.

"You know how to bill me," I said, knowing I couldn't say no. Well, I could, but I needed them to like me.

An hour later, the vampire and a new guy, a young werewolf, brought out several boxes, everything wrapped and packed. I looked at the gun boxes, then at the vampire, who pointed at his new assistant.

"He'll help you carry everything," the vampire said with a smile.

"Fantastic," I mumbled. "Sammy, get yours. It's small."

Grabbing two of the gun cases, I left Mateo and the werewolf to grab the rest. I led them back to the elevator, where Sammy had to finally help since the werewolf couldn't leave with us. Luckily, the walk to my BMW was short, and we handled it without any humans seeing us.

The drive home was quiet. In the end, everyone had gotten what they wanted. I had a moment to finally talk to Sammy without Raphael around, breathing down our necks, and they both got weapons they could say belonged to them. Not to the community, just them. And I was going to teach them how to use everything they got. Mateo was easy since he already knew how to shoot, but Sammy was going to force me to brush up on skills I had let go to waste years ago.

When I parked at the compound, I intended to let them figure out how to get everything home.

"Hey, thanks for talking things out with me, Sammy." I wanted to say it before she had the chance to get out of the car. "It's a delicate situation. I'll try to let him down easy this time. I was hoping a clean break would be... optimal, but..."

"He's so into you, Kaliya. This is going to be messy, no matter what." She pushed her blonde hair out of her face. "At least I understand why it's so messy now. I can't protect him when he keeps trying something that won't work. I thought you were trying to...It doesn't matter. I'll see you at training tomorrow."

"Yeah..." I watched them leave, glad Raphael wasn't around. I had purposefully not told him how the trip was going. So, when I once again drove away from the compound, he had no idea I had even been there.

16

CHAPTER SIXTEEN

I had to clean and sharpen them before they were useful, but I brought my old set of chakrams with me the next day. I normally kept them on the wall, a showpiece and an interesting part of my collection, but today, I was finally going to try using them.

"I saw everything you bought for Mateo and Sammy," Raphael said as I walked into the gym. He was sitting to the side on one of the benches, relaxed and not really looking at me. I pretended not to be startled. Normally, he wasn't in the gym when I arrived in the morning. My fangs dropped down, and need rushed through me at the sight of him, lounging like he owned the place.

He does own the place. He owns this gym and every other building within a mile of here, I bet, and he fucking knows it, which only makes me want him more.

"Let me pay you back."

Not even a hello. Just straight to the point today. At least I have a damn good poker face.

"It's fine." I dropped my bag on the bench next to him,

trying my best not to sound excited to see him or as if I was ready to drape myself all over him. "I have money. It's not a problem."

"Kaliya, let me pay you back." When he finally looked at me, his eyes trailed over me and pinpointed my wrist, finding the bangle still there.

I couldn't bear to take it off—mixed signals. I was good at sending them.

"It's fine," I repeated. "I wanted to do something nice for them. If you're really invested in this, I need you to set up a training area for Sammy and me. Just some posts for her to aim at so we're not destroying punching bags or the natural vegetation. I don't want to kill any cacti."

"Let me set that up and pay you back for half of it," he countered.

"Deal." I chuckled. "It was two point six million. Mateo's new toys are all spelled. That's expensive."

"Half?" He blanched.

"No, all of it. You owe me one point three million if you really want to pay that. Don't worry, though. I have *old* money. It's easier for me to afford these sorts of purchases." My wealth was backed up with piles of gold, jewels, and other precious objects. I could probably take one of the ancient family heirloom necklaces and sell it for more than my bill from the Market trip. I wouldn't since I didn't need to, but it was always an option.

"Really, the only thing I need is somewhere...to use these." I opened my bag and showed him my simple chakrams. I only brought four larger ones, single for throwing. "While I'm working with Sammy, I'll send Mateo to his desert shooting range to practice. I'm thinking of splitting their training. Monday, Wednesday, Friday as a group, learning hand-to-hand skills, sparring, interrogation techniques, all that. Then on Tuesday and Thursday, I'll check in with them on their personal goals, the things they want to learn."

"Sounds good," he agreed with an impressed smile. "You know, Sammy came home talking all about your trip. Said it was interesting to see the sort of treatment you get from other supernaturals."

"Yeah, we were able to cut in line." I chuckled.

He got up slowly and filled my personal space.

"So, what exactly do you need? I'll make it happen by the afternoon. It's Tuesday, so you'll need it."

With Sammy's confirmation, it was easy to see his game now. He didn't need to try so hard. If I had an ounce less self-control, I would have already crawled back into his bed, begging for him to be with me. Still, it was really sweet of him to try so hard for me. No one ever tried hard for me.

He's going to make this even harder the second time around, isn't he? He is.

"I was hoping for a few tall wooden posts, cemented into the ground, so we don't knock them down. They're going to get cut up, but again, I would rather have her throwing sharp things at a post instead of the local cacti. The ecosystem here is fragile."

"I never thought you would be protective over some cacti," he teased.

"Some species are going extinct," I retorted, huffing indignantly. "I like living here. If it's destroyed, then it loses all of its beauty."

"I'll get those posts up," he promised, smiling indulgently. "Anything else I can do for you?"

"No, thank you."

He leaned in and kissed my cheek. Apparently, I had let him know that was okay now. I just let it happen, deciding it wasn't too much of a big deal.

Me, the queen of mixed signals.

After he left and the cambions arrived, morning training went quickly. They were all refreshed and excited after a long week off. Gabrielle watched in case I got hurt, but aside from that, everything was fairly uneventful. Once they were gone, I skipped lunch and went outside with my chakrams, hoping to find something to practice on.

"Over here!" Raphael called, standing in a group of werewolves about a hundred meters away.

I chuckled at the two posts already standing. Someone thought to attach another piece of timber between them. It made a nice H-shape that could make for great practice.

"I told them what you needed it for, and they had some lumber they could use," Raphael explained, pointing at the new structure.

"It'll put us a few days behind on one of the homes, but we can easily replace it. We asked one of the fae to come by and get the concrete set quickly," a werewolf explained with a knowing smile as if he knew what it looked like for a man to do something for his girlfriend, fiancée, or wife just because she wanted it done. It was just as indulgent as Raphael's smile. "Should be good to use."

"And since you have your chakrams..." Raphael looked down obviously, then backed away. "Why don't you show us why you needed the posts?"

I chuckled, nodding. As I turned away, I saw that Sammy was already there, her eyes hungry. She had come early and was going to get a demonstration.

"Clear the area. I'd prefer if you stayed behind me. I'm a bit rusty." I didn't want to take any chances.

The small crowd moved back, with Raphael staying at the front, keeping the best view. Sammy came closer to me, but she didn't try to jump in as I counted twenty meters from the new target. A shorter distance was better to start with.

I brought four, but I dropped two. I didn't want to take a chance cutting myself, trying to throw two. I threw them, one overhead throw and one side throw. They embedded in the wood, not exactly where I wanted them but close enough. I grabbed the second pair and threw them in rapid succession, hitting just below the first two. With those, I added a bit more power, trying to stay true to my target and a wrist flick to really give them speed.

"Sammy," I ordered, holding my hands out.

It was like riding a bicycle. She fed me the ones she got the day before, and I threw them quickly, sending them all into the wood. Each one dug into the post as if it belonged there, and if it was a person, it would have found bone.

"Like that," I said, once all ten of them were in the target. "That's basic. I don't use them often, but I can get you fatal with them." I directed that at Sammy with a smirk. "That's what we'll be doing. You'll throw, finding how they feel in your hand, practice sending them off, then jumping into sparring situations. Sometimes, you'll be fighting someone up close and see a second opponent—"

"And I would throw the chakram," she said with a grin. "I was watching videos all night."

"Good," I said with a laugh. "Yeah, then you know what we're going for here. Tell me they were real people, not like video games or tv shows. They always go extreme with size and use. These don't come back like boomerangs. You want them in something because you want that something dead."

"Yeah, real people," Sammy confirmed, walking with me to get the weapons out of the post. Once we were out of the hearing range of our male audience, her face changed. "He's going to ask you today or tomorrow. I was hoping to see you before he did. He thinks the bangle was enough to butter you up to let him take you out as a thank you for helping us. You accepted one gift, so why not another? He's not going to let you know it's romantic until you're on the date."

"Fuck me," I mumbled. "Thanks for the warning. How did you find out?"

"Don't say *that*. I'm pretty sure he wants to, and he'll be happy to oblige. But in all seriousness, I heard him talking to someone about it on the phone," Sammy admitted. "He didn't know I could hear him."

I took a deep breath, and with my amazing powers of deduction, I figured out who he would talk to about me. There were only two options, and it certainly wasn't Cassius, which only left one person.

Now it makes sense. She's been pretty clear what she thinks about my boundaries and thinks the reasons for them are stupid. She gave him the coins to go the Market, where he got the bangle.

She knew about the bangle before she ever saw me with it. Damn it.

If I knew one thing about the fae, it was their masterful skill of manipulating people into the positions they wanted those people to be. For months, I half-hoped Sorcha was a good friend and would never do it to me. Worse, I couldn't even bring myself to be mad at her. To ask her to do anything else would be like someone asking me not to enjoy warm weather. It was completely against our nature.

But annoyed? I could do annoyed really well.

"What are you thinking about?" Sammy asked softly.

"Nothing important right now. Let's just keep pretending everything is fine."

I walked back with Sammy and put her in position to try her first throws. In an effort to think about the most pressing issue at hand, my job, I decided to do it instead of tying myself in knots over my friend group, which now had clear battle lines. Cassius would support me while Sorcha was playing for Raphael's team. While it seemed self-important to think, that had to have been why the couple was annoyed with each other during the cookout.

"Okay, Sammy, just throw one," I said, making my voice loud enough to warn everyone around us a blade was about to go hurtling through the air. "Let me see what we're working with, then I'll do form correction."

She let it fly with more power than I had used, and it went halfway into the post.

"Let's,"—the wood creaked—"not throw them that hard," I said with a chuckle. "I don't want to go into the desert looking for it if you go through the nice post these werewolves installed for us."

"My bad," she mumbled, grabbing a second chakram.

Her form was amateur but similar to mine. She held back a little on the next one, but it still went nearly as deep as the first.

"Well, you have good aim..."

I went to her, correcting her stance. Feet shoulder-width apart was a good way to keep balance. I showed her wrist flicks and how to hold them. On the third throw, she cut her hand, and I watched it heal before letting her throw another. I made her do it right. She could heal, but that didn't mean she could be sloppy.

It took thirty minutes of ignoring the werewolves and Raphael, but eventually, they wandered off. Well, the werewolves wandered off, not Raphael. His stamina for hovering was outstanding. Apparently, only a few days without incident wasn't enough to get him to leave us be and stop breathing down our necks.

"Why these?" he asked after another twenty minutes.

"I wanted to throw something, and they looked cool," Sammy answered nonchalantly. "You were right to hire Kaliya. Apparently, she grew up with these." Sammy's smile was genuine, and her words sounded honest. Then she side-eyed me. "It was probably just luck, though."

"Funny," I snorted, shaking my head, then looked at Raphael with a smile. "She's too good at hand-to-hand to force her to use a sword all the time. It's useful, and I'll make sure she learns, but giving her something to cover her vulnerability ranged is good to focus on. So, when she picked these out, I agreed to brush up and teach her what I know."

"Good. Sounds like the trip to the Market did you some good." Raphael grinned at Sammy. "I'll let you two work on this and see if Mateo needs anything. I can't believe he just bought more guns. He's going to need an armory at this rate."

"Oh, you're going to need one of those, anyway." I laughed as he walked away, then looked at Sammy the moment he was out of sight. "He's too easy to talk to."

"Yeah, he firmly thinks you're going to get back with him, that you won't be able to resist him and all this." Sammy elbowed me. "Will you? Seriously, the way you look at him..."

"I'll be fine. I just need a moment to set a firm boundary with him, and I don't want to do that here."

"Why not?" Sammy grabbed one of my chakrams and threw it, turning away from me in the process. I checked the throw and saw she hit the middle post connected to the other two.

"This is his place. The same reason I don't want him in my house. It's too...personal. I want us to be on equal footing, I guess. It seems easier. If I do it here, I'll have to think about it every time I come back."

As it was, I wasn't sure if I could ever go back to Cassius' house without thinking about what I said to Raphael that day. It was one of the reasons I didn't visit Cassius, and it had nothing to do with the fae.

"Oh, good point. That would feel awkward, wouldn't it?" Sammy nodded as she threw another chakram. "Well, sooner rather than later, please. I know you aren't trying, but from the outside, it kind of feels like you're leading him on. You know how you feel, and he doesn't."

"Yes, he does," I snapped, offended by how she could say that. It pricked my pride. I wasn't purposefully doing anything. "I did break it off."

"I mean, yeah, but..." she reached out and grabbed my arm, pulling it up to force me to look at the pretty bangle. "You're wearing it."

"Yeah..." I sighed. "It's too pretty to take off, and it...it looks like me."

"Does it?" Sammy frowned.

"Yeah..." I reached out and touched it with my free hand, then Sammy let me go. "Want to see?"

"Sure."

I shifted right there, then coiled around her legs before moving farther away and lifted up, spreading my hood in a display.

She went down on one knee, looking me over like an inspection, her expression curious and amazed. When she backed off again, I shifted back into my human form and opened my mouth to show her my fangs.

"I'm not human," I reminded her as she reached out and tried to touch them. I moved my head back. "My venom is deadly. Let's not try to touch the fangs."

"How deadly are they?"

"People normally bleed out within fifteen minutes or less." I worked to put them away, but with the scent of Raphael on my tongue, it was hard. The struggle to get them under control was always ten times worse when he'd been around. "There's no antivenom, so I don't practice with them. A strike as a snake is more instinctual than a trained technique."

"So, you...you use them," Sammy said, her eyes going wide.

"I've killed people with them, in both this form and as a snake. I've even eaten as a snake when the going was tough. Those weren't proud times, but I was a starving teenager."

"Fuck..." Sammy slumped. "You went through some hard shit, didn't you?"

I shrugged.

"Life sucks, then you die," I mumbled. "Let's get back to training."

17

CHAPTER SEVENTEEN

Hours later, I sent Sammy off and found myself with Gabrielle and Raphael.

"Do we want to give her another demonstration to warm up?" he asked, leaning in so I couldn't avoid him or his scent as it washed over me.

"No, that was a one-time deal," I said with a small smile but kept my words firm, even though his flirtatious words really got to me. My fangs dropped hard into my mouth, and a drop of venom threatened to drop onto my tongue. Before he could say anything, I decided to do the best thing to turn him off and spit onto the dirt to my right, away from him, but not trying to hide what I did.

I was not, under any circumstances, going to take the risk of ingesting my own venom. The bright sun would evaporate my spit, and the venom would sink into the earth, but it was a small enough amount that it was no danger to anyone.

"You need to milk those?" he asked, suddenly curious.

"What?" I frowned at him,

"You spit out your venom. You never spit otherwise," he said with a smirk. "Well, unless there's blood in your mouth, but there's no reason for that unless you bit your own tongue."

"Fuck, you are way too observant," I muttered, turning away from him and walking quickly to Gabrielle. She was still tying her damn shoes, had been for what felt like twenty minutes. As she saw me approaching, her eyes went wide.

As I approached her, I realized he was right. Since I got him out of my house, my venom had produced more slowly. I hadn't milked my fangs and released any since I started working at the compound, where I constantly saw him. That was nearly three weeks ago. With him around, I needed to get rid of excess venom once a week.

I was at max capacity and had been too distracted to do anything about it.

"Come on. We don't have all evening," I said to her, holding out a hand.

She groaned and took my hand. I pulled her to her feet, then moved a step farther, grabbing her waist and tossing her over my shoulder. Her squeal of surprise pierced my ears, but I was going to use every chance I had to take her by surprise. That was what she needed.

Her struggle was enough to make me put her down after ten feet and go for a different hold, yanking an arm behind her back to get leverage. Her wings popped into existence and spread open, knocking me onto my ass, the surprise catching me off guard as I saw stars—her magic, those gold glowing orbs that dissipated quickly.

When I blinked and cleared them from my vision, she was standing next to Raphael.

"Good job," I said, grinning because I couldn't stop myself. "Who gave you that idea?"

"Cassius," she answered. "I mean...I should have thought of it on my own, but yeah, I was telling him about my training with you, and he offered some pointers."

"I was hoping you would figure it out on your own," I admitted as I got to my feet again. "I mean, the whole point of your training is teaching you to give a hit and figure out what you can do at the moment to protect yourself. No one is ever going to ask you to fight for them, not like a cambion or me, but I think everyone would sleep easier at night if they knew you could defend yourself."

"I was always told I...couldn't do anything," she said softly.

"You can tell her everything," Raphael encouraged, looking over Gabrielle's head to me. "Kaliya might know a thing or two about it."

"I might," I agreed gently. "When I was a little kid, my parents taught me the basics to fight just in case, and my mom...she wanted me to be able to kill. Looking back, I think she saw that I was always going to be a fighter, but when I was young, I don't think I really saw it. She was the female leader of the nagas, and I was her precious daughter who shouldn't know pain, hurt, or anything else." I shrugged nonchalantly but talking about my family wasn't easy.

"When she was murdered, I was found on the run

and taken in by another naga, the male ruler. He didn't let me use a sword or practice, and I…I almost believed him when he said women just didn't do that sort of thing." I sighed, pushing my hair from my face. "It wasn't until he tried to marry me off and everything felt so wrong, I ran away. I wanted to find out who killed my parents and brothers, and I didn't think he wasn't working on that enough. I wanted more.

"I didn't know how to do anything until a man named Hisao told me I was powerful. I was seventeen, and I was broken, but he saw me as a predator and taught me to be one."

"I'm not a predator, though," she countered.

"But you are," I replied, shaking my head in sadness. "Gabrielle, what do you think real angels are like?"

"They're beautiful healers—"

"Oh, no," I groaned. "Raphael, you haven't said anything to her yet?" I gave him a look of dismay.

"It's not like I know nearly as much as you or have any experience in the matter," he pointed out. "Only what I read, and we know how trustworthy some of that can be. I also just never knew when to bring it up."

It was another reminder Raphael was new to this leader thing, and Gabrielle wasn't technically one of his. She was unique and taking shelter with the cambions, the only people she knew.

So, I decided to be the one who dropped the hard reality.

"Angels are brutal killers of beauty and pain," I explained blandly, imagining myself reading a dry text and not destroying the reality of a young woman who truly believed she was a powerless healer. "They're monstrous in a different way than demons. They're perfection in a sense, and they want all things to be in their rigid image. They're beings of virtue, and if you toe the line of *sin*, they will find fault with you. Normally, summoning one leads to the death of everyone in the area. No one is perfect enough for them. People usually summon them to punish those who aren't righteous in whatever way they think needs to be addressed. It never works out for anyone in the end." Making it all the more astounding Gabrielle existed. Her mother had been with an angel, got pregnant, and survived to give birth.

"Certain angels cover certain things or so says writing. We don't know much beyond what they do when they're on this plane. They have their own, and we're all perfectly okay if they stay there."

"They killed people?" Gabrielle blinked, and I wondered what was going through her mind. I was well accustomed to death, but she was so fucking naïve and innocent, I couldn't help wondering what she was thinking.

"Every time they show up here, yeah," I answered, shrugging. "Though, I would kill someone, too, if I was ripped out of my home to deal with the problems of another species before I could go home. Maybe that's what makes them so vicious here. We don't really know. Demons, angels, the gods—the only thing we know about any of them is their interactions with our world."

"So, you're saying I could...fight." She seemed uncomfortable.

"You can do anything you want," I said softly.

"Anything at all. Just like the rest of us. We all have free will to make those decisions."

Regardless of biology and fate.

She nodded.

We continued her training, and by the time it was over, I was feeling a little better about her. Her entire world was changing, the stakes were high, she was scared, and I understood all of that.

"You know, for a shut-in who doesn't like people, you're really good with them," Raphael said softly.

"All I can do is talk from personal experience," I said, wiping my forehead off. Sweat was dripping everywhere, and it was getting uncomfortable, but this was the life of training a dozen people to fight, all day, five days a week in Arizona. "I've never met someone who has to overcome as much conditioning. They really made sure she felt useless and weak. I know it seems ridiculous because we keep telling her it's not true, but she's going to need a lot of time before her instincts believe us. We just need to keep feeding her more and more information, telling her she's powerful and helping her believe it. It's the only way to break the mental gaslighting they did to her."

"Yeah." He was sad. So was I at the thought of the life she must have led, kept alone and powerless.

Alone and powerless were two of my worst fears. Alone I could manage, powerless was terrifying, but in a combination, the idea gave me chills. Been there, done that, didn't even get a fucking t-shirt. Not like I wanted one. It would have been covered in my family's blood.

It was a dark thought, but I snorted at the morbid humor.

"What?" Raphael frowned at me.

"I was just thinking about something. It's awful and about me. Don't worry about it."

"You thinking something awful about yourself? I'm not surprised." He chuckled as I reached out to hit him in the gut, a playful move I should have stopped. He grabbed my wrist and pulled it up. "I love how this bangle looks on you. I'm glad you're still wearing it." He made a mock show of pulling my wrist up to his eye level and looking it over.

"It's beautiful and a thoughtful gift. It would be rude of me if I just put it in a jewelry box and forgot about it." It was also a bit of ego since the snake looked like me.

Beyond that, it was from *him*.

I tugged my wrist away.

"I need to head out." Thinking of my family made me think of that rakshasa. Thinking of the rakshasa made me remember the risks I was unwilling to take. Being close to Raphael was dangerous for him, and I couldn't allow that.

"Before you go, I wanted to ask you something."

Here we go.

"What's up?" I played innocent.

"I wanted to take you out to dinner this weekend. Just the two of us, to catch up from the last few months and as a thank you for everything you've been doing here. Casual, between friends and rulers, I guess. I bet some werewolf would see us together and tell Wagner I'm loyal to other people in Phoenix, and I don't need him."

Oh, he's doing this well. It's politically savvy, making it clear we're just friends, and this is a casual outing. Smart man. If I didn't know any better, I would have fallen for it.

"Okay. Tell me the time and place, and I'll meet you there," I promised, casually accepting, refusing to give him any hint if I was excited.

"I expected more of a fight," he admitted.

"I don't see why." With a shrug, I went to grab my bag. "We're always surrounded by people, and I know better than to tell you no because I'm not worth it." *Ha-ha.* "I did what I had to do to help your people, and if you want to stuff me with an expensive meal, I'll survive. It's easier than arguing with you like the time with the yogurt."

"Seven o'clock, Binkley's."

I raised an eyebrow. Binkley's was one of the most expensive restaurants in Phoenix. I rarely ate there, but I knew it was a good spot.

"Okay," I agreed softly. "Saturday, seven, Binkley's. Got it but feel free to remind me before the week is over."

"I will," he promised with a small smile that promised sin and screams. I didn't think he even realized he was doing it, but it sent a shot of warning and lust through me.

He wasn't going to keep it casual, but I needed privacy with him outside of the compound if I was going to finally put a stop to his little game. I didn't want to embarrass him in front of his people. I could only hope he would thank me for that later. We obviously needed to have a long conversation.

I made it home unscathed and sighed as I fell into my bed. As I laid there, all I could think about was how my life was crashing together. I didn't like talking about my family so much, and I didn't like that Raphael couldn't let me go.

My phone buzzed, and I checked it with a groan. The text was from Adhar, who was checking in on my hunt for the rakshasa. I called and put him on speaker.

"I'm stuck," I told him with a snap. "I thought you didn't care."

"Someone tested our boundaries in the last twenty-four hours," he explained, his voice shaking. "No one broke in, but we're planning another move. I'm asking because you're looking into him, and we're suddenly getting tested. I don't know if they line up, but they might."

I hissed.

"What else are you trying to say?" I asked. I sat up in the bed and grabbed the phone as the blood rushed out of my head.

The timing was bad, he was right about that. I still had open inquiries all over the world about the rakshasa. They were either anonymous or with people who would never reveal me, other people working for the Tribunal.

Still, the timing was very bad.

There was always more with Adhar.

"If it happens anymore, I might finally request you come back to India. Not as my wayward charge, but as the ruling female of the nagas. We would need your particular kind of help."

"I would come," I said without hesitation. I hadn't been back to India in over a century, but if they were in danger, I would go without even thinking about the consequences. I would drop everything to make sure they were safe. I wouldn't let my choices fall back on them. "You keep me updated, and if you feel like it's something you can't handle, you let me know. Got it?"

"Thank you. You know how these things go. They test for a few weeks—sometimes months—looking for weaknesses, well before they strike. Sometimes, it's just curious supernaturals who brush the boundaries accidentally and want to know why they're there. Nakul is in a decent enough place to investigate further with me. It hasn't happened to anyone else yet, so we're positive the babies are safe."

"Good. Yeah, keep me posted," I said softly. "Stay safe, Adhar."

"You as well, Kaliya."

We hung up. We didn't like each other, but the fact he reached out to see if I would go help them was something of an improvement.

It also made my nightmares worse that night.

18

CHAPTER EIGHTEEN

The week seemed to drag by, but Adhar told me every day, no one had tested them again. Neither he nor Nakul found any evidence of who the potential problem could be or where they went. That was concerning, and they were on high alert.

I was thinking of ways to let down Raphael. Something Adhar wouldn't agree with, but if he asked me to go to India to help him, there really wasn't much he could say about Raphael. It would be hard to have a mate in Arizona while I was on the other side of the planet.

By the time Saturday came, I felt as if I'd been beaten up, and I still had to get into one more fight before the marathon was over.

I tried not to dress too fancy for dinner with Raphael. I went for a nice pair of pants and a simple blouse, throwing a leather jacket over it. My jewelry was how I always kept it. I was presentable enough to fit in at Binkley's but not enough to look like I was expecting romance.

I finally forced myself to take the bangle off, leaving it on my bathroom counter. I was trying to anticipate how this would play out, and wearing it would only work against me.

I can't let this continue. I need to put an end to it.

I was a stubborn woman, there was no doubt about it.

As I got ready, my phone started going off, and I groaned to see texts from Sorcha, asking me for pictures of what I would wear and if I was nervous.

Kaliya: It's not a date.

Sorcha: Bullshit. You're going to look hot. He's super into you. You know it's going to go that way. Don't play coy.

Kaliya: Yeah, I do know it's going to go that way because someone else warned me. I also figured out that you've been feeding him advice on how to get me back. We're going to have a long talk about that once this is over. You don't get to meddle in my life like that, Sorcha.

Sorcha: Busted. Fine, we'll talk. Look, I'm just trying to make sure you're happy. You were happy with him, and I know he's into you. I just want to see that. You deserve him, and he cares a lot about you.

I rolled my eyes and ignored my phone after that and got in my car with it on silent. I couldn't focus on Sorcha yet. I needed to worry about Raphael.

I was there fifteen minutes early, and he still beat me. He was waiting at the front door of the restaurant, grinning when he saw me walk up. There was no missing the small bouquet of flowers in his hands or his crisp, black suit.

"You look beautiful," he said softly.

"I underdressed." I looked him over, my mouth watering. My pulse jumped as he shifted, displaying powerful muscle hidden under the façade of civility. I remembered removing his shirt to reveal those hard muscles in my bedroom. They were all there, under the suit. I could have them. All I had to do was play along. "You said this was casual," I accused softly, meeting his eyes.

"I lied," he crooned, leaning down. "I knew you would never say yes otherwise."

It was his immediate admission that pissed me off. He couldn't even wait for us to sit down at the table or just let the mood play out. No, he wanted me to know what this was and made no effort to hide it now that he had me out of the desert and in the city with him.

"Knowing that should have warned you not to try this," I snapped. "Damn it, Raphael. I gave you a chance to prove me wrong, and you didn't just go beyond what I thought—I'm pretty sure the line you crossed is in another state."

"Prove you wrong? So, you had the assumption this was what was going on?" He frowned deeply.

"Obviously," I hissed. "I'm not an idiot."

"Yet you went along with it," he growled in return.

"I wasn't going to be an ass in the middle of your home. You put a girl in a weird position when you play nice host, and I'm a contractor you're paying," I fired back, pretty pissed off. "Fucking really?"

"Kaliya!" He snarled as I turned on my heel and stormed away, headed for my car. I was leaving. I didn't have to indulge him.

He ran after me and cut me off before I got there.

"Why?" I demanded. "I thought I made it clear we were over. I haven't changed my mind."

"Hear me out," he said softly, pleading with me, and I couldn't bring myself to walk around him. "I can't stop thinking about you. Sure, there are a lot of people who tell me to find anyone else, but I can't. I look at women, and I think of you. I close my eyes, and I see your face. I can feel you from across the desert, stalking around your home, doing who knows what. I know the exact days you left your home. I was hoping we could talk about this tonight. It's been a few weeks of us seeing each other again, and I felt you needed to know how I feel. I was hoping it would go a little smoother, so you could understand, I think you're it for me." He threw the flowers to the side, letting them land somewhere I couldn't see. I didn't really care. He leaned in and filled my space, his scent invading my sense.

I couldn't breathe well enough to say anything.

"I know nagas mate for life, and you're not too keen on finding that person. That's fine with me because you don't need that person. I'm right here, and I don't think I can survive without you anymore. When you were gone, I was angry at everyone and everything. I would beg Sorcha and Cassius for updates on you. I would ask them to tell you to come see me. I was fucking pathetic, and I hated it. Then...then I saw you at that restaurant, and everything seemed to fall in place again." He took a deep breath. "I think you're my mate, and I was trying to do this the right way, by...winning you back instead of forcing you to move and keeping you. Let me tell you, that's an urge I have pretty fucking frequently."

I looked around for humans before I finally found my voice. No one was paying us any mind. Humans were pretty good at ignoring monsters. We naturally made them uncomfortable.

I turned to him and looked into those damn chocolate brown eyes, gathering all of my courage, and prayed it was enough.

"No," I whispered softly. "We can't do this."

His snarl sent shivers down my spine.

"Don't say that to me."

"I have to," I said, feeling the tears begin to prick in my eyes. "I have to, Raphael, because I love you, and I'm not stupid enough to risk your life. For once in my life, I'm thinking about someone else and what they need. I know it hurts you, it hurts me, too, but I really can't take the risk. Not with you. I love you too much to take the risk."

I don't know how the words stumbled out, but they were the truth.

"You love me?" he asked, leaning in more. His lips were in the perfect range for me to claim, so I said another terrible truth.

"You're too good for me to ruin. I won't do it." I stepped back. "Don't make me leave. Don't make me never see you again because I'll do it. I'll run where you can't find me—"

"There is nowhere on this fucking planet I wouldn't be able to find you," he growled softly, matching my move. "I fucking need you in my life, Kaliya. Something in here is telling me I need you and *want* you in it."

"I'm not good enough for you, and neither is the world I live in," I said, trying my damnedest to be strong. "I'm a toxic mess who's going to destroy you. Ask anyone who's known me for longer than the minute you have. Any therapist would tell you to drop this. I'm not someone you can fix, Raphael."

"I'm not looking to fix you. I'm looking to be by your side for all the fucking crazy that you are," he snapped.

"Fucking crazy?" I laughed. "You don't know fucking crazy...not yet. You don't know why I'm doing any of this. You have no idea what sort of danger you would be in if I gave up and let you keep me. It's better that way! Don't think it's fucking easy for me to walk away. It kills me to know I could have you, but it would put you at risk, and there's nothing I could do to stop it—"

I felt the prick in my thigh. I looked down, stunned to find a little syringe sticking out of me.

Oh no.

I pulled it out as the mysterious something coursed through my veins and began to make me feel sluggish. I held it up for Raphael, then saw he had two in his arm and was listing to the side in shock. Whatever was slowing me down was also going through his veins and doing its dirty work.

I tried to shift and found it impossible. Something was blocking me from my magic, and I hadn't even realized it. We were being ambushed, and there was nothing we could do to stop it.

"That was all *very* touching, but I don't have all evening."

I recognized that voice.

Man-eater. Beast.

The rakshasa.

I watched as Raphael sagged and hit the ground.

I turned, but my legs went out at the same time, my knees bashing into concrete as I saw him walking up. I tried to fight it. I wasn't drowsy, but my body wouldn't cooperate. My eyes were wide open as my face slammed into the ground.

The rakshasa walked closer, his pace unconcerned. He knelt beside me, taking the syringe out of my hand.

"I heard you've been looking for me. You didn't need to try so hard. I was always close by," he said as if I was a lost friend or lover. His fingers grazed my cheek, tender and gentle. There was no animosity in him, even though we both knew he and I were enemies. It was cruel and terrifying. He had all the power.

And he knew it.

I couldn't move my mouth to offer a witty retort. I couldn't blink or wiggle my fingers. I was completely paralyzed in the position I had fallen. It was uncomfortable, but it wasn't why my eyes filled with tears.

No, no, no.

I heard rustling, saw feet moving around me. A shadow moved over me, and I saw Raphael's feet dragging on the ground, but the rakshasa stayed right next to me, continuing to caress my cheek.

Where are humans? Why isn't anyone wondering what's

happening? This is taking too long. Someone should have noticed this by now.

No, he's a master of illusions. They would see something completely different.

Finally, the rakshasa picked me up, carrying me as though I was a child, and took me to a large black van.

"He's secure?" he asked someone.

"Yes, sir."

Professionals. He has professionals. Okay. Good to know.

Thinking about that kept me from having a full panic attack, but I knew it was a useless endeavor. Already my pulse was racing, and my breathing grew shallower. Whatever paralyzing agent he had used was enough to take away my control, but it didn't rob my body of its ability to do what it thought it had to.

He loaded me into the van, even clipping in my seat belt. He put no other restraints on me, even held me upright as someone slammed the door shut, and it made my limp body rock.

Then the van was moving, and the only thing I could do was scream inside my own head.

19

CHAPTER NINETEEN

"Do you know how long I've waited for this chance?" he asked softly, sitting in front of me. The van wasn't like a passenger van parents used. It was a bench on each side of the back, facing the other side. "When I saw you in the Mygi facility, I knew this was coming. I just had to be patient. Finding you wasn't hard. I've known where you've lived every moment of your life, except for some small periods of time where you fell off the map, and no one knew where you were." He chuckled. "No one had ever hidden from me so well. Normally, it's quite easy for me to find someone, but you...When you were young, you mastered the art of disappearing. Once, when I failed to capture you as a child and the next time after you ran away from the other nagas."

Do you think I care, asshole? Do you? Or are you just chatting to fill the silent air?

I couldn't look away from him as he looked over his long claw-like nails. His face had a strange animalistic quality, and two long, feline fangs hung over his bottom lip. He wasn't trying to be human. He was the monster he wanted to be and saw no reason to try to be anything else. He even lounged like a cat, his legs stretched out, taking up more space to intimidate me and whoever else was there.

My heart raced as I tried to figure out a plan, but really, I was caught in my own mind, and there was nothing else to do but think. Think or listen to him.

Powerless. I was completely powerless.

"Losing you for those few years got me in a lot of trouble, but the best...hunts, they take time and strategy."

I fought my own body, trying to say something, anything.

"You have been one of my best hunts," he said with a proud smile. "I had to learn, adapt...evolve. You forced me to catch up with the modern world and play on your level. And what a level that is." He reached out and touched my cheek again, his claw adding a bite to the touch, a threat. "You disappeared as a child and came back a woman, but not just any woman. I've never fought the cat in Japan. I have no reason to, but you...you were one of his protégés when you finally showed your face again. A warrior better than your parents could have ever dreamed. Better than any naga I had ever faced. I knew I was going to have to be patient with you."

Oh fuck. I had a stalker and never knew it.

My breathing stuttered in real fear, as no matter how much I tried to control it, my body had its own plans.

His fingers grabbed my jaw and moved my head, so I could see the back of the van.

"Then you found him," the rakshasa said, moving to sit next to me. "And my patient hunt had to speed up a little. I needed to learn more. I had to call in old favors, so did my employer." His fingers tightened. "You found your mate, and that's what's going to kill you in the end. I was willing to wait longer, let you grow stronger, but this...this was a turn of events we couldn't allow."

We. He's working for someone. I already knew that. I was hoping to use him to find out who.

My mind ran in circles until it came to a screeching halt on the part I was avoiding most of all.

They know about Raphael.

One of those fucking tears started rolling down my cheek. He wiped it away with his thumb.

"Ah...don't cry," he murmured. "Your mother didn't. She went out with a bloody scream that made my ears ring. Not that you can do that right now, but tears don't suit you."

Another fell, and his hand grew tighter.

"You should have kept him better hidden," he taunted softly, his words a whisper in my ear. "The moment you saw me, you should have never seen him again. Did you think you could hide him while he was still in your life? I was in that lab because I had a suspicion he was your mate. You helping him, well, that was almost proof. Almost. You were never one to have friends you would help so...passionately. I've watched you for years. I know everything about you, but this one, you let him live in your house. You showed him off to your little witch. You introduced him to your old lover."

He turned my face back to him. I had no choice but to

stare him in the eye, his feral, feline-like eyes taking in every detail of my face.

"Do you know what really gave it away?" he asked softly. "You left him the moment you knew I was out there, but you didn't go far. No, you started hunting *me* but hovered around him, close enough to help him. There was no winning for you. If you had stayed close to him, you would have mated him, and I would have come. You left him because you were *scared* for him, and I came, anyway. I just had to bide my time until I could grab you both because there's never been a naga who could actually resist the chance to mate. I knew I'd catch you two together outside of your little protected homes, eventually."

I knew I had fucked up. He didn't need to tell me.

"After that, I just needed a way to catch you without risking any of my team." He smirked. "That wasn't too hard. A way to neutralize you both." He snapped his fingers. "So easy. So many challenges for so many years, and it was that easy. Maybe I always gave you too much credit."

He released me with a small shove, enough for my body to list to the side, and my shoulder hit the bench with a thud. Gravity did the rest. I rolled, and my face hit the floor next to the awful fucking cage where my mate was. I couldn't see his face, but from the sound of the way the rakshasa was talking, he was also paralyzed.

Which meant he had to have heard all of that.

I wanted to tell him everything would be okay, but it wouldn't be. My body wasn't working through the drug nearly fast enough, and from the looks of things, neither was his. Our captor didn't seem to be that worried about it. He would have taken into account how to create the right agent to paralyze us both for as long as he needed. To not do so would have been an oversight the rakshasa didn't seem capable of.

We need a fucking miracle, and I don't think one is going to come.

The van just kept rolling to wherever it was taking us, and there was nothing I could do to stop it. There was nothing anyone could do. Our friends probably didn't even know we were missing yet, and it could take days for them to even consider it. If Raphael and I didn't get in touch for a couple of days, they would assume we were at my place, wrapped around each other, having a great time. They wouldn't interrupt.

Sammy might. Fuck, the emotionally unstable, uncontrollable one. She would be fucking pissed if I took Raphael home. She would go to my house to rip my fucking head off because I told her that I wouldn't get back together with him.

Because, and this is some fucking irony, it was too dangerous for me to be with him.

I would have laughed at the hopelessness if I could.

Finally, the van stopped, and the unload was quicker than the load. The back opened, and three guys pulled out Raphael's cage, taking him out of my view. The rakshasa picked me up again and carried me behind them, but I couldn't look around and see where we were. Still in the desert, for sure, but I had no idea where.

I was taken to a house, down a set of stairs, placed in a chair, my hands strapped down, then my ankles.

Raphael's cage was placed nearby with a thud. While the upstairs, from what I saw, seemed like a normal house, the basement was a prison or a lab. From my view, I could see things all over the table. They had to have cooked up whatever they used on me here.

The rakshasa wasted no time, humming to himself as he waved the others away.

"I have it from here. I need to do a verification while you call our employer," he said once he was done prepping a plastic cup with a cotton top. I knew what that was. I used them myself. He was going to milk my venom. He wouldn't get that much. I had milked earlier in the week and again on Friday, but that didn't matter. Even a drop could do what I figured he was planning.

He grabbed a stainless-steel rod and walked over to me again.

"Normally, I talk to my team a lot, but..." He smiled at me. "I have you, and you won't be dying any time soon. Well, you will be, but I won't be the one to kill you. All this hunting and you don't get to be my kill." He sighed heavily as though he regretted that.

Fuck you.

He opened my mouth and shoved the steel rod to the roof of my mouth. With no finesse or gentleness, he worked my fangs down, where they perfectly sat because I had no ability to pull them back. Then he shoved the cup, angled it, and made the fangs pierce the cotton. He threw the rod away, then pressed his index finger and thumb to my sinuses on either side of my nose, right where my venom sacs were. He knew what he was doing, and that scared the fuck out of me. Not that I needed much to be scared in this situation.

"Your mother cursed you," he said softly. "I'll never understand it. She finally had a daughter, and she cursed you. Is that motherly love to you?"

Is that pity, asshole?

"A single thing like a name, yet seeing how you turned out, it makes so much sense. She thought naming you after one of the most powerful of the nagas would make you strong. It did, but only because she named you thusly. Her decision is what brought on the events that led us here." His eyes moved to the cage. I wished desperately to see Raphael, but he was out of my line of sight. "Irony or coincidence? We'll never know, but I do love the poetry. The universe is not often so perfect in its symmetry."

Obviously, he knew more than me because I didn't understand a lick of what he was talking about. I was named after Kaliya of the legend where the powerful naga had been chased from his home by Garuda and was later killed by Krishna. For humans, it was a story of triumph over evil. For nagas, it was a story of mistakes and loss.

Yeah, my name was loaded with a troubled history. What I didn't understand was the poetry thing.

My fangs felt dry by the time he pulled the cup away. Inside was enough venom to kill several people. When I was near Raphael, I made more. He got what he wanted from me and turned his back on me.

"You have no idea what I'm talking about, of course. You will soon enough." He shook my venom around, then got a syringe, filled it, and attached a needle to the end. "Since I am about to do this to you, I will give you a gift." He turned and smiled over his shoulder. "How does that sound?"

I stared blankly at him.

He put the needle down, then spun my chair until I could see Raphael. He went to Raphael and moved him until my mate and I were able to stare at each other.

He was awake, and he had no expression.

There were so many things I would have said to him in that moment.

I'm sorry.

I love you.

I never wanted this to happen.

This is what I was running from.

The rakshasa grabbed his little deadly needle, then Raphael's arm. Without any word, he shoved it into Raphael's arm and pushed my venom into my mate.

He was mine now. Live or die, Raphael was mine for the rest of eternity, and it wasn't romantic, sweet, or even an accident. We had been robbed of the choice.

Raphael groaned as my venom shot through his veins, and even from my position, I could see him grow hard in his suit.

"Verified," the rakshasa said without surprise. "Just as we thought. You've done what only one other naga in history ever has. Well, we must finish this. He'll want you to be complete when he kills you."

Who? And what the fuck are you talking about?

He drew some of Raphael's blood, now mixed with my venom, and came back to me.

Mating was an exchange. With two nagas, it was only venom, though a little blood always made it through, thanks to the whole biting part. If it was a naga and a human, or anything else, thanks to what Raphael was, it was venom and blood from the other person. I never knew if the blood was symbolic or important, but it had always been done that way, and it seemed the rakshasa intended to fully give me my mate.

He injected Raphael's blood into my body, and it felt like lightning tearing through my veins. I was trapped in a painful, electric hell as it bonded me to Raphael completely.

Oh shit, this is a cambion thing. I am *his mate, aren't I?*

A whimper of pain and pleasure made its way out of my throat. I began to sweat, my skin growing cold, thanks to the air blowing through the room. I shook uncontrollably as it worked a course through every single piece of me.

"Now, Kaliya Sahni of the nagas, you are mated to a demon-spawn, and it will make you one of the most powerful nagas to ever live. Congratulations. Too bad it's the very thing you'll die for," the rakshasa said, spreading his hands.

The tears fell freely as I stared at my mate, and the pain slowly left me. On his cheek, I saw one roll down his face.

Then I blacked out.

20

CHAPTER TWENTY

A beautiful woman ran in front of me, laughing as I chased her. She was everything to me. Perfection in flesh, a soul so pure and wonderful, I couldn't stop myself but go to her like a moth to bright light. The flame that was her passion was my warmth on cold evenings and the balm that eased my troubled mind.

She was love, life, and everything I had ever wanted. My fangs ached at the thought of sinking into her and claiming her as my own, to have her in my arms and under my mouth. That was why I chased. She was to be my mate if she accepted me, and we both knew it.

Finally, she stopped and laughed, letting me catch her. I spun her around, holding her to my chest as we laughed and laughed.

She was so perfect, and when her eyes flashed red and black, I knew she was done playing hard to get. Her grip on my shoulders tightened, and I went to my knees for her, accepting her and all her power. Now, she wanted to really play, *and I was more than willing to oblige.*

I finally found the right moment to ask her, on my knees before her. The urge was too strong to resist. If she would not have me, then I needed to leave and never return.

"I love you, Rama. Please, let us have eternity together."

Her expression changed, her fire changing from sensual to pure.

"Eternity is such a long time."

"Yes, and I want it with you."

She bit her bottom lip, then I got all I needed. She nodded, and I struck, biting her tender inner thigh.

MY EYES FLEW OPEN, and the rakshasa was still standing in front of me, frowning deeply.

"Well, that wasn't what I expected to happen," he said softly.

I could remember every detail of the dream, looking over everything as if it was a memory and not a hazy dream—the beautiful woman and her cambion eyes. My fangs aching to go into her, to sink my body into hers and never leave. I thought of my hands as I held her and the chest she had leaned into.

They had been masculine. It hadn't been me. It was someone else, another naga with a cambion mate.

Add in the new strange feeling, and I wasn't sure what to think about anything anymore. In all my years of hearing about it, no one had described mating the way it had just happened. That meant it had to be rooted in Raphael's heritage as a cambion as well.

"I wish you could speak, but it's much too dangerous to free you. It'll be a mystery I might never know the answer to. Hmmm." He dismissed it and straightened up. I was once again given the sight of my mate sitting in a cage where I couldn't help him.

The rakshasa left us. I heard the sound of steps on stairs and the muffled voices of people above us. They walked around, something going on, then at least two of them were headed back downstairs.

"He gave us leave to kill the male?" the rakshasa asked benignly.

"Yes, sir."

The new power in my blood spiked. It felt like it was going to tear me apart from the inside, and I was helpless to stop it.

"Good. I don't want to have to keep both of them on my hands. One is enough, and he only wants her. He's just a security risk now."

"Maybe we should consider dumping him. He's the ruler of a species. Consider the attention we would get from people like the Tribunal."

"The cambions will never know what happened to him once we destroy the body. I'm not concerned about the others. If we let him live, he will remember and never leave us be. He'll want revenge for what he lost. We can't risk it." The rakshasa laughed. "And I don't care about the Tribunal. My people aren't a member of their little clubhouse. They don't have any power over *me*. I made sure of it."

The rakshasa came into view with one of his people. My mouth was still open, and the taste of everyone in the air finally hit my tongue, the thick taste of magic coating it. This team member was a witch, probably one of the reasons I had no access to my ability to shift and why their paralyzing compound was so damn effective for so long.

The rakshasa's grin made his fangs pronounced and turned the bemused expression into a threat.

"If you're so worried about the Tribunal, you know how to leave my employment."

"I don't wish to leave your service," the witch said, lowering his head.

"Good." The rakshasa patted his cheek, and the witch didn't even flinch. His cold eyes seemed unbothered by the touch and betrayed nothing about feelings except that he was completely loyal to his master. With something unspoken decided, the rakshasa went to Raphael's cage and opened the door, sliding it upward.

"Time to get rid of you. You're no longer needed."

I screamed, and no one heard me. Not a single sound penetrated the silence left by the rakshasa after his words.

I watched him grab Raphael and pull him out of the cage, leaving him on the floor.

Power continued humming in my veins, trying its best, and I fought to move anything, even a finger or a toe.

No. Take me. Kill me and let him go, please. You can't do this. I promised myself I would keep him safe. You can't do this to me. Anyone but him. I'll give you everyone. I'll give you all the nagas. I don't fucking care. Just not him. Please, not him.

The rakshasa lifted his hand, and an axe formed, stretched over his head.

My fingers curled on the armrest, and I gasped.

The rakshasa stopped, his eyes going wide.

I hissed viciously.

The world blurred around me as I freed myself from the restraints through a series of shifts between forms. There were no thoughts as the new power in me drove me to defend my mate.

I wasn't in control.

Blood splattered the walls. Furniture was thrown around.

I blacked out as destruction and death reigned.

I WAS A WARRIOR, and my enemies fell to my feet, unable to withstand the onslaught of my blades. They couldn't defeat me, for I was one of the most powerful of my kind. I would not give up my home for them nor my mate. My family would know peace and safety, and not even the gods could force me to change my path.

I HISSED as I reached out and grabbed my mate, pulling him across the floor.

Mine.

I held him close, breathing in his scent, then bit him hard on his neck, ignoring the blood that covered us both. If there was even a drop of venom left, I gave it to Raphael.

Mine.

He didn't respond, and I hissed again, lowering him to the ground before I searched for a solution. There were many options—so many vials, drugs, and needles. I had no idea where to start.

A low laugh made me swing around and bare my fangs.

"You'll...*never*...figure out...which one...can fix him," the rakshasa said as blood gurgled and poured out of his mouth.

I lunged for him, grabbing the front of his shirt, and dragged him up the wall, holding him high and letting him choke on his own blood.

"Tell me!" I roared in a language I hadn't spoken in years—Vedic Sanskrit, an old language, not even nagas regularly used it anymore—yet it came out of my mouth as if I was born to use it and had never spoken in anything else.

"Why?" he asked, also slipping into Vedic Sanskrit. "Why should I give you what you want? We're enemies, Kaliya. I do not help my enemies."

I roared and threw him across the room. Before he could try to move a finger, I rushed for him again and threw him across the room, working out my rage. He would answer me. I could make his death last hours if I had to.

When I went to him a third time, he weakly lifted a hand.

"You don't need to kill me. I will help you. I will be loyal to you." He was pleading now, begging for his life.

"No," I hissed. I reached out and grabbed whatever was hanging out of him and squeezed. His screaming roar was weak and filled with pain, and I *loved* it. He *deserved* this.

He'd made me powerless. He locked me inside my own body and took away my choices.

He was going to suffer—for a very long time.

"Beg harder," I hissed in his ear.

He did. The words tumbled from his lips like a waterfall, a force that could not be stopped, mixed with the blood of his broken body.

None of them were how to fix Raphael. Nothing proved his newfound loyalty.

"You don't know, do you?" I hissed.

"We never made a cure."

That was all I needed to hear.

Finally, I had enough and ripped him to pieces, throwing limbs across the room as I screamed. My blood screamed for vengeance, and I was going to have it. I was going to make sure there was nothing that could put this rakshasa back together.

When it was over, I turned to my mate, where I had left him lying on the floor, slowly picked him up, and moved toward the stairs, heading up with ease as if my body was rejuvenated. There was no ache in my bones, and I had energy to spare. I took him outside and sat him down next to the van. It was pitch black outside, but the stars were beautiful. I tilted his head to view them.

I needed to fix him, and I didn't know how, but I had all this *power*. I reached for it, hissing as it formed in my hand, red swirls of magic—my power—then shoved my hand into his chest, the only thing I could think of, and he gasped, his body beginning to convulse. It lasted for what felt like minutes.

During that time, reality sank in, and horror filled me as I moved back from him—horror not of him, but myself.

I looked at my hands to see the long black claws extending from my fingertips instead of the usual, black-painted fingernails. I tried to move again and realized I wasn't on my feet. I corrected that quickly and staggered away as the power receded. Every moment, I was feeling more like myself, which left me more scared of what I had just done.

I vomited nearly ten feet away from Raphael and the van. I could barely breathe as I heard him grunt and groan. I heard him hit the van and turned to see him tapping it and checking the doors for anything unlocked. He wouldn't even look at me.

I didn't even know how I felt, so I could only imagine what was going on in Raphael's mind.

Straightening, I went back inside and searched everything, going through the pockets of pants on legs severed from the rest of their bodies. It was already beginning to smell in the warm Arizona night. Eventually, I had wallets from every one of our captors, papers and instructions, and the keys to the van.

Raphael didn't come in to help, and I couldn't fault him. I didn't remember how I did all of this, but I knew I did. He'd been a bystander, trapped in himself.

When I came back out, I dumped everything I found on the ground, then headed back in. He was already on his way to look at everything I had brought out, so I didn't concern myself. He knew me. He would make sure it made its way into the van.

Inside, I collected every piece of wood furniture I could, found the small kitchen and cut the gas line to the range. After that, I found matches and lighters.

Nothing of this place would remain when I was done.

I started a small fire in the basement, another in the kitchen as the gas continued to leak, then another at the front door.

Going back to the van, I pointed to the passenger's seat, forcing Raphael to move out of the driver's seat. He'd already turned on the engine and was ready to drive, but I needed to drive. I needed to keep doing something.

I got in and hit the gas.

We left the burning building in the desert and tried to find our way home—without a word spoken.

21

CHAPTER TWENTY-ONE

When I found a road sign, it finally gave me my bearings. I turned to head for the city, not wanting to go home—home was vulnerable and dangerous. Raphael didn't question my decision. He said nothing at all, staring out the side window of the van with an unreadable expression.

I stopped at Cassius' gate and watched it slowly open as it recognized its visitors. I pulled into the driveway to see both my fae friends coming outside in a hurry. They had known tonight's plans, and coming by to see them certainly hadn't been part of those plans. They knew something was wrong. I could see it on their faces through the dark-tinted windows.

Raphael got out, and his appearance made Sorcha stop in shock, but Cassius kept coming for me. When I got out, he was only a few feet away, and I watched him take in the blood that covered me and the blank expression on my face.

"Come inside," he said softly, reaching to take my arm

and guide me. I took a staggered step towards him, wanting his friendship, trusting him with my life.

Raphael's explosive snarl stopped us both short.

"*Mine*," he growled from the other side of the van. It was the first word he had spoken since I helped him, since we had been attacked—since we had been in the middle of a terrible argument where no one had been the winner, and we both would have walked away hurt.

Cassius' face went through a number of emotions—shock, fear, fury. He didn't like being told who he could and couldn't touch, especially when he was trying to help. He was, after all, a prince, and obviously, things were a little rough with him and Raphael. I didn't know how I missed that before, although Cassius had warned me in his own way.

"I'm trying to help—"

"Let me help Kaliya," Sorcha said softly, coming between everyone. "You help Raphael get inside."

Cassius stared at me long and hard before he followed my mate inside, leaving Sorcha and me alone in the driveway. She approached me cautiously.

"What happened?" she asked gently, reaching out to touch my shoulder.

I jerked away, unable to bear being touched. The rakshasa was dead, but the way he had caressed me was going to haunt me for years to come.

"I spent the evening in hell," I answered, speaking English for the first time since I had come to. It felt foreign in my mouth as if it wasn't supposed to be there, and my accent was thick, which bothered me.

Sorcha's eyebrows furrowed. Whether it was my

statement or my accent, I didn't know. I normally sounded like a generic American.

"That doesn't answer the question."

"I don't know if I can answer the question." It was all too raw, and there was this big piece missing.

I slaughtered them, and I don't even remember it. How am I supposed to explain that to her? How do I tell someone I killed half a dozen men and only remember one of them?

"Okay. Come inside and have a glass of water. Sit down, and we'll get this figured out." She started backing away, and the urge to do something hit me. I grabbed her and pulled her closer to me.

"Never meddle in my life again," I whispered. Power rushed through me, adding oomph to my words. "*Never again.*"

She shivered, and I released her, walking past her to head inside. She followed me but kept her distance.

Cassius was waiting for us in the dining room, and Raphael was nowhere to be seen.

"Where is he?" I asked, gesturing around the empty room.

"He went to the room I keep for him and locked himself in," Cassius explained. "He didn't want to scare my staff, and he's not fit for company, so he decided to remove himself. That leaves you to tell me why you are in my house, covered in blood again. I want the entire truth, Kaliya."

"I'm not at fault," I snapped. "I told everyone it wasn't safe for Raphael and me, and you were the only one who listened. So, don't fucking stand there and throw blame at me. I fucking warned you, and you believed me. Maybe you should take it up with your wife and Raphael!" I was screaming at the end, pointing at the woman who stood to the side, her head down.

He shadow-stepped to me and grabbed my shoulders.

"I didn't say you were at fault," he whispered passionately into my ear. Slowly, his arms wrapped around me in a hug. "I'm sorry. I don't like this. I just want to know how I can help. I need to know what happened."

I leaned into him. He was safe. Cassius was a friend with no expectations. His touch didn't bother me. He had nothing to do with what happened tonight. He had fought for me because we had history. We knew what it meant to be alone, without family and support.

He cared for me and I for him, and for a moment, I let that protect me. There was nothing more he wanted than to hold me for a moment.

Everything I have worked so hard for is gone. Raphael will never be safe. Not like this.

Cassius being my most loyal friend was enough to get me to answer the hardest question.

What happened?

"They forced us to mate," I whispered into his shoulder. He tensed, and his hold grew tighter. "The rakshasa...he's been watching us. He captured us as we argued, kept humans from seeing what was happening, and paralyzed us with something. I was awake for all of it. He loaded us in a van and took us...He took us to where he was working, milked my venom, then shot it into Raphael. Neither of us could fight back." I started to shake as I remembered the feeling. It wasn't the first time someone had robbed me of my ability to defend myself. I had promised myself no one would ever do it to me again.

I failed. I had been helpless to stop it.

"Then he took Raphael's blood and put it in me," I continued. "It's done. We can't go back now."

"How did you get out?"

"The drug wore off, and I fought back," I said softly. "The blood is theirs. They're all dead. I didn't leave anyone alive." I couldn't tell them what I didn't remember, how I killed them. I only knew the aftermath, which wasn't something I was comfortable sharing.

"Okay..." Cassius slowly released me, tentative because honestly, neither of us was sure if I was stable enough to stand alone. "Shower and stay the night in your room if you want. I can take you home tomorrow."

I shook my head slowly. I needed to get to work.

"Kaliya?"

"I have their names," I whispered. "I have a bunch of their stuff in the van. I need to..." I started walking, but I was slow and sluggish. I was safe with Cassius, and my body was beginning to remind me I was tapped out.

"Tomorrow," he said softly, guiding me to something stable, and the closest thing there was had to be a wall. He didn't bother trying to get me to sit in a chair.

"Wait...if you and Raphael are mated now, doesn't your venom..."

Sorcha sank back when I looked at her.

"Yes," I answered, leaning on the wall. "But,"—I shook my head—"I don't know what to feel or what's going through his head tonight. I'm going to get to work, then...

then I'm going to find a way to fix this. Need to figure out what to do next."

"What are you going to work on?" Cassius asked, pushing my sticky hair aside. He leaned in close as I remained quiet. "Kaliya, answer me."

"They were employed. I was supposed to be kept alive...I think I was supposed to meet the employer but getting out with Raphael was more important. I need to find him and..." My head throbbed, and I fought it, refusing to blackout again.

"You need one night to rest," Cassius said gently. "Come on. Don't push yourself. You know you're not in a good place to continue this fight right now. Get some sleep, and we'll talk in the morning about everything we can do to help you. We'll bring everything in and start sorting through it. Do you want us to read it and start taking notes?"

"Thank you."

I was able to walk on my own, but both fae hovered until I made it through the door to my room and closed it.

Stripping my ruined clothing, I stumbled into the bathroom, my heart feeling weak as I turned on the hot water. Once I was under, I barely moved, leaning on the wall to soak and ignore the red and brown blood going down the drain.

I felt him in the building. As I finally got a private moment to figure out what was different about me, things came to the forefront. I could feel him pacing around. I didn't know what he was feeling, but just down the hall, he was pacing.

Feeling the new interesting power, I was able to call

the wispy red tendrils into my palm. Once they dissipated, I felt weak. As I sagged against the shower wall, *he* started moving, leaving his room.

I didn't move from where I was as he entered my room, which I had foolishly not locked. He stopped outside the bathroom door and said nothing, but there was an acute awareness. We knew the other was there.

Cutting off the water, I dried off, then wrapped my hair.

He didn't back away as my hand wrapped on the doorknob and slowly pulled it open.

"Can I do something for you?" I asked him, looking up to see his messy hair and cambion eyes.

"Explain," he said, his voice taut and strained.

"Which part?" I scoffed and walked around him, throwing my towel to the side as I went to the dresser to find something to wear. His hands grabbed my hips and held me in place. He wasn't nearly as weak as I was at that moment. I wouldn't move his hands until he decided to let me go. While Sorcha's touch had repulsed me, and Cassius' had been clean with no expectations, Raphael's touch was warm and rough, with a long list of expectations. If it had been a different night, they would have thrilled me even as I ran from them.

Tonight, I just wanted to pretend as if none of this had happened.

"Which part?" I asked again, refusing to lean back into him and that urge was a difficult fight all on it's own. "The part where we were taken by a supernatural, who had stalked me my entire life, and I didn't even know it? The part where you found out you were my mate? Or is this the moment I get to say *I told you so*? That being with me was dangerous, and this was so much worse than I thought it could even be. The part where I've known you were my mate from the day I stopped you from going to mass? That I knew you were my mate when you shot at me in that dark, dirty apartment covered in beer bottles? That I've *always known*, even as I watched you kiss, then kill someone from the lab? That I left you, knowing it was a last-ditch effort to protect you? Which part, Raphael?"

"All of it," he answered. He tugged me into him harder, reminding me that he had my venom flowing through his veins. It could take hours to wear off, and until then, he was stuck with a need that would keep him up all night. "And this."

"Well, I don't have the mental or emotional energy for this conversation," I snapped. "I certainly don't have the physical energy for *that*."

"How much of what we had was real? Answer that, then. Truthfully."

"All of it," I whispered. "I just...held back. I didn't tell you everything because I always hoped I could cut you loose, and you could have your own life. I wanted you to be happy without me."

"Why?" he growled in my ear.

"I told you. I never wanted to mate. It was too dangerous, and..." I blinked back tears of exhaustion. I refused to be broken-hearted over his fury. I was too tired. He had come to me, demanding to be in my life. I didn't drag him into this. I tried so fucking hard to keep him out of this.

"So, it had nothing to do with me." He released me,

and I was left cold. His insult cut me deep because he had no idea—none at all.

I turned and shoved him weakly. He didn't budge, but the shove was only the weak physical part of my emotional turmoil.

"It had everything to do with you!" I screamed. "You were always too good for me! I wasn't going to fucking ruin you! And now I have!" I was shaking as I stopped screaming. Here I was, naked, tired, and weak, screaming at the man who I would give my life for.

His face was a stone wall.

"Get out," I pleaded. "Just go. Be mad at me somewhere else. I can't do this tonight."

"No," he growled.

"We were just abducted off the street, and I watched my nightmares play out in real-time! I don't have it in me to deal with this right now, Raphael!"

"That's a perfectly good reason...for me not to go anywhere," he said, reaching out to touch my cheek. I pushed his hand away.

"Please," I begged softly.

"We're *mates* now, Kaliya. There's no going back. If there was, you would already be working on it. As far as I'm concerned, we're dealing with this, then going to bed. No more secrets, no more lies. Tomorrow, we're going to talk about what our new normal will be."

"Why?" It was my turn to ask such a simple question and hope.

"You said you love me." He ran a hand through his messy hair. "I might be fucking furious with how you never told me the truth, but it doesn't change the fact I will burn this world to the ground to be with you."

"You—"

"Shut the fuck up," he snarled.

He grabbed my face and slammed his lips to mine.

22

CHAPTER TWENTY-TWO

Oxygen. His kiss was oxygen, and I had stopped breathing for too long.

No, not that. It was more than that.

I had never even taken a breath.

I thought I didn't have the energy, but his kiss was fuel for my body, and I wanted all of it.

His grip was firm, and there was no denying the anger in his kiss—pulling my hair as he held my head in place, pressing his body against mine, rigid from anger—but I melted into it. My shaking hands wrapped around his neck, and I clung to him, looking for stability because the future felt too uncertain.

This was the first time I ever kissed him...or anyone. Decades of experience doing a lot of things, and my first kiss was with my mate during an argument, and he was so much better at it. He possessed me with his lips as his tongue explored my mouth, feeling my fangs, trailing over them, and sending sparks through me.

I have nothing to lose now. It's done, and I might as well take this. Might as well be selfish and keep him. Risk his life every day. He fucking wants that, so he's going to get it.

I knew there was no going back for me. If he wanted me, he was going to get all of me.

Palming my breast, he pushed me back into the dresser. He shoved a thigh between my legs, and a moan erupted from me as he moved it against me, a promise of what he was going to do. His lips pulled away from mine, and he used his grip in my hair to pull my head back so he could kiss down my neck.

"Bite me again," he growled.

"What?" I was hazy with lust as his lips made a line over my collarbones.

His eyes met mine as he angled my face to his thick neck.

"Bite me again," he demanded.

I didn't resist. I had no venom left in me, but I struck, and he groaned as he worked his hips between my legs and pressed his bulge against me. I ran my hands through his hair and over his back and chest as he pushed against me.

When I retreated, he lifted me and tossed me onto the bed. Before I could move into a more comfortable position, he grabbed my ankles and pulled me to the edge. His expression was something I could only describe as furious and desperate.

"Raph, condoms." I put my hands up, and he leaned down to kiss me. His growl was annoyed with me. "We need them now. Please. Please, just do it for me."

He yanked open the bedside drawer faster than I could follow, fishing around inside, and I could hear things rattling around. Then he had one and tore it open with his teeth. Shoving his sweatpants down, he rolled it on and thrust into me without any more preparation. I groaned as he filled me and held still for a long time. His chest was heaving as he stood there, deep inside me, his entire presence crowding all my senses.

He moved, fast and hard, full of the righteous fury I knew he was trying to expel. I accepted every bit of it, wrapping my legs around his waist and clinging to the bed as he tried to kill me with his touch. He leaned down, wrapping a hand in my hair once again, his mouth hovering over mine. I screamed until he silenced me with a brutal kiss that scorched me from his heat. He bit my lip as he pulled away.

I came first, shattering as he fucked me with a single-minded determination. As the bed slid on the floor, I was only half there, floating away as he took me. Pulling out, he moved me, placing me in the center of the bed and getting on with me. He rolled me over onto my stomach and pushed in deeper, groaning as he ran his hands over my back. Taking me harder and harder, his hand slid between my legs and rubbed, trying to build me up again. It worked so well.

When I lost myself to pleasure a second time, he went with me, growling as he finished over me.

Then he was gone, and I was left with an awful lonely and empty feeling as if he had just walked away from me forever. I heard the snap of him ripping the condom off.

"Fuck," he snarled as he walked into the bathroom. Water started to run a moment later.

"What? I thought you wanted this." I had wanted it, as much as I had wanted to avoid it for the rest of eternity.

"I'm still hard," he growled.

"It'll fade," I promised, trying not to let my eyes drift closed. "I can't..."

He came back to the bed and laid next to me, staring as if he was trying to figure me out.

"Get some sleep," he whispered, leaning forward to kiss my forehead. "We'll talk about everything in the morning."

"No," I said, groaning as I pushed myself up. Sleep sounded great but now I was confused too. "No. You wanted to talk, so we're going to talk. You don't seem okay with this."

"I thought I wouldn't be angry with you once it was over," he growled softly. "And that's not the case. This was exactly what I wanted. Me and you, but..." He sat up and swung his legs off the bed, putting his head in his hands. "I'm still fucking pissed at you. You kept this massive secret from me, and I found out when it was too late to do anything about it."

"Would you have let me walk away if I told you the entire truth?" I asked softly.

"No," he snarled. "I can't..." He pulled his hair. "I don't know what's real anymore. Did you only like me because I was your mate? Did I only like you for the same reason?"

"I don't know," I whispered honestly.

"I need to know," he said gravely, looking back at me. "Or I don't know...if I can..."

"You wanted freedom, and I tried to give it to you.

You're the one who chased *me*, saying I was probably your mate, so you don't get to take your anger out on me."

His snarl made my chest shake. Pulling my knees to my chest, I rested my cheek on them.

"I get it. I never liked the idea of having my mate chosen for me. Some mates among my people learned to like each other, learned to love. I wanted to save you from this, from me..."

"Are you about to say you're a terrible person, and I should have wanted another woman?" he asked, still looking at me over his shoulder. "I've had fucking enough of that talk."

"Tell me, is it you who thinks I'm perfect or the mating?" I hissed. "Or am I perfect because I'm your mate?"

Standing, he glared at me, then crawled across the bed until our noses were nearly touching.

"I've never thought you were perfect. I think you're damaged and alone all the fucking time. Even when we were together, you have this headspace you would go in to be alone. You hate yourself, and I'm tired of seeing it."

"Hard not to hate yourself when your parents and siblings died, but you didn't. Hard not to hate yourself when you're a failure of a ruler who can't even protect her mate from her enemies."

He kissed me, but this time, it wasn't angry but heartbreakingly soft.

"You did protect me," he murmured on my lips. "You did, Kaliya. You don't get to hate yourself for that. And when your family died, you were a *child*. You have survivor's guilt, but I bet everyone in your family was fucking praying you would escape, and you did. They would be so proud of you for escaping." He touched my cheek and pressed his lips to mine again.

"What about being angry about this?" I asked, feeling hollow.

"I think..." He sighed and put his forehead to mine. "Being your partner feels natural. If I walk out that door, my world would tilt, and everything would feel off-kilter until I'm back here again. We'll figure out what's real on our own."

"My feelings aren't from mating," I offered. "Naga mating...is biological. We're not required to like our mates, just to be with them."

"With you, I'll be able to figure out if we're the same," he whispered, kissing me again. "I'm still mad at you. It's not forcing me to let what you did go, so I guess that's a plus."

"I wanted to protect you—"

"While I appreciate the sentiment, it really doesn't change how I feel," he said as his grip grew a little stronger. "Now, you need some sleep."

"Are you going to stay?" I asked in a small voice.

"I have nowhere else to go. I was thinking of calling my people, so they know something happened. Think you can sleep through that, or should I go to Cassius's office?"

"I'll sleep through it."

I cleaned up before getting under my blankets. Raphael sat on the bed next to me, toying with his cellphone, the screen broken. Our captors had been so unconcerned with getting caught, they had left them on us. Even though the screen was broken, Raphael was able to make the call.

"Mateo?" he said softly, using his free hand to brush my hair. I fought to stay awake until he was done, my back to him, so he couldn't tell. I didn't want to wake up and realize he was gone. "I'm staying at Cassius' place tonight. Yeah, there was a...an incident," he said diplomatically. He gently tugged a bit of my hair, and I couldn't stop the small groan. "Go to sleep," he ordered. Then it was back to the call. "Yes, I am talking to Kaliya. Look, things got complicated. We were abducted and... No, I don't need you to come here...We're safe. Everything is going to be fine."

I sure as fuck hope so. I don't know if I can handle 'not fine' after a night like tonight.

The conversation went on as Raphael gave a condensed version of events. I didn't want to listen any longer, didn't want to think about any of it. My eyes grew heavy next to his warmth, and I drifted asleep.

"Do you love me?" she asked coyly, her lips pressed against my ear, teasing and soft.

"More than anything," I promised, reaching out to pull her fully onto my lap, but she ducked and seemed suddenly shy. We were still new to this, and she wasn't what I had expected from a mate. She liked to be in control of everything, so she could understand what was happening between us.

I laid back, letting her tumble and laugh on my chest, but it gave her what she wanted—power. I could be powerless for a moment with her. She threw one of those beautiful long legs over and straddled me, her eyes flashing red and black in excitement. She ran her hands over my chest, making a pleased sound that made me excited in return. I ran my hand up that exposed leg, groaning at how soft she was under my touch.

Between us, power crackled. I was already a powerful warrior when I met her, and she was deceptively strong. We didn't live in a world willing to recognize her for what she was, but I knew. I recognized a powerful warrior and strong leader when I saw one.

Now, we were even more. Whatever twist of fate brought us together only made us stronger.

She leaned down, her black hair veiling us as her lips touched mine.

23

CHAPTER TWENTY-THREE

I woke up slowly, my body still aching from the punishment of the night before.

Well, it wasn't all punishment.

I reached out and found him, leaning into his back and absorbing his heat.

Or maybe it was, and I just liked it too much to care.

He didn't stir, and I had no idea what the time was, so I was careful not to wake him as I got up, biting back a groan when I put my feet down. My mind was awake, but my legs weren't. I pressed on when my stomach made an uncomfortable gurgle. I had skipped a few chances to eat Friday and Saturday, so I was hungry enough to eat with Raphael. Making my way into the bathroom, I stretched out my arms, brushed my hair and teeth, then went to find something to wear, checking the time before I walked out. It was breakfast time, which meant I could put something into my stomach without having to bother anyone off their normal schedule. I could have woken up Raphael, but he deserved some sleep. He knew where I would be the moment he woke up, so I quietly shut the door and left. I found Leith standing in my hall as if he had been waiting.

"Will Master Raphael be joining us?" he asked, his face deceptively blank.

"Maybe. He's still asleep, and I couldn't bring myself—"

He took a step forward, then another, each less tentative. I was stunned when he reached out and hugged me, an awkward, stiff gesture of kindness. I closed my eyes and hugged him back.

"You always have a home here," he reminded me as he pulled away. "It's always a pleasure to have you here with us."

"Oh, so you do like me!" I teased, trying to smile. "Thank you. Cassius didn't ask you to say that, did he?"

"Your arrival last night meant I had to be woken up, so I wasn't far while you explained what happened to Lord Cassius and Lady Sorcha. I'm sorry I didn't announce myself. I felt like I should be close in case anything was needed, but I didn't think you needed any more people around you than was necessary."

"Oh." I gestured for him to lead the way. "Breakfast would be wonderful. And you did nothing wrong. It is what it is, right?"

He nodded briskly, then walked to the dining room. There were other eating spaces in the mansion where Cassius lived, but he was a minimalist. He liked the dining room, and he used it and only it unless we were hanging out in the kitchen because Terry was off.

"Are they..."

"They are awake, yes. During breakfast, they've been working on the things you brought home. We also put the van away and wrote down all the important details about it, so they're on hand."

"Yeah, set that thing on fire the moment you get the chance," I said. He nodded once more, and I entered the dining room. He didn't follow me. I had a feeling he was going to wait in the hall until Raphael was awake.

"Kaliya..." Cassius looked up from whatever he was reading. "I would ask if you slept well..."

"I slept," I mumbled. "Well?" I shook my hand. I couldn't give a firm answer. Between the complete upheaval of my life in the last twelve hours and the dream...

I'd tried not to think about it when I woke up, but once again, remembered every detail about the cambion woman and the male body I had. I didn't know what or who it was about. There was a chance I could piece it together if I could think straight for longer than ten minutes, but I was fried.

"It's not my place to ask, but how are things between you and Raphael?" Sorcha looked up, her moon-grey eyes filled with guilt.

"We're going to figure it out," I said as I sat down. She grabbed the plate from in front of me and served me before I had the chance to do it myself. When the plate was put down in front of me again, I had a large meal to make my way through, full of eggs, bacon, and more. If it was served at breakfast, there was a chance it was on my plate. "Thank you, and..." I sighed. "I'm mad at you, but we're still friends. I know you didn't think any of this would happen."

"Thank you," she said, going back to her own seat. "I just...I wanted you to be happy."

"Well, you had loftier goals than I ever did," I mumbled, my appetite fleeing.

"Feel free to say I told you so," she said, pushing her food around with her fork. "You were right. Someone was going to target both of you, and you were trying to protect yourself and Raphael. I shouldn't have encouraged him, but I didn't put much...faith in your estimation of the problem. I thought you were just running from your feelings and making excuses. I'm so sorry."

"It's done, Sorcha." I didn't want to have this conversation. "Cassius—"

"I'm not getting into this," he said softly, his eyes back on the sheet of paper he was holding. "I'm not in the mood to have this conversation for a second time."

"He's angry with me," Sorcha said with a sad expression. "He warned me, too. He said you knew the problems that plagued the nagas better than anyone, and I should trust your judgment on the matter."

"I don't want my problems to come between you two," I said as pain hit the back of my throat and my chest tightened.

It was never supposed to happen like this.

"I've already forgiven her," Cassius said as he dropped the paper onto the table. "She did what she thought would make her friend happy."

"I really don't have many friends, so I'm going to mess up sometimes. I just never thought I would mess up this much. You would think that being...what I am would make me a bit wiser."

"Look, you couldn't have possibly known...I didn't even..." I sighed heavily, leaning back in my seat. "He'd been stalking me for years, and I had no idea," I whispered, looking away from them to the window. The soft glow of morning coming in was like a balm. The night had been so long and so terrible, but it was another new day, and I had survived to see it. I had to be grateful for something.

"How long?" Cassius was suddenly more attentive.

"Before you and I even met," I answered with a brittle smile. "He knew about you. He knew about Hisao training me." I wrapped my arms around myself. I could make some educated guesses, thanks to what he said and inferred. "He went to that lab to see the cambions because he knew about Raphael and me. I think he wanted to know what Raphael was and how to work with it so he could capture us, eventually. There was never any hope for us to escape this, and I..." I lowered my head. "I have no idea."

There was a small kernel of anger. I wanted blood—revenge—but first, I needed to get over the aftermath. My head was in the wrong place, but it wouldn't be for long, then my hunt would begin.

Raphael walked in and silently took the seat next to me. He didn't lean over to kiss me good morning. I didn't know I had wanted it until it never came. Cassius was the one who got and made his plate for him, even though Raphael gave no indication he wanted to eat.

"Thank you," he said, but like me, he didn't touch the

food yet. "You were all talking about the rakshasa and last night, right?"

"Yes," Sorcha confirmed, more nervous than I think anyone else at the table. Odd, since she was the most powerful at the table, by my estimation.

We had been such a tight-knit group only five months ago. We stumbled, and we made mistakes, but we trusted each other. At that moment, it seemed like everyone was waiting for a bomb to go off. We just didn't know who that bomb would be. Me or Raphael? Maybe Cassius. He was capable of it.

"What are you thinking about?" he asked me, leaning over to make sure I knew who he was talking to. "Eat your breakfast."

"Don't...start telling me what to do," I said, rubbing my temples. "And...I think rehashing all of last night is useful, but only because I want to figure out what to do next. I had planned to capture the rakshasa, not kill him. I needed answers, and now I can't get them from the source."

"We have everything you grabbed. If there're answers there, we'll find them. Just like we did with Raphael and helping him with Mygi. Speaking of..." He grabbed a sheet of paper and held it out. "Leith helped us last night. He did a write-up of every person you had identification for. Obviously, they were fakes, but something we can start with. We can track identity to identity, find out who they were talking to, where they bought their equipment."

I thought about Raphael's phone as I looked over the sheet of paper. I didn't recognize the names because they didn't use any names around me. But they let Raphael keep his phone. They had been incredibly confident, and that had made them a little sloppy. They thought they would live through the night and leave two dead bodies behind with no evidence. That hadn't been how things had gone down, which meant we could hopefully capitalize on those errors.

"We'll find something," I said with a surety I shouldn't have, but I really believed we would find something.

"Maybe we should talk about the parts of last night you don't remember," Raphael said softly, taking the piece of paper from me and setting it aside.

"What?" Cassius's sharp attention flicked between me and my mate.

"I blacked out a couple of times after we were forcibly mated," I explained.

"When you mean forcibly mated..." Sorcha was a touch paler than normal.

"They milked my venom and injected it into Raphael. Then they took his blood and injected it into me. It was all very clinical," I said quickly, dispelling any ideas she was having. "Consummation is a choice, not a requirement, so they left us paralyzed and helpless through the entire thing. Thank the gods."

"You were blacking out?" Cassius narrowed his eyes. "You've never done that, not even drunk. You always remember something."

"Yeah." I wasn't sure how much I should tell them about the visions, dreams, or whatever they were. It was clearly important, but it was definitely a naga thing, which meant the best person to ask was Adhar. I needed answers on that front. "But I blacked out. Mating was...painful."

Raphael made an odd choking noise.

"It was. Your blood was like fire or lightning running through me. It fucking hurt. Sorry, but that's the truth of the matter. It...freaked me out because I never heard of another naga feeling that when they take a human mate, so it must be something to do with you being a cambion. I think it made me pass out." I went with the truth, so he could understand. If it was a cambion thing, he needed to tell everyone else so they knew when they met their potential mates. Going into something blind sucked.

"And it gave you new powers," he said, rubbing his face.

I lifted my hand so Cassius and Sorcha could see instead of me needing to explain. I summoned the power humming in my veins, and the wispy red energy swirled and danced, then closed my hand.

"I don't really know all of what it does, obviously. I... shoved it into Raphael, and it cleared him of whatever was paralyzing him."

"I think it jumpstarted my system. That's what it felt like," he said, rubbing his chest right where I had hit him with it.

"I was moving on instinct. I didn't know I could do it until I did. Something was wrong with me. Something is still wrong with me."

"No," Raphael whispered. "You were magnificent. I should have said that last night, but there were other things we needed to talk about. You two should have seen her. The rakshasa was going to cut my head off. I wasn't needed once they confirmed Kaliya and I were mates. They wanted to keep her for their boss, but I was useless. The moment he raised that axe, she jumped into action."

"What did I do?" I asked softly.

"You don't remember?" he asked, frowning down at me.

I shook my head.

"You..." Raphael pushed a hand through his hair, now worried about me. "You did that thing. You said nagas lost a lot of power over the years, but you...you were like half-snake. From the waist down, I guess, and you wore armor I had never seen before. It just showed up. You had this scary red glow, and you tackled him. The axe went into the wall, and he tried clawing you. He was shapeshifting and trying to fight you, but you were relentless. You eviscerated him, then you killed the other one with your...tail?"

"Tail works," I whispered, staring at my food in horror. I had awoken the old power? Or did Raphael's blood?

"When someone else came down the stairs, you tore his arms off, then his head. I didn't see exactly how you did it, just remember seeing the body parts flying past me."

I felt sick.

I felt *powerful.*

The pleasure I took in destroying them flashed through my mind. I closed my eyes, seeing snippets of what Raphael described. I had butchered them, screaming in fury as they came for me. Between every kill, I went back to Raphael, checking on him, hovering over him defensively until the next one decided to hurt us.

My life was taking a very strange turn, and I would have to meet it head-on. I wasn't ready, but I knew it didn't matter. Visions, the old powers, the new ones—I didn't have much of an option. I couldn't run, not if I wanted answers.

"When did you start coming back?" he asked me.

"When I thought they were all dead and wanted to help you," I answered. "Then...then I tortured the rakshasa. I..." Clenching my fists, I remembered how different I felt at that moment. "I carried you upstairs and outside. I guess I didn't want to think about it. I realized I wasn't walking on my feet after I put you down. Things started to catch up with me then. I've killed a lot of people, but I've never...never been a full-on monster. I've never been that powerful. It shook me, which is why I vomited. Well, one of the reasons."

"They put you in a vulnerable position, and you watched someone you care about nearly die," Cassius said gently. "No one here is going to blame you for losing whatever contents you had in your stomach."

I rubbed my face and nodded. He was right.

"I'm still a little rattled," I admitted. "But I'll get over it. We have shit to do. Raphael, you were calling the cambions. What did they say?"

"I explained as much as I felt comfortable over the phone. I'm going to sit down with them later today."

"I'd like to be there. Sammy is going to be furious with me, and I want a chance to explain this to her myself."

"Oh?"

"Yeah. She and I were starting to bond over the goal of keeping us apart," I explained, smiling ruefully. Sorcha chuckled across the table.

"We made a team, so you made one. Smart."

"I thought so, too, and I never wanted to take one of her punches again. My team was better." I couldn't resist the hollow laugh that bubbled up inside. "All for naught."

"It was," Sorcha agreed. "Only Raphael and I were on the same page on our side. You also had Cassius."

"Is that why you and Sammy started getting along? So you could keep us apart?"

"Yup." I didn't see a reason to lie about it.

He shook his head slowly, then finally started eating his breakfast. "Women," he muttered before shoving an entire strip of bacon into his mouth. Cassius chuckled.

It was a good sign. Everyone relaxed a degree, and it felt more normal. We ate together, enjoying each other's company. I was still a little more on edge than everyone else, but I was also focused.

Raphael and I will figure this out. I'm going to make someone pay for this. And I'm going to find answers about what is happening to me.

I had a new goal, which gave me a new resolve.

24

CHAPTER TWENTY-FOUR

"Let's make a list," Cassius said, grabbing a pen from his pile of stuff on the table. "I want to know exactly what we're planning on doing and when. We can streamline it, meet back here if needed or at Kaliya's home once we're done."

"You don't need to get into all of this, Cassius. You've already helped enough." I didn't want to see more of my friends risk themselves for me.

"There's no such thing as helping enough," he said benignly as he wrote something down. "Raphael needs to talk to the cambions. Kaliya?"

"I'll be there, and I also need to talk to Adhar. That'll take me home, and I can take Raphael with me, then you two could meet us there. And we need to go get our vehicles from last night—"

"That's been handled," Sorcha said softly. "Leith, Cassius, and I made that trip after you both went to bed. They're outside in the driveway."

"Thanks. Can you bring all of this with you? Or

maybe I should just take it with me." I reached out and pushed some papers around.

"You can take it all," Cassius said, continuing to scribble down our little list. "We've already scanned it all. The originals should stay with you."

"Okay." I reached out, putting the papers into a better pile. Leith arrived with a sandwich bag and threw in the smaller items—IDs, credit cards, and other wallet items—then took the pile from me.

"I'll put this in a folder, and it will be waiting for you in your car," he said, bowing his head and leaving.

"Thanks, Leith," I called out as he disappeared.

"We'll reconvene to continue the search into who did this once we all arrive at Kaliya's home," Cassius said, tapping the pen on his expensive dining table. "What time would you like us to arrive?"

"After lunch," I answered. "I'll send you a text when you can start the drive over. We don't know how long it'll take with the cambions, and I definitely don't know how much Adhar and I will need to talk."

"Why Adhar?" Sorcha frowned. "He's the...male ruler, isn't he?"

"Yeah, um, earlier this week..." I groaned. "I need to call him right now, actually. Earlier this week, they had someone test his defenses, and Nakul went to check it out. They didn't figure out who or what it was. He said he would get ahold of me in case they needed me."

"A distraction? Or a coordinated hit?" Cassius asked softly.

"Could be anything. I don't even remember where my phone is. Fuck."

Sorcha jumped up and jogged out of the room, coming back with my phone.

"We found it in your car. I put it on a charger here. Sorry, I should have thought about it when you woke up."

I took the phone and gave her a one-armed hug.

"Don't feel bad. There's a lot happening right now." I checked the screen. No missed calls except Sammy. Of course, Sammy was trying to get a hold of me. I texted her, promising an explanation when Raphael and I made it to the compound. Then I texted Adhar, telling him I needed to speak to him within a few hours about an evolving emergency. Even though I was safe, whenever a naga was attacked for being a naga, it was high alert, and I made sure he understood we were on high alert. He replied instantly, promising to keep himself available and to get in touch with everyone to make sure they boarded up their windows and kept their heads down.

"Okay, nagas know something is going on," I said, putting my phone away. "Adhar didn't have anything last night. We have people test the security all the time."

"Then why was this one a big deal?" I could hear Raphael's frown.

"I was trying to find the rakshasa, and Adhar was concerned I poked the bear, in a manner of speaking." I stood and stretched. "Let's get moving and get the pressing stuff done."

"I'm not comfortable with you driving after you've had black outs," Raphael said as he and everyone at the table stood as well, all eyes on me.

"I'll be fine. If I can kill a bunch of people during one of them, driving home should be a cinch." I was going to drive my own car. They weren't going to take that away from me. Slipping easily from one thought to another, I turned to Cassius. "While you're waiting on us, do you think you can keep going through everything? And destroy the van?"

"Of course. By the time you see us again, I'll have a full report on everything you took from them. Do you think we can go see the location where they held you? Do you remember the trip?"

"I set it on fire," I said softly. "It needed to burn."

"That's fine. There still might be something, and we can do a post-cleanup. We can't have human authorities finding bones there down the road." Cassius held out his pen.

I tried to retrace my steps to Cassius' house. I had been on autopilot.

"Shit," I mumbled. "I don't really—"

"I had my phone on me," Raphael said. "Maybe its movements are tracked?"

"Do you have an app that does that?" I frowned up at him.

"Every cambion does, just in case," he said with a shrug. "Here." He started typing on his phone, then put it in front of me.

Sure enough, the app tracked the phone's location over twenty-four hours. This wasn't a consumer app, but tech he must have asked for when he was dealing with security issues the cambions were facing. He could, from his own phone, track the movement of every cambion as long as they had their phone on them, including himself.

"Who else has access to this?" I asked softly. It was

dangerous information.

"Only the cambions. Cole manages the admin, so we didn't need to use the company who developed it to track all of us."

"Good." With the app, it was easy for me to write the correct directions for Cassius and Sorcha, then hand them over to them once I was done. "You'll find it. It wasn't far from the road, and hopefully, it'll look like a charred corpse of a building now."

"We'll get on this," he promised. "You two head out. Call if anything happens, okay?"

"We will." I patted his shoulder, then hugged Sorcha. Raphael shook their hands. Leith was waiting at the door with our keys.

"Drive safely," he ordered both of us. "Your other things are in your car," he told me directly.

"Thanks."

I went to get in my car, but Raphael grabbed me.

"I didn't want to do this at the table," he murmured, then kissed me until I was pressed up against my BMW, my heart pounding, my skin feverish as his hot hands found every inch of me that was exposed.

"You could have," I said with a weird flutter in my stomach. "I mean, we're not hiding anything anymore."

Or running from it.

"You've never liked PDA," he reminded me. "So, I wasn't going to push you. Drive safely. I'll meet you at the compound."

He backed away slowly, and I got into my BMW. As I started driving and hit the on-ramp for the freeway, Adhar called me, and I put him through the speakers.

"I need to know more about this high alert," he said, a touch frantically. "Everyone is in full lockdown and in their safe rooms for the next forty-eight hours. I need to tell them something. They all think the others have been hurt, and the children are in danger."

"I was abducted by the rakshasa. He tried to kill my mate. I killed him. We're safe for now, I think, but we have some things to manage before I can have a longer conversation."

"Okay."

"Oh, and I mated. Well, the rakshasa forced the mate bond on us." No reason not to tell him. "I'm having blackouts and seeing things. I know that's not normal. Can you look into that before we talk later? Maybe some previous naga had this problem or something similar."

"Certainly..." He seemed apprehensive. "Do I offer my congratulations or my condolences?"

"We'll see. Let me think about that." I hung up on him and hit the gas as I entered the freeway. Then Sammy called, and I groaned as I answered.

"You said—"

"We were forced, Sammy. We couldn't stop it," I explained quickly, cutting off her accusation of betrayal. "He was waiting for us to be vulnerable to capture us. We're working on it. We're going to figure out what the hell is going on. But none of it will change the fact Raphael and I are now mated. There's no going back."

"You said he *wasn't* your mate," she snarled into her phone, causing all sorts of weird disruption to my speakers. "You lied to me."

"Yes," I whispered. "I did. I couldn't...I couldn't trust

he wouldn't force you to tell him what you knew, and I...I wanted you to feel confident I could manage him. I was doing just fine until we were abducted." My throat was thick as I tried to explain. I had built a new friendship on a lie—again. "I didn't want this to happen."

"Raphael said he's on his way so he can explain what happened. I can't believe you two were taken, and you're coming back without...anyone even knowing it fucking happened. We had no fucking idea until Raphael called Mateo. When he didn't come home early and called instead, I thought you had given in."

"Our captors took precautions and had some understanding that no one would look for us quickly. Luckily, Raphael and I know how to get out of a tough situation," I said, the shame of how I lied to her giving way to hollowness. I was resigned that no matter how good my plans were, how hard I worked, I would never actually win. For other people, I could, but when it came to my own problems, they would always cut a swath of destruction, and I was powerless to stop it. It would always be like this now, maybe not frequently or even soon, but it would happen.

Unless I found the answers I needed. I tightened my grip on the steering wheel. The rakshasa had opened up so many questions, and I needed to know the answers before I could move forward.

"Yeah..." Sammy trailed off. "Mateo is asking me to get off the phone. Look, thanks for telling me what really happened, but I don't like being lied to. I thought...you and I were actually going to be friends. I was looking forward to it."

"Sammy—"

She hung up on me.

I drove in silence and beat Raphael to the compound. Getting out of my car, I saw the cambions watching me from afar, waiting for their warlord to return. None of them approached me, and I certainly didn't wave. I leaned on the back of my BMW, keeping them where I could see them. There was a strangeness as if I was meeting my boyfriend's disapproving family, but we'd already eloped, and they couldn't do anything to break us up.

When Raphael arrived only a few minutes later, he parked next to me and got out. Before he did anything else, he looked between me and the cambions. His heavy sigh told me a lot. Was he really hoping they would be happy with this?

As I started to walk, I blacked out again, the world melting away as I lost consciousness.

"Are you ready to meet them?" she asked, looping her arm in mine. I held her close once she gave me that leverage and leaned down to kiss the top of her head.

"To meet your parents? A man is never ready for that," I joked. "You said your parents would understand what's happening between us."

"My parents have a mate bond," she said with a wise nod. "They'll know there's no fighting this. I just want everyone to meet. You don't need my father's approval. He can't take me away from you."

Walking down the stone path, we were nearly there, but I

was grateful for her reassurance. I had always expected to mate with another naga, a woman who would understand or a human I had to steal away for eternity. Instead, I got this unique, beautiful creature, and she was all mine. We didn't just complement each other like any of the mated pairs I knew. We truly made each other better.

She stopped at the front door and knocked, politeness I didn't expect since this was the home where she grew up.

"My daughter," her mother said with a loving smile as she opened the door, then gasped as she saw me. "Is this him?"

Her mother seemed totally human.

"This is my mate!" She pushed me forward. "Tell father he was right. A little blood and now he's mine forever." There was something predatory and possessive about those words. It excited me, even though I was trapped under the gaze of the mature woman who had raised my mate.

"Well, come in, and we'll all get to know each other," her mother said, pulling the door open wider. "Your father went off to do something. He'll return by nightfall. Are you willing to stay the night?"

"If you'll have us," I said politely, bowing my head in submission to the woman of this house.

"My home is always open to family," she replied in kind, touching my cheek and earning a growl from her daughter. Her mother laughed as she released me. "Oh, yes, just like your father, aren't you?"

"Yes, I am," my lovely mate said, her eyes red and black as she grabbed me possessively and led me into the charming home.

25

CHAPTER TWENTY-FIVE

"Kaliya?" Raphael was holding me, his arm tight around my waist and my chest, making sure I didn't slide down onto the gravel. We were still in the parking lot, and my back was still pressed against my warm car.

"I'm fine," I said, shaking my head, trying to clear the memories. Her mother—now I was meeting the parents. Fuck.

"Are you?" he asked, leaning down to put his forehead against mine.

"I don't know. That's why I want to talk to Adhar."

"What's happening?"

"We should talk to the cambions—"

"You come first right now. None of them are trying to black out and meet the ground."

"I'm having...visions, memories, but they aren't mine. They're from another naga who mated a cambion. I have my suspicions, but I really want to talk to Adhar about it."

"I'm driving you home later."

"Yeah, that might be for the best," I agreed, rubbing my temples as I pushed away from the car. "There's nothing we can do right now. I'll just stay close to you in case it happens again."

"Another naga and a cambion, huh? So, this has happened before."

"Apparently, I think. Maybe it's a weird interaction of our blood. There's magic at work, and I don't have all the answers. We're in uncharted waters as far as I'm concerned."

My suspicions didn't make any more sense than the visions, so I didn't want to voice them until I had a real expert. I didn't want to share my theories and give them an impression of something that was probably wrong. I knew a lot about nagas. They were my people. I was one of them. Adhar, on the other hand, was an expert at naga history in a way I wasn't. He was a keeper of that important information—the old legends and stories, and their truthful origins, diaries from previous generations—and had lived through some of it. He was an old naga, but those first few generations lived longer and had fewer children because the numbers were so high. It was complicated, and I wasn't an expert in the history.

"Okay, we'll focus on this, then get to your place." He walked with me to the cambions. There were no werewolves or fae working, but I didn't put much thought into that. Them being gone was nice, which was all that mattered.

"Are you both okay?" Gabrielle asked, coming forward first. "Anything need to be healed?"

"No, I don't think so," I said, waving her off. If I had

even a bruise, I would have let her. Anything to wash off what had happened the night before. Not the sex with Raphael. That had been fantastic. What led to it? If I could forget it happened, I would—in a heartbeat.

"Let's head inside the gym," Raphael ordered. "It has enough space for all of us to talk this out."

The group shuffled along. Sammy stayed as far away from me as she could, her head down. I had lied to her, and I couldn't expect her to forgive me. For the mating, for the danger, maybe since she knew I had been trying to avoid that.

But not for lying to her.

Stephan ordered some cambions to grab chairs for everyone. After fifteen minutes, we were all sitting down. Raphael was in front of his people, and I sat to the side and a little behind him, trying to be small and out of the way, but also in a place they could ask me questions.

"Kaliya and I are mates," he announced. "Last night, we were abducted by her enemies, and they were planning to kill both of us."

"It's a naga thing," I added. "We have enemies. Someone is trying to drive my kind to extinction." I had mentioned it and knew Raphael had mentioned it before, but I had this crushing need to mention it again, so everyone realized this wasn't a joke.

"This won't change what we're doing here. However, I do want to have my mate in my life, so I'm going to move in with her."

"No." I sat up straighter. "You can stay here weekdays and come see me on the weekends. Just for now, Raphael. Don't force them to live without you yet."

"You don't live with your people. I'll be thirty minutes away. Your people are on the other side of the world."

"My people are in their homeland, and we have two rulers, not one. Adhar takes care of the day-to-day things in India. He never turns off his phone in case one of them needs something. We're an established people with several estates and generations of wealth built up. You and everyone here, you're just finding your feet. You need to be here to do that for them. I refuse to take priority over them."

"If I don't move in with you, it could be several more months before we could live together when my home is done," he reminded me.

I opened, then closed my mouth, and his face changed as he realized I wasn't talking about moving in with him yet.

"This is one of those things you think we should take slow," he said softly, narrowing his eyes.

"I mean…I built an entire life and my own home. I'm not incredibly keen on just throwing it away. Moving in together doesn't need to be right now. We've barely known each other for a year. We're mates now, and I want to make it work, but…"

"Okay, we'll come back to this. I'll spend the weekends with you, and it's not like you won't be here at the compound every day, anyway."

"Exactly. I'll still be training the cambions, and we'll see each other all the time. I just want to make sure everyone has time to adjust."

"Including you."

"Including me."

"Fine. You all heard that? Good." He didn't seem happy with me, but it was something we would need to talk about. There was so much we needed to talk about, so many kinks to work out. The choice had been stripped away from both of us, and we had no plan for how it would play out. I certainly had never considered the day I would mate Raphael. These were all reasons I had been fighting it so hard. We both had responsibilities and lives, and I was used to my freedom. Living on another compound...that would be hard for me.

"So, are you her mate, or is she yours?" Cole asked, looking between us.

"Both," he answered. "I'm immune to her venom, and...Kaliya, you might have a better idea about this than I do."

I did, but it had really been confirmed by the visions.

"Your blood. When you meet your mate, give them your blood. It makes you fertile with the person. I don't know the logistics of it, but Raphael's blood did something to me, and I think it's a cambion thing. It certainly isn't naga, or maybe it's a combination of the two."

"Will all our mates be nagas?" That was Sammy, glaring at me from the back.

"I sure as fuck hope not," I mumbled. "I think humans are also a possibility."

Raphael looked over his shoulder at me again. I tapped the side of my head.

"I'm rolling with the visions I've been having," I explained to him. "The cambion mate of the previous naga I'm seeing, she had a human mother. I think. But her mother said she was just like her father. So..." I shrugged. "I'm trying. You'll need to tell them what you felt with me if they're going to go out looking for mates."

"Yeah, they already know. This is just confirmation." He turned back to the group. Some seemed greedy for knowledge, while others seemed scared or distrustful. This was a lot, and it was happening backward. Normally, people learned the general rules before they were confronted with an anomaly. Raphael and I were an anomaly and the only thing the cambions had to go on.

"So, what now?"

"Well, we need to increase security on the compound. I told you I didn't want to do patrols, but we're going to start. We're already doing a buddy system for those who need to leave for whatever reason, and I won't be leaving the compound without at least Mateo or Sammy—"

"Unless you're coming to my house. I don't need Mateo and Sammy sitting in my living room, and I have good security." Raphael turned to me again as I spoke.

"We should probably put a patrol on your house—"

"No." I didn't back down under the weight of his stare. "When someone comes into my house, I have safe rooms and weapons. I also have every right to kill them where they stand, and I will. My security is better now than it's ever been. I won't have cambions going all the way to my place just to wander around. There's not enough of you to do that for more than one location, anyway. Which, let me say, would make it even more impossible for you to move in with me."

His lips twitched in anger.

"Then move in here, and this won't be a problem," he

said softly. "Today. We'll get everything you need and bring it here. We'll shuffle some people around, so we're not crowded."

"We'll talk about it later."

He growled softly.

"So, things are going to change, but not all that much and not all right now," he said, his mouth tight, the words said with so much control, I knew he was thinking about shaking me until I saw things his way. He wouldn't, not in front of others. This was the confidence I knew he had. Now, he was used to being in charge of something and had, so far, made all the right decisions for his people. He was quickly becoming an exceptional leader.

But he would not rule me.

"What can we do to stop this from happening?" Cole asked.

"Mating?" I frowned.

"No, you were taken without us even knowing."

"Oh. Well, Raphael showed me the apps you have to track each other. You want to be in charge of the tech here, start monitoring them. If someone is not where you figured they would be, give them a call or text. If they don't answer in a reasonable time, release the dogs of war. Go get them. There's no such thing as too paranoid in our world." I smiled as Raphael growled softly again. "Can you do that?"

"Yeah. I'll monitor when people are gone. I probably should have been doing that, anyway." He sheepishly rubbed the back of his neck, his face flushed with embarrassment.

"This would be more involved. They would need to

tell you where they're going, so you know where they should be. Make a sign-in and sign-out, with a reason for leaving. It's going to annoy everyone, but it's important. A lot of nagas were lost over the centuries for not telling people where they were going. They just never came back. I don't want to see it happen to all of you."

"How many are we talking about?" Cole asked softly.

"Hundreds. There used to be hundreds of us. Most were lost to petty conflicts, war, and humans over the years, and we never had children fast enough to keep our numbers up. Then we started realizing there was a pattern. We lost people to the black market trading of our body parts. Then there're the ones who are trying to wipe us out. They were the pattern. Entire families just gone when no one checked on them often enough. When I was born, there were less than twenty of us left. By the time I became an adult, there were less than ten. Not including babies, there are more cambions in the world than nagas. So, take it from me, start protecting your own with every resource, sooner rather than later."

"We'll start now. I'm going to head to Kaliya's, probably for the night, but I'll be back tomorrow. We'll work with Cassius and Sorcha to figure out who and what was really behind the attack on us. Cole, you'll be on duty tonight. Pick one person to do a shift change, so you can get some sleep, and we're always watched. This could be the security measure we need, so you know I'm safe over the weekends with Kaliya. Consider this a test run."

"Yes, sir."

Twenty minutes later, I was back at my car, my hands

shoved into my pockets as I waited. Raphael was filling out a thrown-together sign-out sheet, then ruffled Cole's hair before he got into the driver's seat.

I got in next and let him drive us away.

Time for me to address my half of this problem. Time to talk to Adhar and try to get some damn answers.

26

CHAPTER TWENTY-SIX

I spared no time getting comfortable when we got home, marching into my back office while shooting back an order for Raphael.

"Tell Cassius and Sorcha they can head over!"

"I will," he said from the living room, where I heard papers being shuffled around. He had brought in the stolen documents and identification we would need.

I texted Adhar, warning him I was going to call any moment. He didn't reply, but I saw the little notification he read the text. I didn't close my office door, leaving it open for Raphael to come in if he wanted. He was my mate, which meant all naga secrets were his secrets now. I would eventually have to introduce him to Adhar and all the others. It was only proper, but I wasn't going to force it. If he wanted to come in, the door was open. It was an invitation he could join in.

I called Adhar and waited for him to answer. It took several rings, but he eventually showed up in front of me, looking tired.

"Kaliya, you look better than I expected." He gave me a wry smile.

"You should have seen me when I escaped last night," I replied with a dry chuckle. "You would have seen exactly what you expected."

"Was it bad?"

"Yeah." I rubbed my arms and leaned on my desk. "The rakshasa and his team were waiting for us to come into the open. I haven't been seen publicly with my mate in months. Not alone, anyway."

"Who was normally with you?"

"Cassius and his wife, and it was just the once. You know who Cassius is, right?"

"King Brion's son, yes. I know who he is and your history with him." Adhar pulled up a chair and sat down. I knew I didn't have a reason to be surprised. Adhar was a ruler of the nagas and had probably met all the Tribunal at some point. My mother did more of the public duties, then I had a direct line to them, so I had never seen Adhar interact with the Tribunal, and we never spoke about who he knew. "We don't need to talk about last night or how it happened if you don't want to."

"You never told anyone about Raphael and me, did you?" I needed to ask. Seeing him, knowing how he was about mating and continuing the species, I couldn't resist asking.

"Nakul, who talks to no one and lives with me. He heard us talking through the door. Also, he had met your Raphael, and I wanted to know more." Adhar sighed. "I would never leak the identity of your mate to anyone. I don't fault you for asking, but I would never."

"I just...it happened so fast. The rakshasa pretty much said he had figured it out on his own, but you know, we're trained to be paranoid."

"No, *you* were trained to be paranoid by your parents and the life you've decided to live since their murders. The rest of us are just survivors, doing our best to live every day like people aren't out to get us."

"You live in a compound you haven't left for more than a few hours in a century," I countered. "And the last time you left that compound for more than a day was to track me down when I was twelve, and my parents had been butchered."

"Sixteen," he corrected softly. "When you ran away, I spent months searching for you."

"Oh, you never told me that." I rubbed my arms, feeling vulnerable, like the teen girl I had been when I ran. "Why didn't you ever tell me that?"

"I was just grateful for the day you finally reached out to us. You didn't need to know the rest. There was no reason for you to know. We've never been compatible people, Kaliya, and we have our disagreements, but...you were a child who had lost everything, and I could not take the role of a parent. When you finally reached out, I decided this was one thing I would not make you feel guilty about." He shook his head sadly, looking away from the camera for a moment.

"That's beside the point. I apologize for bringing up the past. You have found your mate, were attacked by our enemies, and now you are mated. The mating has been... strange for you. Have you considered it has something to do with his blood? He's not human."

"I mean, he is human," I said softly, thinking about it. "When he's not using his powers, he smells and presents fully human in all ways. The moon cursed catch something in his scent they think stinks, but you would never know he's not human if you met him. I still can't catch his cambion nature when he's not actively using it." I tapped my foot. "I think cambions are less one type of species and more a two-natured individual. They are human, and they are demon. That combination makes them a cambion, which is unique, but there are two definitive parts, not so much a perfect blending of two halves. Does that make sense? Maybe if I had met Raphael before they activated his demonic nature, he would have been my normal, human mate."

"Very interesting theory." Adhar frowned but nodded. "We can look into it further once we understand the more pressing parts of your situation. Still, there is a part of him that is not human and is a demon. That must be playing some part in this. You've been having blackouts, yes? Tell me about them, please."

"Yeah, and they're always...visions or something, but not just from the blackouts. I'm getting them in my dreams." I rubbed my temples again as I had so many times in the last twenty-four hours. "They're...moments from another naga's life. Another naga who had been mated to a cambion. They're always...weirdly like whatever situation I'm in. I was thinking about how seeing the cambions after it happened felt like meeting his family, and they didn't approve. Then the blackout was the naga and his mate literally meeting her mom.

When I blacked out while fighting, it was him fighting, and he was a warrior." I lowered my head, closing my eyes as it settled in me. This was exactly what I thought it was, and I knew Adhar was going to agree with me.

"Kaliya."

"It's just never happened before, has it? I mean, we're reincarnations, but..." I groaned and leaned over to put my elbows on my knees.

"It's never happened before, but that doesn't mean it cannot happen," he said softly. "You are regaining memories from a previous life, but because it's coming slowly, it's giving you a hard time. I'm not sure what would be better. Remembering all your previous life at once and potentially losing your current self to your old one, or remembering in pieces, which can put you in a dangerous position. From what you describe, you're seeing memories of your previous life or one of your previous lives. There's a chance you have multiple reincarnations behind you."

I straightened again and looked at him desperately.

"Do you know who?"

"I have no idea. The ability to track it was lost a long time ago." He clasped his hands. "Your mother...she was working on something to do with it, but she never told me the results of her efforts. I believe she never broke any ground with her theories. She gave all of you names of first-generation nagas of great power, but I never took it seriously. Roshni's middle name is Vasu. It's traditional to give names of the previous generations to the new one."

"My oldest brother was named Vasuki," I said softly,

playing with the things on my desk. "But he certainly wasn't Vasuki. In any life." I rolled my eyes.

"Exactly," Adhar agreed. "I think it's dangerous, but you might need to find someone who can unlock the rest of your memories if you want to know who it is. Unless you're lucky enough to catch his name or her name in a memory. All we can do is theorize and look through the old scripture, but many nagas didn't write down their lives. Others did it for them, oftentimes after they died."

"Of course, they didn't. They were powerful and thought they would be immortal," I said, shrugging. "Why would they? Sure, they would tell tales of their epic feats, but the small things? No one cared, even though they're the parts that matter."

"They had too much pride," Adhar agreed. "Find a witch. A witch would be your best bet. Someone you trust. It's dangerous, and I want you to be careful, but if the universe has decided to gift you with the memories of your past life, I believe you are going on a journey of self-discovery."

"Therefore, even if you did know something, you won't tell me. You want me to figure it out myself. Adhar, we're a few thousand years past the 'mystical journey' era of the world. We have our survival to work on. If you know something, I need to know."

"Ah, it's never too late for a mystical journey, and a mystical journey may give you the keys to survival. To be given the answers is easy. I don't have any to give you, but if you search for them, you will grow in the process, which will prepare you for the answers you may find," he retorted with a small smile. "You would not be the first naga to go on such a personal quest."

I nodded slowly. I needed to figure this out, needed to know the secrets of my past life. I didn't really care who it was, but they had mated a cambion, and that cambion had also known things about what she was that Raphael and I were only guessing about.

Then there was everything the rakshasa had said, terrifying implications.

Cursed with a name. I didn't like that *at all.*

"Will you bring him to India?" Adhar asked, then grew worried again. He turned to the door and sighed. "Hold that thought. May Nakul come in? He is hovering."

"Sure."

My uncle walked in without Adhar needing to get the door. He looked at Adhar with a frown, then at me, his eyes moving as if he was studying the screen.

"Niece," he said softly, touching the screen under the camera.

"Uncle."

"You look well."

"I am well. You seem...better."

"Every day is better, but some days can be very bad," he said with a raw, vulnerable honesty that made my heart squeeze. "I knew that male was your mate, and now I hear you have him for eternity. Congratulations."

I tried to school my reaction, but something about the interaction bugged me. Not in a troubling way, but a realization about the two men on the screen. I pushed the thought away, deciding to come back to it later.

"Thank you."

"And children? Will we have more children soon? I'm excited to continue being an uncle. I know we've had our...differences, but I shall be a better uncle to the next generation. I swear it on my honor."

Oof. Nakul, the situation is way more complicated than you just being a better uncle.

"I'm sure Kaliya and Raphael will attempt to have children when they are ready," Adhar said softly, reaching out to touch Nakul's shoulder and pull him back. "Their mating is as complicated as Kaliya's mind. Nothing is a straight road. Let's not burden them with responsibilities that can wait. We have many dangers, and Kaliya doesn't live in the safety of one of our estates."

"Ah, they'll have children. It'll be too hard to resist," Nakul retorted with a grin.

"Hmmm." I didn't say anything, tapping my foot. Adhar sighed and moved Nakul to sit back with him, so neither of them was crowding the camera.

"So, what were the two of you talking about?" Nakul asked as he sat in a chair offered by Adhar.

"Oh, we'll...continue this later," I said quickly. I wasn't comfortable talking about it in front of Nakul. Nakul wasn't a man I would call trustworthy or good. He was complicated. He lost his mind over the deaths of his wife and child, then became a serial killer. While in prison for that, after Cassius and I had caught him, he had been mentally violated and used as an unwilling assassin to kill me.

I wouldn't be telling him anything about the strangeness in my life.

Adhar caught my meaning.

"We shall. Let's—"

"Hey," Raphael said from the door of my office. I hadn't been paying attention to catch him walking up. Nakul and Adhar had been my focus.

"Hey," I said, suddenly nervous as he walked farther into the room. "Um..." I glanced at the screen as he came up to me and leaned down. "I'm on a call."

He growled and kissed me, anyway.

Adhar cleared his throat, making Raphael break the kiss. I took my chance and grabbed Raphael's hips to turn him toward the screen and camera.

"Adhar, this is Raphael, my mate and the warlord of the cambions. Raphael, this is Adhar, the male ruler of the nagas. Raphael, Nakul, you already know each other."

"It's a pleasure to finally meet you, Raphael," Adhar greeted, bowing his head.

"The feeling is mutual," Raphael said, looking over his shoulder at me. "Cassius and Sorcha said they would be here in an hour."

I didn't miss how he said absolutely nothing to Nakul. There was the time Nakul had repeatedly stabbed me in Cassius' kitchen that probably left a sour taste in my mate's mouth when it came to my uncle. At that point, Raphael had known Nakul was a mad serial killer. The entire situation was complicated.

My entire life was complicated.

"Would you be willing to answer any questions—"

"No," Raphael answered stiffly, then I felt him relax under my fingertips as I massaged his hips. "Not right now. There's a lot going on, and I need to focus on it. I'll be more willing to talk once I know Kaliya and I are safe, and my cambions won't be caught in the crossfire."

"Of course," Adhar agreed, nodding quickly. I got the sneaking suspicion my mate was not what he expected. Adhar was used to being the respected elder to the mates. Then again, right now, all the mates were human women who needed to be brought into the fold, educated, and protected. Raphael was none of those things. He was strong and a leader in his own right.

"Then I shall let you both go..." Something came to his mind. "Give me one moment." He left the room in a hurry.

"What's going on?" Raphael asked me.

"I don't know. We were talking, then Nakul interrupted us—"

"What were you talking about?" my uncle asked, his eyes narrowing on me and my mate.

"None of your business," I retorted, losing my patience for the nosiness.

Adhar came back in as the rest of us stayed in the uncomfortable silence I had caused. He held out a beautiful carved box.

"Your mother wanted you to have this when you mated." He held it awkwardly, then put it down on his desk. "I'm sure we can find a way to get it to you."

"We will," I agreed. "You mentioned I should find a witch. Do you think you could get it to Devika? She and Mom were friends. I can meet her at the Market."

"I can certainly pass this along to Devika," Adhar agreed. "I shall leave you two to meet the fae. Kaliya, we can talk more later when you have time. I will keep myself available to you. Just give me a warning if you intend to call so I can wake up."

"Thanks. Stay safe." I hung up the call as Raphael turned to me and wrapped his arms around my waist.

27

CHAPTER TWENTY-SEVEN

"That was interesting," he commented. "What did you and Adhar talk about? Why do you need a witch?"

"We're pretty sure I'm seeing visions of a past life," I explained. "I need to figure out who it is. Whoever I was before had answers. The cambions he knew, they knew what they were, and he had time to figure out this." I lifted my hand and called my power. "I don't even know what it does or what it means."

Raphael reached out to it, and it danced over his skin, not hurting him.

"How does it feel to you? To me, it's just...power."

"I don't know if I could describe it yet. We'll play with it more and see if we can figure anything out." He leaned into me.

"You know, I'm not used to not having the answers. When it comes to what I am, I've always been really confident. I know what a naga is and what nagas can do. I never thought I would have to wade through a sudden new revelation. It was strange enough finding out my mate wasn't going to be human or naga. There's *never* been a case of it before, but I'm seeing visions of a naga with a cambion mate. She had to have hidden her powers well if no one else figured it out to write it down."

"I can tell it has you rattled," he whispered, those soft lips grazing the top of my ear.

"Well, there's a lot that has me rattled right now." I turned to him and sighed, putting my head on his chest. "I'm sorry I never told you. I didn't know what to do except protect you and thought I could only trust doing that by keeping it a secret. I didn't think people were going to put it together based on what they did see of us. Obviously, the rakshasa, and whoever he was working for, knew nagas and cambions could mate. They just needed to make sure you were what they thought you were. That means I'm dealing with someone who knows things about my species even Adhar doesn't know, and..." I pulled away, running my hand through my hair. "I've been fooling myself to think I could control this, and I'm sorry I tried."

"I can't say you're forgiven, but I'm willing to make this work. I'll help you find the answers. I just need you to trust me to be able to fight for myself. After everything you did for me, just let me do the same for you. It burns a little that you were discovering all the secrets of the cambions, but I had no idea you were holding on to this massive secret. Did you think I didn't need to know that our species could be together?"

"It wasn't..." I leaned on my desk again. "It started out...I figured I would send you away, you would meet someone else, and everything would be fine. After a while, my plan changed from getting rid of you completely to finding the bad guys, defeat them, then maybe, we would have a chance," I admitted. That had always been a thought at the back of my mind. The idea that just *maybe* it would be safe enough to be with him. I had told Adhar as much months ago.

"The four months you didn't see me? I was here, working endlessly on finding that motherfucker before he came back for me. Use him to get to his boss. Finish this. I finally had a lead, but it went cold, and I didn't stop. Cassius and Sorcha heard from Paden. He was worried about me, so they were worried about me. They came here with Leith, cleaned my house, and forced me to go to dinner with them."

"And they had invited me to dinner to give you a job," Raphael said softly, nodding. "You know, Cassius kept telling me to hire someone else. That he didn't see why I wanted you so bad."

"He knew you and Sorcha were trying to get us back together."

"Wouldn't he want his ex to be happy with someone?" Raphael frowned.

"He would want his ex to live the life she wants to live and wouldn't appreciate people ignoring her wishes. Only he took my warnings seriously," I said with a bit more snappiness than deserved. "Sorry. After the Sammy incident, he came over and was furious."

"Yeah. I got an earful over the phone," Raphael said with a sigh. "Especially after you went to bed that night, and he was on his way home." He ran a hand through his hair, looking away from me. "He was right about one thing. I didn't take you seriously. I didn't think anyone would come after us or try to fuck with me because of the spotlight on us. I figured my position would deter your enemies. It was pretty arrogant thinking, and I'm sorry." He leaned on the desk next to me. "Truthfully, I thought if I hadn't seen your enemies yet, maybe you were paranoid and using it as an excuse to get away from me. Or I wasn't good enough and needed to prove myself. In the end, all of it just made me not really care about what you had going on in your own life and made me selfish. I wanted you and didn't see the big deal."

They were words I wanted to hear, needed to hear.

Validation. I rarely got it. Outsiders never really understood, but finally, some of them did. The ones I cared for the most understood why I had done it all.

Instead of being happy that I was finally recognized for being right about my problems, it fucking *hurt*. It had taken our choices being stolen from us to prove it. I never wanted *that*.

"I think that's what made me so angry last night," he continued in a whisper. "That you were right. If it wasn't for your sudden...power, I would have died last night in the exact situation you were trying to avoid. You wanted to keep me safe from your enemies, and I was fucking helpless against them. They're like you. They thought of all the contingency plans, came in knowing exactly what they were going to do, and executed that plan. The only thing we had going for us was something we didn't even know about."

"It sucks being right." I started to walk out of the

room. With Cassius and Sorcha coming soon, I wanted to finally get into all the stuff we found, and I wanted to get a hold of Devika. So much to do and so many answers I needed to find.

"Wait," Raphael called. I turned back to him, wondering what he was going to surprise me with this time. "I need to know if you'll accept my apology for... dismissing your fears."

"I don't know yet," I answered honestly. "I mean, I probably do, but,"—I pointed at the Board—"people have called me crazy and paranoid for years. Knowing you completely disregarded my fears, knowing you thought the same, hurts worse than I thought it would. Not just because you did it, but because you learned your lesson in the hardest way. I never wanted you to get hurt, Raphael. I have to get over the fact this blew up in my face, that decades of work and warnings were useless.

"We're out now. Everyone is going to know we're mates, which will keep a massive target on our backs. We're rulers of separate species, and both will suffer because of this." I closed my eyes. "Yeah, even without the politics, it just hurts to hear the man I've fallen in love with didn't take me seriously." I blinked several times, covering my eyes with a hand. "And he nearly died for it."

I walked away, leaving him in my office as I wiped my eyes.

Paranoid. Crazy. Insane. Irresponsible. Senseless. Obsessed. Troubled.

Don't worry about Kaliya. She's insane. Thinks everyone is out to get her.

Kaliya, don't go finding conspiracies where there aren't any.

Stop trying to make this bigger than it is.

There's no secret organization trying to kill off the nagas.

You're losing your mind.

You've gone too far.

I sat down on the couch and stared at the evidence. It would all go on the Board soon, but first, I needed to catalog it and see what I actually stole. My hands were shaking as I picked up the top piece of paper and found it hard to read. I wiped my eyes again and sighed before I dropped it and tried to focus—every insult, every dismissal, every well-meaning but hurtful comment.

No one had ever believed me. Cassius might have taken my paranoia seriously, but even he hated the Board.

Now, I was staring the truth in the face, and I was right. Someone was out there pulling strings, and the validation I finally felt was completely smothered by the pain. I couldn't laugh in the faces of the people I cared about. I didn't even want to.

Some part of me had always hoped I would be wrong.

I *hated* being right. None of this was the way it was supposed to be. I was supposed to find my enemies and destroy them before they could hurt anyone else. And when I took their heads to Adhar, he was supposed to finally give me the respect I deserved.

I was never supposed to be the victim again. I was never supposed to watch an axe hoisted over my mate's head. It was never supposed to be that close.

Raphael came in after nearly twenty minutes.

"What do you think?" he asked softly.

"I haven't even started looking," I admitted.

"Want me to tell you what I read?" he asked, sitting across from me, where I would have to avoid looking at him, but he wasn't close enough to touch.

What a fucking mess. We both disregarded each other's feelings, and both of us are trying to figure out what that means going forward.

"Um...sure," I said, trying to focus.

"The rakshasa was going by the name Mehar, and I'm sorry, but I can't pronounce the last name. Cassius already ran him through searches with the Tribunal and found nothing. He stayed under the radar. He made a note..." Raphael shuffled the papers. "Mehar was probably only working on this, and the rest of his interests were completely legal. Then he wrote 'personal' with a question mark. You never met him, though."

"Maybe personal against the nagas as a whole," I said, leaning on my hand. "Something someone in our species did upset him, and he was an easy partner to whoever paid him. He probably rarely left India, which would help him stay low. If he only left to chase after me, there's no reason to think anyone outside India would know who he is. Or he had people who worked under him to keep his face from being recognized over the years."

"Yeah. He had a known witch, a known vampire, and a..." He held out the paper. "Cassius didn't say for the last one. Tribunal knows it's definitely a supernatural and wrote some information on him once, but they never gave him a species classification. Some of the notes are pretty funny. Red eyes? Like me or like vampires?"

"Yeah, tons of species have red eyes," I said softly. "I wonder if it's..." I frowned. "Some sort of demon nature to them. Vampires have a demonic relation to cambions. It would make sense if demonic blood mixed into a variety of things over the years. Fucking weird."

"As a snake, you have red eyes," he pointed out.

"Not the same color red, but yeah, it's pretty close," I agreed. "The Tribunal doesn't know what this guy is, which means they didn't know because he's rare and probably not a subject of the Tribunal. The same problem with the rakshasas. I only recognize them because they're like me. We all come from the same place. There was no way I wouldn't recognize one." I shrugged. "Or they just never got a close enough look at him to identify him. That happens a lot. Let me see the notes on this one."

"Why don't you fill out their information for them?" he asked as he handed me the sheet of paper, and I began to read it thoroughly.

"Because I'm lazy? The idea of secrecy runs deep, and helping them identify the myriad creatures in India reminds me too much of home, I guess, back to lessons I got from my parents and brothers and Adhar. I spent decades trying not to think about those. Then I just never got around to it." There was nothing in the information that could tell me what this last guy was. Not that it mattered, he was dead. I recognized his face in the picture and knew I had torn it off his body.

I dropped it on the table.

"Let's just wait for Cassius," I said with a sigh. "I'm going to leave the moment I get word from Devika. Do you want to come? I need to figure out who and what I'm seeing, and it really can't wait. I can't...black out in another fight."

"I was worried you wouldn't ask. Of course, I'll go. You'll need someone to watch your back. I'm uncomfortable with you going back out in public alone." He rubbed the back of his neck, no longer looking at me. "Someone could try to grab you again, and we don't know what that new power of yours does or if you can do the snake thing again, and what if they use the same stuff we were hit with last night?"

"And now you're learning," I said with a rueful smile. "Join me in the land of complete paranoia. It's a great time."

28

CHAPTER TWENTY-EIGHT

When Cassius arrived, Raphael let him and Sorcha inside. I was growing more anxious with every passing minute. I hadn't had a vision since the late morning incident in front of the cambions. It was like waiting on the other shoe to drop.

If Devika was willing to help me, she would have her hands on something from my mother. I understood why Adhar had never brought up the gift left for me. I would have held it against him for keeping it from me before I mated. I was older and hopefully wiser because I couldn't summon the anger. My mother had left it behind with explicit instructions, and he'd only respected those instructions. Or maybe I was just beyond caring. Adhar was Adhar. I had always written him off as an asshole who thought he knew everything, but as things got worse and I was forced to look at myself and my own faults, I was beginning to see beyond his.

He stuck up for me with Nakul and knows me well enough

to know how bad this situation was for me, how uncomfortable it is to finally have a mate.

I twisted my hands together as Cassius sat down in one of my chairs at the dining table behind me. Sorcha looked at me, then at Raphael.

"How long has she been like this?" Sorcha asked him softly.

"On and off since we left your place," he answered. "There's a lot on her mind, not just all of this." Raphael picked up the folder and took it out of the living room.

On any other day, I would have been drooling over everything in that folder. On any other day, I wouldn't be having visions of a past life.

"I'm going to...take a walk, I think," I said softly. My heart wasn't in it. Not my hunt for my enemies nor the new information I could use. None of it. The twisted hunt I'd been on for decades soured on my tongue. They had finally hit me again where it hurt and had damn near taken everything from me. Fear of death, not for myself, but for Raphael, was a hell of a deterrent.

"Do you want company?" Cassius asked.

"No." I left out the back and headed into the desert. My security would alert me to anyone coming to visit, no matter where I was on the property.

I just wanted to stand in the desert while my life felt as if it was being turned upside down. The desert never changed, harsh and beautiful, even with the storm clouds rolling through the sky. It was late in the year for a storm, but it wasn't unheard of. It would be full of lightning and thunder from the look of it.

Once I was out of sight from the house, I summoned

the red magic to my hand and tried to manipulate it. It did nothing for me, so I let it disappear. Then I tried to shift forms, not to my snake but to the *other*. I hadn't had a chance to tell Adhar about that, not with the appearance of Nakul. I couldn't trust this sort of knowledge with someone as unstable as my uncle.

Nothing happened. Whatever burst of power and rage I felt while being held captive was gone. Standing in the desert, the only thing I learned was I really needed my memories of my past life. Closing my eyes, I tried to summon one. I could remember every detail of what I had already seen, but I couldn't summon a new one. How was it to meet her father, another cambion, who probably had answers? What did people call me?

I kicked a rock in frustration when nothing came to me.

My skin felt too tight. Something was off, and I could blame it on the mating, the rakshasa, or the memories of the past, both my current and my previous lifetime. It was probably a combination of all of it. I was *scared*. I remembered how different I felt using those abilities and killing the team who had taken us. I hadn't felt like myself.

For the first time in my life, I found myself wondering if I really wanted to go any deeper, to stop looking for answers, and just fighting for my life and surviving.

I mean, what if the answers only make it worse? What do I do then? How do I keep them safe?

"Kaliya," Raphael called out in the distance. "We might have something."

I walked back slowly, leaving the thoughts in the

desert, where they would hopefully shrivel and die under the sun.

"What?" I asked, going inside to find him already seated at the dining room table.

"Sorcha and I went back to the place you were being held. Your fire didn't completely destroy it, so we were able to grab a few more items of note, hopefully, things you would be interested in," Cassius explained. He pointed to a box on the table. "Sorcha and I were sorting them out when Raphael noticed it."

My mate held up a pendant on a golden chain.

"Do you recognize it?" he asked softly. "I've seen this one before. In her shop."

I took it from him slowly, noting the beautiful metalwork involved, and could taste the magic radiating from it. It was of a tiger, beautiful and fierce.

"This is Devika's work," I said softly, flipping it over for confirmation, her very tiny way of signing each piece she made. She didn't use her name, but there were always three little dots. To be sure, I took the pendant with me to my bedroom and grabbed the bangle Raphael had given me. Same tiny signature. Then I checked another necklace I had from her. It was all the same. When I walked back out, I put the pendant down.

"We can ask her who she sold it to," I said, finally taking the fourth chair at the table. "Lots of people go to her. Let's hope she remembers this piece. If it was sold in her shop in the Market, there's a chance her apprentice sold it and will most likely not remember. She gets dozens of people interested in her jewelry every day."

"It's worth a shot. You already want to visit her," Raphael pointed out.

"It is worth a shot," I agreed. "What else do we have?"

"These are something we can give to Monica," Cassius said, showing me vials from the basement. "Have her break down what they are. If you're not comfortable with our local witch, we can ask Tristan."

"Who's Tri—"

"A witch Tribunal Investigator with a specialty in magical objects," I answered quickly for my mate. "Monica is fine. Tristan is always busy with his own shit, and I can trust Monica. Her silence is easy to buy, and she has no political relationship to anyone who matters."

"I'll send them along," Cassius promised, then set them aside. "Aside from interesting objects and fake identities, I haven't found any connections to other criminals. The one unknown, Raphael said he mentioned it to you, but it seems like that is a dead end."

"They were professionals, so I guess they wouldn't leave anything stupid lying around. They were sloppy in some areas, overconfident they were completely fine, but I guess some things they didn't skimp on. There are two options to find out who the rakshasa is. Hoping he bought this directly from Devika or going to the rakshasas and hoping they can identify him from a picture."

"You mean you never gave them a sketch? Why not?" Cassius snapped as if he was pissed off I had missed it or just surprised, probably something between the two. Honestly, I was too tired to summon a strong reaction.

"Adhar didn't want me to piss off their rulers. I wasn't

allowed to go to the rakshasa leader until I had more than my own memories and circumstantial evidence of a crime he committed against the nagas. One witness from another race, who is also a ruler, and you know, considered crazy? Yeah, they would have just been pissed off, then we could have a situation on our hands that was even worse. Adhar and I went back and forth, but in the end, I agreed to follow his orders. Even then, the rakshasa leader is in India, and it would have been stupid to send Adhar. So, it just never happened."

"Ah, politics. The unavoidable problem with investigations," Cassius said, relaxing. "Forgive my tone. It's just, you never miss the little details. I thought you would have already gone to the rakshasas."

"They're not easy to find. They're not Tribunal, so I don't know who their leaders are. That's a completely different hunt."

"Then we should go to India," Raphael said, frowning at the table. "If the answers are there, we should go."

"He's right, Kaliya." Cassius gave me a sad look.

I took a deep breath and tapped the side of my head.

"Let me figure this out first. I can't go in front of the rakshasas' leadership if I can't keep my head on straight. And gods forbid I lose it like I did when we were captured. I could be responsible for killing a lot of people and have no idea how to stop it."

"That does complicate things," Sorcha agreed, nodding sagely.

"We're going to Devika. She's an Indian witch, a friend of my mother, who has always been a help to the nagas. She and Adhar have finally started talking again, so if she knows who she sold this to, hopefully, she will tell us. She also might know some magic that can help me."

"Yeah, all signs point to Devika," Raphael agreed. "Do we wait on her to reach out or try to find her at the Market and hope she already has the package from Adhar?"

"Adhar will let me know when he's passed it along, then we'll go during her business hours."

"How do business hours work in the Market?" Raphael frowned. "I just realized time zones are a thing, but she's always there when I need to find her, during our regular days. It must be the middle of the night for her, though, if she lives in India."

"On days she's not in the Market, her clients in her region would find her at her home," I explained. "Her Market hours are based on the rest of the world. She tries to capitalize on when the Market is the most crowded."

"One day, I'll get to see it," Cassius said softly, shaking his head.

"Poor guy," Sorcha murmured, rubbing his arm. "I gave it up for you, so it's not like you're missing too much."

I snorted. Of course, Sorcha had been at least once or twice. It didn't surprise me Cassius had never gone, but I had never pinned him as someone who secretly wanted to go.

"Do you want us to stay, or do you think you're going to be safe here?" Cassius asked, leaning back in his seat, looking only at me.

"You can hang out here. Let's have dinner and watch

some movies or something." I was groping for some bit of normalcy. I wanted a quiet evening, and for the first time since we'd all met, there were no secrets between us, at least not between Raphael and me.

"That's a wonderful idea," Sorcha agreed with a smile. "And drinks. We definitely have to drink."

"Agreed," I said with a chuckle.

We broke into my stash of whiskey while Raphael and Cassius worked in the kitchen in silence. While they cooked, Sorcha and I looked for the first movie to watch.

I needed it.

It was a surprisingly better day than the last. Cassius and Sorcha found they fit in the loveseat together, while through the night, I slowly leaned into Raphael and ended up draped over him like a blanket.

It was nearly midnight when my phone started going off.

"I got it. I'm up," Sorcha said from behind me, where she was making more popcorn. She held it out to me over the back of the couch, and I checked it while she whistled happily. We were still up since I'd made no indication I was ready to sleep. Everyone else was staying up in solidarity.

"It's Devika. She got the package from Adhar and wants to meet at the back of her shop when she's next open. That would be tomorrow." I stared at the message, my heart pounding. That was fast. Adhar must have hidden the package for her, and she wasted no time getting it. Normally, these things took up to a week to get done.

"Are you sure you want to do this?" Raphael asked

me, pushing some of my hair out of the way so we could see each other.

"I have to," I said softly, locking my phone, then gently tossing it onto the coffee table. No one jumped at the noise it made because an explosion happened on the television. "Raphael, I need to know the truth about what's happening to me, and those answers are right here. I just need some help getting to them." I tapped the side of my head. "Old memories, new powers…I *need* answers."

"Okay. Guess that means we need to get some sleep. I'm going to message my people and tell them I won't be back tomorrow unless you don't keep clothing for me like Cassius. Then I'll need to head back there to change."

My face heated.

"Yeah, I keep some stuff here for you," I admitted, then got off him and the couch. "I couldn't bring myself to throw it out."

"Do you mind if we take the spare room?" Cassius asked as he turned off the television.

"You're more than welcome to it," I said, knowing that meant Raphael was coming to my bedroom with me. It only made sense.

We were official now.

Together, we cleaned up. Cassius stepped outside to check the perimeter, something he'd started doing between the movies. Once he was back inside, we bid each other good night, yawning as the early morning decided to catch up with us.

I was alone with Raphael in *my* room for the first time in months. In my home, my territory, my space. This felt so much more intimate than my guest room at Cassius' mansion. He slowly stripped, methodical in his movements as he prepared himself for bed. Part of me wondered if this was happening a little too fast, but I couldn't tear my eyes away from the defined muscles of his back. Then he revealed his ass, and my mouth grew dry.

Raphael liked to sleep in the nude.

"I'm not going to jump you the moment you get in bed," he said gently, looking over his shoulder to see me standing there, still holding onto the doorknob. "We can just sleep."

I let go of the doorknob, nodding.

"Yeah, of course," I mumbled.

"I've never seen you like this before. It's actually worrying me."

"I've never felt like this before." I pulled off my shirt as he got in bed. I also slept in the nude, but tonight, I left my underwear on and got under the blankets next to him. We kept as much of the bed between us as we possibly could.

"Have you ever felt something close?" he asked, rolling onto his side to stare at me.

I thought about it, keeping my eyes on the ceiling.

"Once. There was one time in my life where I felt so out of my depth. Hisao rescued me at seventeen and took me to his home in Japan. The entire trip, I was stuck between wanting to run for my life because I didn't know who he or anyone else was. It's the same confusion, not knowing the future or where to go next. I just had to trust my instincts, and they were telling me Hisao was okay." I turned my head to look at him, drowning in his warm chocolate brown eyes.

"That's what I'm trying to do right. Trust my instincts. My instincts are telling me this is what I need to do. It's not exactly the same, but it's the closest thing I have that can relate." I closed my eyes. "And…being paralyzed like that reminded me of what happened when I was grabbed as a teen, living alone on the streets and trying to find information about what happened to my parents. Paralyzed, unable to protect myself…" I blinked back tears. It was literally my worst fear.

"Come here," he whispered.

I rolled and went into his chest. His body heat comforted me as his large hands rubbed my back, calming me. If I hadn't needed him before, I certainly needed him now. Without him, sleep would have been impossible, but he was there. Just as long as he kept holding me, everything may be okay. Just maybe.

29

CHAPTER TWENTY-NINE

We were meant to be together. Every day, I grew more used to the idea. While she wasn't the mate I always expected to find, it didn't matter. She was better. Her power was glorious, powerful enough to protect herself and those she loved, just like me. Her soft skin tempted me to stay in bed with her for the rest of our eternal lives, and her eyes...I wanted to lose myself in them.

"My love, we need to get up," she said with a small laugh as I pushed my face against her stomach, nuzzling her, tasting and smelling her. All I wanted was to drown in her.

"No," I hissed before nipping her hip. "I think we should stay right here."

"We're introducing your brother and my father today. Remember? We're supposed to be figuring out how this happened and how it's changed you. Our kinds have never mated before. We promised to make this introduction to help ease tensions between our families."

I shook my head. I didn't care how much it changed me.

"Your father changed your mother," I reminded her. "It's

not that pressing. They can wait." She moaned as I ran a hand between her legs.

"Oh, yes, they can wait," she agreed.

She was everything to me. She was the reason I would destroy this world if I had to. She was more important than what was happening to me. I was growing more powerful, and I had no worries about it. It only meant I could defend her better, and one day maybe we could have a family, and our children would also be safe.

I succeeded in losing myself to her for the entire morning, laughing with each other as we continued to learn each other's bodies.

I WOKE up with my hands on his bare body, and one of his hands found their way to my ass, sneaking under the thin layer of protection.

"They loved each other so much," I whispered, still feeling that as I came back to my reality.

"I would hope so," he murmured, kissing my forehead. "Another dream? You were sleeping so deeply, I didn't think you would have one."

"I would take these dreams over the nightmares any day." I got up slowly, stretching before I even made it off the bed. "Come on. We have a big day ahead of us."

"Hey, Cassius," Raphael said as we walked out of the back, dressed in sweats and tanks to get breakfast.

"Good morning," Cassius said from where he sat alone at my dining table. He was on his phone, seeming to be checking his emails. He was a bit haughty as he looked up, something I knew wasn't really him but the accidental air he always gave off. "You both look better."

"One day at a time, right?" I gave him a tight smile. I was still drained, but there was a new, small electric pulse of energy I was going to cling to with all my might.

He nodded, his face softening.

"I wanted to ask for a favor." Raphael went into the kitchen as I sat across from Cassius. The fridge opened, and he came back with three yogurts and a protein shake, putting them in front of me. "Do you think you or Sorcha could stay with the cambions today?"

"I can. Sorcha had to leave early this morning and stranded me. I'll need you to drop me off, or I can have Leith drive here and shuffle me between here and there."

"We'll drive you. What's going on?" Sorcha wasn't one to abandon her husband.

"It's nothing important. Her parents called and asked for money." Cassius gave me a tight smile. "Like they have several times since she moved to the right side of the law, and her money became legitimate."

"Oooh, rough."

"She always takes their calls, but she rarely gives them money. She uses the calls as an excuse to talk to them because they normally stay in our realm. I got left behind because I wanted to make sure you didn't need anything, and it seems you needed something." He put his phone down and leaned back. "I think someone wants you to eat, and you should," he pointed out as Raphael started on his own breakfast.

"Don't start," I hissed across the table as I ripped open the first yogurt container, then the protein shake. In the last twenty-four hours, I had eaten more than I had the week before. Something was burning my energy faster than I could replenish because I was hungry. The moment cool yogurt touched my tongue, I focused on the food and didn't stop until everything was finished.

"Interesting," Cassius said softly, watching me.

"Yeah, think about how much she ate last night and yesterday for breakfast." Raphael came back to the table with a plate of eggs and bacon.

I stole a piece of bacon.

"Yeah, it's weird," I agreed.

Raphael did something quickly, and I yelped in pain as the knife he held ran across the top of my hand.

"What the fuck?" I demanded, pulling it close.

Cassius's magic filled the room, adding a layer of danger. It was a threat without the words.

"Look at your hand," he said softly.

I glared at him, then looked down. Cassius handed me a paper towel, and I cleaned off the blood to see it had already stopped bleeding and was quickly scabbing.

"It'll be healed in an hour," Raphael mumbled. "I couldn't find the right moment to bring it up yesterday and was still trying to figure out if it was that or maybe I had been mistaken. I saw you get injured while we were captive, but by the time we got into the van, there was no sign of it. And now you're eating more than ever. I figured you were burning calories like cambions do, which requires upkeep."

"Well, well," Cassius said thoughtfully. He reached out, and I offered him my hand. We watched as it slowly knitted. "You picked up some cambion talents."

My dream from the night before suddenly came to mind, and I felt another wave of anxiety and strangeness —it had to be a coincidence, had to be.

"I guess so," I whispered. "This means the demon part of cambion blood completely alters physiology. That would explain how you bond your mates if you think about it. If, say Cole gave his blood to his mate, she would change into something closer to him."

"Yeah, that's a good theory," Raphael agreed. "We'll go with it. The only way we can know more is for one of our cambions to finally find their mate."

"Our?"

"Our nagas, too," he said with an arrogant smile. "What? Did you think I wouldn't think about how we're rulers of two different species? In my opinion, if you need anything, my people are your people."

"I won't offer up the nagas like that. Sorry." I smiled, guilty. "I just don't know them well enough to know what they would think about this."

"I can't wait to meet them," he said softly, leaning in closer, his lips drifting over mine.

"I'm still at the table," Cassius said. "What time are we leaving?"

I chuckled as Raphael turned a glare on the fae noble.

"Once we're done getting ready. The sooner we hit the road, the better." I cleaned up my trash and went to get ready, constantly looking down at my hand. I didn't heal as fast as a cambion—I could watch them heal, and it was alarming—but I was certainly healing fast enough to make a considerable difference. It was already passing through the swelling phase.

While it was very useful, it did nothing to help my anxiety. I was *changing*. The last time my body changed was when my hair went completely white. That was nearly a century ago.

I stepped into the shower, and Raphael joined once I was under the hot water, his hands moving over my skin.

"I freaked you out," he whispered in my ear, heating me up just as effectively as the water and steam.

"Not you specifically," I countered, turning my head to let the water run over my face. "Let's just get ready and see if we can find some answers."

"Do you have any theories? You've been surprisingly closed-lipped, taking everything cautiously. That's not like you. You're normally shooting off ideas faster than I can process them."

"My *name* cursed me. That's what the rakshasa said," I whispered. "I don't want to be the reincarnation of a naga who...who was killed like that. I don't want that on my shoulders. I've liked never knowing who my past life or lives were, Raphael, and..." I shook my head. "My mother wouldn't have been so stupid to name me after who I was before. She would never purposefully put that target on my back, would she?" I turned to him, letting out that fear. "Would she?"

"I never knew her," he reminded me, touching my cheek.

Getting out of the shower first, I got dressed as he finished up. We met Cassius at my BMW, and once again, I let Raphael drive. At the cambion compound, Raphael spent twenty minutes making it very clear to his people Cassius was in charge, while Cassius promised he would let them have the day off. The only thing they needed to worry about was security. Cassius would deal with the construction teams that had already arrived to start another day of work.

"Do we want to take Sammy or Mateo?" Raphael asked me before he was done talking to them. "They've both offered."

"No," I answered. "I want them to keep everyone here safe. Leave them here because it's not their fight."

He nodded and went back to them. After a few more minutes, he shook Cassius' hand, said goodbye to everyone, and got back in the car.

The drive was long and quiet. There was really nothing else to say.

"Fuck, I'm so nervous," I admitted as we parked in Phoenix. "Not just to do this, but what if someone tries to grab us again? What if we're not safe?"

"I asked if we wanted protection," he reminded me as he cut the engine. "But we need to do this. Now that we know they're close, they won't get the drop on us again."

"You're right." I was too wary for someone to try the same stunt twice and succeed.

I got out of the car, hyper-vigilant. I jumped as humans walked by, watching for strange cars, especially ones big enough to hide Raphael and me. When we got to the elevator, I put my back against a wall, so I could see anyone who might come by.

The elevator came, and we entered the Market. Violence in the Market wasn't illegal, but it was frowned on, especially in public spaces. I knew if I stood in the middle of the main "road," it was unlikely anyone would come after me, so I kept Raphael and me there. It also kept us out of the small crowds around the different shops lining the sides.

Once we reached Devika, though, I was ready to get out of sight. Holding Raphael's hand, as any couple would, people were staring as though we had two heads. I was holding it so we weren't separated, but it left a lasting impression.

"Want to really give them a show?" Raphael asked as some of those watchful stares began to feel as if they were burning holes in the back of my head.

"Let's not draw any more attention to ourselves," I replied, trying to get through the people.

"But I want to," he murmured, leaning down to kiss me when I was forced to stop our forward movement to let someone pass. His free hand made its way around my back and held me there. In the middle of the crowd, Raphael was making a scene, making sure everyone knew who belonged to who and that the cambions and the nagas were now intricately tied together in ways that couldn't be undone.

The view for those around us who knew who we were was probably scandalous. Someone was going to write about this online. Everyone in the world was going to know within twenty-four hours if they cared—forty-eight to seventy-two hours for those who didn't.

When he released me, I was more than a little breathless.

"Raph."

"If we're open and honest about it, more people would find it strange if we both go missing at the same time," he pointed out. "It'll either make people curious enough to look into it or force the Tribunal's hand. They can't have the optics of two loyal rulers of different species suddenly disappearing or being assassinated."

"Oh, you really are starting to think like me." I continued walking, and finally, we were at Devika's, but it was closed. "Shit."

"What is it? Where is she?"

"She's probably here but didn't want to open to meet us," I mumbled. I walked around Devika's stall, which was positioned outside the building representing India and a few other countries of the subcontinent. Going through the building gave me a side entrance into her stall through a downstairs door that wasn't a portal in and out of the Market.

"Devika?" I called, my anxiety growing as I walked in. "Are you here?"

"Yes, in the back." I saw her head poke out between two curtains. "I figured since you were coming by for something important, I would remain closed. I knew you would rush to get here the moment you could."

"Thank you so much," I said, relieved to see her. I led Raphael to the back curtains with me, and Devika allowed us through.

I licked my lips, a habit I would never lose. I could taste her, seemingly human as all witches were, and her apprentice was around as well, and there were hints of her magic as if she had used it recently. Not uncommon.

Then the softest taste of rakshasa. It set me on edge, but I tried to focus on my goal.

Probably a previous customer. She serves everyone.

"I swore to Adhar on my life to pass this along to you," she said, lifting the box I had seen on camera only the day before. I took it from her, pulling it to my chest and closing my eyes for a moment.

"Thank you," I whispered.

"Don't thank me," Devika said. My eyes opened, and I watched her walk to the back of the room. "You'll make me feel guilty about this. The only reason I agreed to give you that box was because it would get you here."

My hands started to shake. I put the box down very slowly. I reached for a weapon, the katana at my waist, but Devika held out a hand, and I could no longer move my hands.

"I liked your mother...and you," she said, pulling open the curtain into the deepest room, where I could get no thermal read. She revealed three rakshasas, their scents and heat signatures masked from me. "But you were never supposed to survive your mating."

30

CHAPTER THIRTY

I hissed as I tried to pull my hands and feet from their invisible chains. Raphael snarled behind me as the rakshasas came closer.

"You must have killed Mehar," one hissed, a female, a rakshasi. Like naga and nagini, they also used a female version of their species. "That's the only way you could be here right now."

"Yeah, I did," I snapped. "I tore him open and gave him an anatomy lesson. Then I ripped his limbs off. Maybe he shouldn't have tried to kill me."

"I can't hold them for long, so don't play with your food, maneaters," Devika snapped. "Do your little tricks and manage this. You'll be well rewarded."

"We don't need your money. She killed my husband," the rakshasi growled, coming closer. I tried to yank my head away, but she grabbed my jaw tightly. Devika disappeared out the back of the room. "Don't play with our food, the witch says. That's the best way to enjoy it."

"Mehar was going to kill me. What did you think would happen to him?" I asked softly.

"He was the king!" she roared, making my ears ache and forcing a wince from me. "He would never waste his time with a petulant naga child."

Fuck. Fuck, fuck, fuck.

Raphael growled viciously as one of the rakshasas came up to him, ripped open his shirt, and left four red lines. The blood slowly turned black, and the wounds healed.

"We're going to kill your mate, then you."

I hissed and turned to my mate to see his eyes red and black. Devika had made a fatal error in her betrayal. She had left us able to call on our powers.

She was right about one thing—she couldn't hold us for long.

The rakshasa male raked his claws over Raphael's face and snarled as the injuries began to heal quickly.

"Raph, I think it's time we really made a scene," I said, grinning at him. "I'll be right here with you the entire time."

"I could hurt a lot of people by accident," he countered as his skin slowly turned to ashen grey as the black veins spread over him completely. While Devika's spell kept his hands at his side, it couldn't stop him from growing taller, his legs getting longer, and his body filling out even more than it already was. The rakshasa in front of him went wide-eyed.

"Fine, we'll do this quickly," the rakshasi snapped. She reached out to grab my head. A simple neck break would end her problems. "Chop off his head. Everyone dies from that." She grabbed my hair instead and forced me to watch as the second rakshasa grabbed my mate from behind and kicked his legs out from underneath him, forcing him to crash onto his knees.

Raphael seemed unperturbed, glaring at the one in front of him, who drew a sword. I could taste the unique scent of him on my tongue, overriding everything in the room. When the rakshasa started his swing, Raphael broke free of whatever was holding him with a roar.

It happened quickly. Raphael grew in size, and the sword only made a minor cut on my demonic mate as he filled the room, then crashed through the ceiling. He batted away the rakshasa and kicked back at the second. The female let me go and started running out of the room. He didn't catch her, turning his attention to me.

He trailed a long black claw down my arm, hooking the invisible cuff on my wrist, and yanked it off. Once the first was gone, the others left with it.

"We need to catch Devika," I said as he leaned down to touch his nose to my forehead. He wasn't so out of control this time, and I didn't have time to question it. The rakshasas were getting to their feet, and I was able to see one morphing into something else—stripes on his skin and a feral look on his face. Then the second jumped out of the wreckage and landed on Raphael's back. I barely had time to move before Raphael and his passenger burst through the next room, then the next. When I looked after them, I saw them in the street, and people were starting to scream.

"He's going to keep your mate busy while we deal with you," the other male said. That was when the female came back as well, having shifted into their more bestial form.

I pulled my katana from its sheath.

"Look at her. Can't even use a respectable weapon of her homeland," the male snarled.

I ignored the jab. What they were missing was the fact this katana was given to me when I had nothing, not even my homeland. When the past started creeping up on me, it was the support I reached for, not anything from India.

What they should have remembered was who trained me to use it.

Roars and screams were the backdrop to our clash as the male rushed me first. He was strong, but I deflected his attack before kicking away the female. I was faster and used it. I ducked under their strong attacks, rolled from their kicks, and sidestepped their onslaught.

I didn't escape unscathed, though. As I was pushed through the wreckage left behind by Raphael, I had nearly a dozen small injuries where I had only just barely gotten out of the way in time. The street was cleared when I stopped, but I could see people trying to hide. There were probably long lines at the doors as well, everyone trying to escape.

A roar broke my concentration, and I cursed as I jumped out of the way of a piece of building. It clipped me and sent me down, nursing what felt like a cracked femur. It crashed into the street, leaving a crater beneath it as Raphael stormed into view again. He must have taken his rider to another street and was now barreling back into the main road.

I didn't have time to recover as the rakshasi brought

her sword down on my injured thigh, sinking it into the ground underneath me. She crouched, with the male watching her back, his eyes on the fight Raphael was in.

"Someone is going to kill you for this," I said as I looked up at her.

"If they can find me," she countered.

"Oh. No, not in the future. I meant right now." I reached down for the sword and grabbed its hilt before she could. Ignoring the pain, I tore it up from the ground as I ripped my leg away. In a rush of power, I was surrounded by red tendrils of magic. I swung the sword and buried it in her neck, then rolled away before the male rakshasa could get to me. He grabbed the female as she fell, and I moved away.

"Mother!" he cried out.

Ah fuck. This is a family affair. Mehar was the king, she was his mate, and these must be the rakshasa princes.

I struggled to get to my feet while he was busy holding onto his dead mother, cradling her. I found my katana, glad to see it survived the destruction of the street around us. Power pulsed through me, knitting my injuries.

"You don't have to keep fighting," I called out to the male. "You can walk away right now and go back to your people. Rule. I can call off my mate if the other one leaves him alone."

"My brother and I will avenge our parents," he snarled, putting down his mother's body.

Yup. The entire fucking family.

I lifted my sword and shifted a foot back, waiting for his attack. He prowled like a beast, his form shifting further into a monster as he approached. He didn't bother to use a weapon. Rakshasas were ferocious killers.

Then I was out of the Market, standing in a jungle. The scent of feral magics on my tongue told me I was in an illusion, his hunting grounds, and he had the upper hand.

I turned slowly, trying to find a sign of my enemy. When I took a step, I heard leaves crunch under my feet and vegetation rustled. His magic was strong. Not every rakshasa could make these sorts of illusions, and they took considerable energy to do so. When I sniffed with my nose, I could smell the damp earth of recent rain and the unique mixture of life from this particular jungle. It was lush and beautiful, but it was all fake. The undercurrent of magic in the air, something I could taste on the tip of my tongue, told me it was all fake.

When I approached a log, I stepped on it and found it was solid. This illusion had cast itself over the real world. He was smart. He just changed my perception of what the real world looked like. An elephant came charging through the woods with a tiger on its back. I jumped to the side as it took out trees bunched together in a thick line with no space between them.

"An *elephant*? You turned my mate into an *elephant*?" I hissed, looking around for my own tiger. I couldn't get any indication of him, not even a heat signature.

I saw a glimpse of it and turned to try to follow it but couldn't keep up. I ran after it, trying to catch its scent, but there was nothing there. It was his magic that made this, and it was hiding him from me.

The pain didn't help, my thigh throbbing as it tried to

heal fast. If it had just been soft tissue damage, it would have been easier to ignore, but the ache went to the bone, which scared me. A strong hit could crack my femur in half.

I needed him to show himself instead of toying with me. As I listened to the "elephant" running around, I knew there was a chance he was helping his brother instead of coming after me. I needed to fix that.

"Are you really so much of a coward?" I called out. "You're the apex predator! I'm just a fucking snake! Come on!"

It worked. I heard him rustle behind me before he jumped. I shifted into a snake to avoid his leap, then reared in a hiss, opening my hood in a warning display. He snarled, walking on all fours, but still seemingly human-shaped, with long feline fangs and terrible claws. My snake form was vulnerable, but it could get one good strike and could fit in places I otherwise couldn't.

"Little snake," he said in a growling way. "So many predators are able to kill you."

Yeah, yeah, but I can take all you motherfuckers down with me.

When he charged again, I shifted and shoved my katana in his chest as he landed on me. His claws raked my arms, but I kept pushing the sword up, tilting my head to avoid his bites. Eventually, with his blood pouring down on me, he died, and the illusion snapped, revealing me on the ground in the Market again.

I rolled him off and worked to stand. It was a good bait and switch, but it would only work once. As I ran for

Raphael and his attacker, still clinging to the back of him, I was blocked by an invisible wall.

"We've contained them," a furious voice said. I turned slowly to see a group of fae standing there. I recognized some of them. The one who spoke stepped forward. I didn't know this one, not by face.

Behind them, people started walking out of the buildings, their faces shocked by the destruction Raphael had caused. The Market would be fine, but it had never been torn up quite this bad.

"I need to—" I needed to start speaking my case *now*.

"They will remain that way until one of them is dead," the de facto leader snapped. "Then we shall kill the other, Executioner Sahni."

The founders of the Market had finally arrived.

And they were pissed.

31

CHAPTER THIRTY-ONE

Some gasped, while others cheered. Most…most were silent. The Market was neutral ground, ruled by a group of ancient criminals who had wanted a space where the rulers couldn't get to them and couldn't control them. This was the first time the two sets of rules would crash into each other, and people could end up dead. Or the Market would be changed forever.

"If you kill my mate, no one will leave here alive," I hissed.

"I don't care if he's your mate," the one in the lead replied. "This is unacceptable behavior, and it will be punished."

"We were baited into the Market and attacked. Self-defense is our *right*. The Market has *never* punished someone for defending themselves."

"We acknowledge your right to self-defense as a Tribunal Executioner. We don't recognize his," the fae said, pointing over my shoulder. "We've never had someone lay waste to everything we've built. That changes everything."

"Why not?" I demanded, taking a step closer to them. "He's protected under the Endangered Species Law. He's also the ruler of the cambions. Are you kidding me?"

"We get to decide which laws of the Tribunal we are willing to recognize," another one of the founders said with a shrug of one shoulder. "And not all of us are comfortable with the likes of one like him."

"If you kill my mate, you are subject to *my* wrath," I said softly, pointing at Raphael, then myself. "You will *not* kill him."

"How do you know the rakshasa won't?" he asked softly.

I turned away from them and met Raphael's gaze. He might have been in demon form, but there was knowledge there. He was in control as best as I could tell.

"He'll beat him," I said confidently. "He heals faster than the rakshasa can hurt him." I put my hand on the invisible wall. "Won't you?"

Raphael grabbed the annoying pest off his shoulder and threw him. It wasn't enough to kill him, which he proved by picking up the rakshasa and slamming him into the invisible wall between us, presenting him to the founders.

And me.

The rakshasa was furious and afraid.

I turned back to the founders of the Market. Not all of them were founders, though. There were a couple who I was certain had claimed their positions later and only took up the title for posterity.

"We can always kill you as well for attacking us, Executioner Sahni."

"No, we can't," another of the founders said, stepping forward. I recognized this one, and he was smart. He didn't throw a single look at me, but I was certain he remembered the portal he had made for us. He had helped us get into the Rockies and find the lab Mygi ran. "And I'm afraid I need to speak out. We also cannot kill Raphael Alvarez."

"Excuse me?" The one who had been in the front turned on the one speaking out against him.

"These two are too close to the fae ruling family," he said softly, leaning toward the one who definitely wanted my mate dead. "Much too close. Listen to me, Niall."

"Are we talking about Cassius?" Niall shook his head. "He married Sorcha. She gave up her coin for nobility and marriage to him. He gave up the throne just because he was mad at his *daddy*. He's not—"

"They're close enough, he used up a favor from me for *her*," the one I knew snapped, pointing at me. "And that's before we get into the fact that Sorcha was a founder of the Market and knows every backdoor in and out. We can't kill a friend of those two. If we kill one or both of them, his blind eye will no longer be so blind. He is far too powerful to disregard. So is she."

Sorcha...Sorcha was a founder? *Oh, she has to tell me about this. Shit, knowing what she is, she could have probably built this place from scratch. And Cassius* knows.

My friends have a lot of secrets.

"Then there's the Tribunal," another of the founders said, stepping forward to back up the one who had helped me, thanks to Cassius. "They all send their people here for the things they need, so long as we don't overstep the bounds. If we completely disregard them, we will go back to being the Black Market for *everyone*, which will destroy our business. We've ridden a very fine line of independence for many years. It is time we show some loyalty to the rulers who haven't sent in their best to destroy us. We can fix this damage in less than a day. We will shut down and get to work. We cannot throw away everything for this pettiness."

There were now clear divides in the ranks of those who ruled the Market. I swung my sword around in my hands, playing with it as I heard Raphael tear something meaty, and screams bounced off the rubble around us. I glanced over my shoulder to see he had torn the rakshasa in half.

"Looks like you have to make a decision," I said softly. I summoned power on my hand and sent it all over my body. "I suggest you think carefully and choose wisely."

I saw the fear in their eyes.

"You may both go, but you will be billed for our time," one of them snapped. "You will also be banned from the Market for one year, starting the moment you leave."

"For threatening my life and the life of my mate, I demand a boon," I said, keeping my chin up. "I need a portal to find the witch, Devika. She ran a shop here. You can probably find a sample of her to help you make me one. I will also like a portal home to use after I take care of this problem."

The one I knew through Cassius started to chuckle.

"You know how to bargain," he said dryly. "You've

been banned from the Market, yet you demand a boon, even though I put my neck out to help you."

"You put a neck out for your business interests, not to help me," I countered.

"Same end result," he retorted.

"How do humans say it?" I put my hand on my chin, humming in thought. "Oh yes. It's the *thought* that *counts*."

Someone foolish started to laugh in the crowd, but it was quickly cut off into a gurgle, and everything went silent again.

"This Devika...she's the one who kicked off the violence in the Market?" he asked, crossing his arms.

"She laid a nice ambush," I confirmed.

"Fine. Two portals." He nodded slowly. "You'll be banned for two years. The second year is for being annoying. You, Cassius, and the rest of your little friend group are like fleas. I accidentally brushed one of you, and now I can't get rid of any of you. Maybe a couple of years will help me forget the lot of you."

I bowed my head respectfully. Then a big black, clawed foot appeared beside me. I rubbed the leg gently.

"Come on, Raphael. We're living to fight another day."

Then I blacked out.

"You fight so well," I said softly as she twisted and spun, dancing with a blade as if she was meant for it.

"I fight so well so I can fight tomorrow," she replied. "The same as you."

. . .

"I'M FINE," I quickly said as Raphael held me. "How long?" I whispered.

"To everyone else, it looked like a dizzy spell," he whispered. "They're too busy directing people out of the Market, so they can start the clean-up. We're being ignored."

"Good," I said, patting his chest. "That's good."

"Yes, it is." He let me go, and I pushed my hair out of my face. "What did you see?"

"Oh, just a small moment. They were both warriors. He was admiring her work with a blade. She was pretty fancy with it."

"Ah. They sound like they were a happy couple," he said softly.

I turned and met his gaze.

"We will be, too," I promised. "But first, Devika and answers. She obviously knows what the fuck is going on. She's been playing double agent. She knew about Mehar being dead, or she wouldn't have brought his family to the Market to kill us. She worked fast."

"Do you think Adhar is okay?" Raphael asked.

That was a horrifying thought.

"I don't know," I admitted. "Oh, shit. I need to get ahold of them."

"Or Devika will tell us," he said with a mean grin.

"Yes." I snapped my fingers and pointed at him. "Yes. I guess we're both okay with a little interrogation."

"I slept with a woman so I could escape the lab, then kissed her and broke her neck. Do you think I have a problem with your...skills?" he asked, raising a single eyebrow.

"You did before…this," I said softly, reaching up to touch one of his horns. He didn't go back to his human form. He was showing everyone that he was a cambion. Taller and more lethal, he was the biggest man in the Market, and everyone was giving us a wide berth.

"I…" He nodded. "I'm still trying to reconcile the five years in and five years out, but this me, with all my memories of both... We all do what we need to do to survive, right?"

"I wonder if that's an opinion you came to or one you learned from me."

"A bit of both." He looked up. "This could lead us to India."

"Yeah."

I was willing to chase Devika to the ends of the earth. Curling a fist, when I opened it, red magic danced on my palm. It had healed me during the fight. The longer I stood there, the less my leg hurt, even though I had torn it open.

"Are you okay with that?"

"We won't be staying long. When I introduce you properly to the nagas, it will be an official trip, and…Shit, the box!" I started jogging for Devika's destroyed shop. Two of the founders were walking around inside it. I grabbed the box from the ground, and they said nothing. It had been a gift from my mother, and I wasn't willing to part with it. They were smart enough not to question my presence.

"Are you excited to see what's in it? Do you want to do that before we go get her?"

I shook my head. It could wait a little longer. My mother was dead. The box wouldn't bring her back.

Devika, on the other hand, was still alive and I could change that.

"Let's just not leave it anywhere," I said softly.

After another hour of waiting, I knew Devika was making ground to get away, and I was growing anxious. Then, the fae who called me annoying found us.

"I'm ready to make your portal. This will take you close to her. Her magic is strong and unique enough to be a homing beacon. Normally, it probably doesn't bother her, but she also thought you would both die today, and no one would go looking for her." He led us to a door deep inside the building. "I'll be using this one. Close your eyes."

I did as he asked and saw the bright light burning through my eyelids.

"Okay, you can open them," he said breathlessly. "To return home,"—he revealed a stick of chalk—"just write down your address on a door, and for one time only, it will open to the main entrance to the structure. It will disintegrate quickly, and I only put enough magic into it for a one-time use."

"You use these to escape places, don't you?"

"Yes. That is from my personal stash. I don't recommend writing your specific address. Write someplace else you can get home from...safely."

I took the chalk and nodded. "Thank you."

"Just tell Cassius it was my pleasure," he said.

"Politics," I mumbled as he walked away.

"Are you going to tell Cassius?" Raphael asked,

crossing his arms as we watched the helpful founder leave.

"Yeah, no reason not to, and then it becomes his problem, not mine." Turning, I shoved the chalk into my pocket and opened the door. His warm hand touched my back, but I knew India was not on the other side of the door. "Well, I'm not going home today, it seems. We're off to Sri Lanka. First guess, this is Piduruthalagala Conservation Forest."

I stepped through the door into the lush forest. When Raphael stepped through behind me, the door slammed shut and disappeared.

"He really wanted us gone," I mumbled, seeing he didn't even give us a door out of the jungle. It was power magic, summoning a door out of nothing. Most fae couldn't do it, having to use real doors if they made portals.

"Does it matter? We should track Devika. Do you think we can?"

I turned and pointed to a small home hidden in the trees.

"Not hard," I said softly. "She's right over there."

As I spoke, Devika walked out of the small home, and her eyes went wide.

32

CHAPTER THIRTY-TWO

"Maybe we should try talking this time," I called out, walking toward her. "I'm getting tired of people trying to kill me but never telling me why."

"What do you want to hear?" she asked boldly, lifting her hands. Magic filled the breeze. "That I was never loyal to the nagas? That I would rather have what he pays me?"

"Who?" I demanded. "Damn it, Devika, don't make me kill you!"

I will, though. This ends with one of us dying.

Devika laughed, and it sounded a century younger than she really was. Gone was the old woman who was finally training an apprentice. She sounded as though she was still as powerful as she had been when I was a child. Her face still had all the wrinkles, but the exhaustion of age was gone.

I started running for her, sword in hand.

"Oh, you haven't put it together yet!" She clapped her hands together once, and the magic in the air grew stronger. I was twenty feet away when the roots grabbed me and threw me back. Raphael had the same problem, landing ten feet behind me.

Devika walked toward us. I jumped up and reached for my sword, but the roots took it from me. I reached for a throwing knife, and it was ripped from my hand.

Raphael roared, and I smelled his change, but when I turned to him, he was being held down. His muscles bunched, and he pulled limb by limb. He even broke a few, but for every one he broke, another two surged from the earth and grabbed him.

"You should have known better than to chase a witch to her home," Devika said softly. "I had hoped letting the rakshasa kill you would keep my hands clean. No one would have known I had to betray the nagas. They knew Mehar was on a mission for an ally, and death was possible. You were supposed to die after he got his hands on you. He confirmed he had you. Confirmed he was going to kill off your mate."

I tried to turn around to see her, judging her distance through her footsteps, but my feet were planted to the ground. I looked down to see my feet were now swallowed in the earth, and roots were creeping onto me. I tugged and pulled, only causing my legs to go two inches deeper. I summoned the red magic and tried to use it, but it was snuffed out by Devika's overwhelming force. She was a centuries-old witch, and I had less than seventy-two hours of practice with my new magic. It was no contest.

"Raphael, stop fighting! They get worse as you fight!" I roared. He stopped struggling. He was still tense, stiffer than a marble statue, but he stopped pulling against the roots, and they stopped adding their weight to him.

"It still might work," she said. "Hiding what I've done. Maybe. Adhar, he knew better than to trust me completely after your mother was gone. He didn't know the extent of it. He won't let anyone near the nagas now. A pity."

Not Devika. Please no.

Denial was a painful thing. I didn't want to believe. She had been such a good friend to my mother.

I looked back down to see the root beginning to crawl up my legs. Others reached out and snatched my hands, pulling them open.

"Why?" I asked as Devika stopped right behind me.

"Power," she answered simply. "Knowledge. Hopefully..." She walked around me and stared me down. "Immortality." A root wrapped around my throat and hoisted my head into a position I couldn't shake. She was holding me out of bite range. "Something *wasted* on you. You don't treat it with enough care. You were always so haphazard with it. When you were a child, I pitied you. It's why I didn't help hunt them down. Killing children who didn't understand...I couldn't be a part of it. But then..." Her fingers tightened. "Then you went off and wasted it. You decided to be this." She shoved my head away. "Being stupid with such a gift when so many of us are constantly fighting for more years. We keep fighting, and you are so willing to throw all yours away. Sometimes, I think that's your real goal. To die and join your family in the next life. That's why you are so reckless."

"I needed answers. I was willing to die for them," I said, trying to control my breathing so the root around my neck wouldn't tighten. It took a force of will I hadn't called upon for a long time. I closed my eyes and focused. I was taught how to survive situations like this. I just needed to remain focused. I was safe and alive as long as I didn't struggle. Hence the danger of these sorts of traps. Survival instinct, the body, the adrenaline—all wanted me to *fight*, the very thing I *couldn't* do.

Not yet.

"You know what's so funny about that?" Devika giggled, and it sounded practically girlish. "You're the only one who can give them to you!" She laughed harder as if I was a comedy act that just absolutely slayed. Standing ovation. Encore. The whole fucking bit. "Only you, you stupid girl! I blocked them from you when you were a child. I can't reverse the spell. Only you can!"

If I know the answers, then I'm not asking the right questions.

Or not trusting my own instincts.

"Why haven't you killed me yet?" I asked softly.

"Mehar wanted to give you to our mutual benefactor. Since he failed and his family couldn't even kill you when I handed you right to them, I will hand you over. It will put me back in his good graces, and he will finally give me what I want. I have you nicely packaged. Mehar wanted to kill the mate, but he can stay, too. I know enough about nagas to know what went wrong with Mehar's plan. He didn't want to keep your Raphael, but a naga will never watch their mate die without giving themselves up first. That brought you to life, didn't it?"

"I won't watch him die."

"I knew the moment you walked into my shop with him that first time. I saw him and said yes, there's a man who can finally bring the great Kaliya to her knees." She brushed a hand over my cheek. "He is all that we ever thought he would be."

"If I'm going to die, can't you at least explain?" I begged, aiming for pleading—desperation. If Devika liked my mother so much, maybe I could play on that.

"No," she answered with a smile, then walked away, heading for her home. "The bonds here won't release you as easily as they did in the Market. I've been saturating this land with my magic for centuries. It's a near-endless reserve for me to pull from. He will come down and be able to feast on you, and I will have a front-row seat."

I closed my eyes again, trying to control my breathing.

I know all the answers.

I searched my memories for something that might seem out of place. Devika said she had blocked the answers from me as a child. It was an important clue, and while Devika was a powerful witch, no one was perfect. I had snuck around the house a lot growing up. My parents were always whispering about something. My mother would often just sit with me, keeping her thoughts to herself, but she watched me.

Nothing stood out—until I remembered the bad parts of my parents. I spent a century only focused on the good. So, I tried to remember the hard parts. That rabbit hole of memories took me to others—my parents always telling me my English needed to be perfect, yet I kept slipping to Sanskrit.

No, I kept slipping into Vedic Sanskrit, just as I did with the rakshasa. It was so easy for me, and they...they forced me to stop. They didn't like it.

I felt a tear roll down my cheek.

She didn't. She couldn't have. Why would she do this to me?

I remembered how she taught me all the old stories, especially telling me all about who she named me after and his beautiful human wife. I had to have been four at the time, and it was the only time she ever mentioned it. My father had stormed into the room, and they got into an argument. I remembered him pointing at me, saying how he couldn't believe his wife would do something like that to their daughter. How he thought it was foolish and dangerous, and I would be the one to pay for it in the end. That was only what I remembered.

It was never mentioned again. But now, I remembered the mysterious wife's name.

Rama. Gods, it was Rama. She was a cambion.

My name was cursed—coincidence.

But it wasn't a coincidence at all. It was the only clue my mother left me.

I laughed as I sat there in Devika's trap. I laughed until I wanted to cry.

My mother had given me the answer as a child, and Devika had somehow blocked it. Now, I would find out soon enough, but there was one thing I knew for certain, and the pieces all fit together.

My name is Kaliya. I am the demon-serpent reborn.

It felt like the dam broke, and I screamed, thrashing as it felt like an entire life was being poured into my head, drowning me. Memories of being trained, memories of Rama, whispered promises, and great battles. My entire previous life was now exposed to me, and so was the death I had suffered.

STOP! It's too much!

I felt the personality of my previous life try to assert itself. He had had an entire lifetime to develop who he was—his strength of will, the depth of his heart, and the prowess he brought to war. He was given the name of the demon-serpent because of the extraordinary powers he had received through his mating to Rama.

"No," I hissed, throwing my eyes open. "This is *my* life."

Maybe I can use you. I will certainly learn from you.

"What are you doing?" Devika screamed, running out. "Kaliya!"

More vines came up, and I sank to my hips in the earth. I was too focused on what was going on inside my own mind. How did one soul reconcile having lived two lives that suddenly meet? Rebirth, reincarnation. It was supposed to offer a clean slate, a new beginning—a chance to do things differently under different circumstances. This was never supposed to happen.

We need to come together. I need my past life, yet this is my turn.

No.

He and I are the same person. These are my *memories.*

I am Kaliya, reborn into new flesh and given a second chance at life. I will not lose it. I will protect my mate, and I will fight for my people.

We're the same person.

Recognizing that and accepting it was all that was needed. Power surged around me as something odd happened—the memories settled, and a wave of acceptance ran through me. The memories became mine. I no longer felt as if they were other. It had been a different time, a different attempt at life. Now, I had a second chance, and I would not lose it.

"Don't make me crush you! I don't know how you broke the block I put on your mind, but I will do it. I will kill you."

"You can try," I said, shuffling through the new memories I felt as if I had known all my life. There was so much familiarity. "You can certainly try."

I summoned power I never thought I had and yanked my arms from the vines, put them to the earth, and pulled myself out of the hole as Devika tried to close it on me and crush my legs.

She frantically tried to call more of her vines to grab me. I threw my hands out and blasted them away, then straightened, glaring at her.

"Well, you've had your chance. Now, it's my turn. But first, you're going to tell me *everything*."

Devika didn't start spilling her secrets as I hoped. Instead, she reached for more of her power and started raising golems. The earth rumbled as it split open and revealed them as they climbed out of their hiding spots. They had to have been made ages ago because creating golems was powerful magic, and they couldn't be built in a mere moment. They raised out of the earth and stood between us. Some were made of wood, a combination of branch and root, others out of rock.

This was an army she had built over her centuries.

"You are powerful, Kaliya, but you are also killable," she said, then began chanting. I grabbed a throwing knife off my hip and threw it. It slipped into the barrier just before it went up and struck her in the shoulder. I would have aimed for the heart, but a golem's shoulder had been in the way. Injured was better than nothing, though. As she grew weaker, so would her magic. She yanked the knife out, a furious expression on her face.

"For that, I will kill your mate," she hissed, holding a hand over the bleeding hole.

Raphael screamed as the roots pulled him down, and the earth began to slowly swallow him one inch at a time. It wasn't the earth that worried me, though. It was the vines and roots, squeezing the life out of him. I jumped into action, only to meet resistance with the golems. A stone golem knocked me away from him, sending me into a tree.

"Raphael, you can push through it!" I yelled, grabbing my sword as I ran for him again. The rush of confidence I had getting out of Devika's trap was fleeing me. This time, I dodged the golem's attack and sliced a wooden one in half as I ran the gauntlet to him. Another tried to tackle me to the ground, but I shifted into a snake and flew underneath it, only to reform on my feet, still running.

I hacked the vines and roots to no avail. For every one I cut, another replaced it. Raphael was little help as he was yanked into a backbend, the roots pulling his arms into a useless position.

I hissed and shifted, but this time, it wasn't to my snake form. Desperate times called for desperate measures. Now, I had the need and the memories to guide me in using these abilities. I reached through the roots and grabbed him, swiping my tail to knock away the golems before they could attack me. One of them stuck a sword in my tail, but I ignored the pain.

"SHIFT!" I screamed.

He grew larger than the roots could contain. When he had tried this earlier, I hadn't been there to stop him from crushing himself. I tore off the roots as he grew. As I relieved pressure on him, others lost the fight and snapped on their own.

Eventually, he was a demon with me, and we turned to face off the golems coming for us. He crushed one with a simple step, its wooden body crumbling from the pressure. I ripped the head off a stone golem and used it to throw into another, knocking it off balance. Golems had to remain whole. The moment they lost a single piece, the magic was useless, and they fell apart. I didn't get the chance to tell Raphael, but we cut an effective path through them.

Together.

Just like my previous life with his mate when they fought together. They kept an eye on each other and learned from one another without ever having to speak a word.

Finally, I was standing outside Devika's barrier, and there were no golems left.

Then the barrier cracked, and Devika's eyes went wide with terror. I turned to see what the witch was looking at, to find her young apprentice, whose name I had forgotten, standing there, her arms outstretched, an expression on her face both horrified and determined.

She was betraying Devika, and that was all I needed to know. I hit the barrier, but it remained only cracked. Then Raphael charged into it, and it shattered.

I shifted back to my feet and walked to Devika.

"Now, you will talk to me," I said softly, grabbing the front of her clothing and hauling her to her feet.

"You were a babe when she finally discovered how to unlock it," Devika answered weakly. "I helped her develop the spell. I figured allowing her to do it would help me determine which of the nagas we needed to target the most."

"And?"

"Well, let's say we got what we wanted but ended up with a child who did things she wasn't supposed to be able to do. I sealed your memories away and instilled in you an avoidance for them. You would brush up against the truth—"

"And I would refuse to believe it," I said softly.

"With your mother dead, part of the way to do the spell is lost," Devika said with a twisted expression. "No one will ever do it again."

"So, my memories...didn't start coming back because I mated."

"Oh, I'm certain the collision with your destiny certainly helped crack the blocks I placed. Part of me wonders if it only ever worked because you were meant for this," Devika said, then she started coughing. There was blood in it. My knife had hit a lung, not enough to quickly drown her in it, but enough to give her pain and problems. She would die before she made it to a healer. She certainly no longer had the strength to heal herself. With the destruction of the golems, the magic of the area felt weak, nearly used up.

"That's it?"

"I am the one who suggested they needed to kill you and your family before this could ever happen. Before your mother could come to me to remove the block and let you out into the world to search for your mate," she whispered. "I just refused to be a part of it. Your stupid mother gave everyone a clear hint you were Kaliya, the serpent-demon. It painted the most beautiful target on your back. I didn't even need to tell anyone about the spell. They just wanted to crush you for having the name. Just like they enjoyed crushing others who took on the old names."

I dropped her to the ground. She started chanting in a language I hadn't yet learned.

"Who hired you and Mehar? Devika, answer me!" I raised my sword. It was all I wanted—one more answer.

"Get away from her!" the young witch screamed. She pushed me aside and shoved a dagger into Devika's heart. "She was casting a death spell. I didn't know if it was on you, your mate, or herself, but..."

I nodded slowly and stepped back.

Devika died, staring up at her apprentice in disbelief.

"This is all yours," I said, gesturing around at the land and the house. "Enjoy it."

"You're not going to kill me, too?" she asked in a small voice. "I...I could have warned you in the Market. I—"

"Don't cross my path again," I said softly, turning

away from her to walk to the house. "You'll live because you helped when you finally got the courage to. That means you get to live to see another day."

"Thank you so much."

I looked back at her to see her on her knees in a groveling position. Raphael stopped beside me, holding a box.

"Kaliya..." He offered it to me, and I took it, feeling tired. "I think it's time we go home."

"Me too," I agreed softly.

33

CHAPTER THIRTY-THREE

We went to the front door of Devika's cabin, and I quickly wrote an address of an abandoned property near my home while also thinking about it, knowing that part was just as important as the writing. The fae hadn't said anything because he had been annoyed with us, and I hadn't thought to call him out since it seemed pointless. The chalk was gone right as I finished the last letter. I knew from there it would be easy to either walk home or call a cambion to get a ride.

When I opened the door, I smiled at the dry heat and stepped through. Raphael came through next. I closed the door on the apprentice still kneeling next to Devika's body. Just to be certain, I opened it again and only saw the decrepit, abandoned farmhouse I knew had always been there.

"How do you feel?" Raphael asked as we walked away from the house.

"I don't know yet. Devika was such a good friend to my mother, and the entire time, she had been working for the enemy, whoever that is. All I know is that this isn't over, not by a long shot. I need to get ahold of Adhar. He needs to know everything. I need to make sure he can make the proper plans to see the nagas into the future."

"Then that's the first thing we'll do," Raphael promised. "And this?" He rapped a knuckle on the box in my hand.

I lifted it up and stared at it. "Yeah, I'm going to look through this, too. Actually, I might do that before I talk to Adhar. He would want me to, even if it means putting off a phone call. Decisions, decisions."

"Whatever you think is best," he said softly, pushing some of my white hair out of my face. My braids were ruined, and my hair was going everywhere. I could only imagine what sort of mess I looked like. "Also, your new powers are surprisingly inconsistent."

"Aren't they?" I chuckled. "With time and practice, I'll get better. Promise. Now..." I tapped the side of my head. "I have all his memories, how he used it, what it could do for him. It's just magic, though it's of demonic origin..." I twirled it around in my hand, and my legs gave out. I was officially tapped out. He helped me sit down comfortably and searched all his pockets for his phone, only to find it nearly broken in half. Then he started to search for mine.

"I've got it," I said, slapping his hands away. I pulled it out and revealed the terribly cracked screen. "Let's hope it still works."

He nodded, powering it on, and tried to navigate without having the ability to do so accurately. Eventually, I heard ringing as he called someone.

"Cassius. We're back. We're at..." He looked at me,

holding out the phone. I rattled off the address, then he put it back to his ear. "Yeah. Yeah. It's a long story. We'll tell you if you can come pick us up. Tell Mateo to drive or something. He's learned how faster than the others. Or you can drive. I don't care...Yeah, meet you soon."

"He's on his way, huh?" I sighed and leaned into my mate. "The work never ends, does it?"

"We need to stop finding ourselves in this kind of position," he said with a laugh.

"We really do, but I have a feeling we're not going to be that lucky until I figure out who is behind it all. Mehar and Devika were both pawns."

"Who used to be an enemy of the nagas?" he asked.

"There are a lot of notable names on that list, and while I wish Devika had the chance to answer the question, I'm not going to stress and try to play the guessing game right now. I'm frustrated, but there are a lot of things I can get done in the next twenty-four hours before I get to that." I reached out and took his hand. "Like we need to really talk about the future. We've tried, but I feel like we haven't been able to make any decisions yet...about us."

"Agreed. I want you to move in. I want to be able to crawl into bed with you every night, and I want you to be the first thing I see in the morning." When I opened my mouth, he put a hand over it. "But the logistics don't work out. You shouldn't have to live with Sammy and Mateo, and they shouldn't lose their space because of me. You were right when you said I couldn't move out because they need me."

I smiled against his hand.

"So, I want you to move in with me when my home is finished, and you can even help me design every inch of it. We'll keep your house for getaways. Actually, now that I think about it, I want you to design every inch of it." He removed his hand slowly.

"Yes. And you're mine on the weekends," I reminded him. "Don't forget that part."

"I'm always yours," he whispered, leaning in. His kiss was soft and full of promise. There was still so much to talk about, but that would be at home.

We went back to waiting on Cassius, who took twenty minutes to arrive. Raphael hauled me up in his arms and carried me to our ride.

"How did you get here?" Cassius asked benignly as Raphael put me in the front seat.

"Um..." I sighed. "We didn't leave the Market in a traditional way. We were attacked. Devika betrayed us..." I shrugged. "You remember the fae who helped us get to Colorado?"

Cassius groaned.

"He says it was his pleasure to help us," Raphael said from the back seat.

"I can't let you two out in public without supervision," he mumbled, hitting the gas and pushing me back into my seat. "I'm going to get those human backpacks used for children. With the leashes. Maybe if someone always has their hands on you, you'll stay out of trouble."

"I doubt it," Raphael muttered. He leaned through the front seats. "I mean, have you met her?" He pointed at me. "She's a magnet for trouble. And she's mouthy. And dangerous. I'm beginning to think she likes when people are trying to kill her."

I knew he was teasing, so I just put my open hand over his face and slowly pushed him back to sit in his own seat.

"Only children try to come between the seats and bother the parents while they're talking," I said with a smile.

"Oh? You think you're one of the parents?" Cassius raised an eyebrow at me.

"I mean—"

"No, you are one of the children. The smaller but older sister who thinks she knows everything and constantly gets everyone else in trouble." I saw a twitch in Cassius' lip. "You lead him out there and unleash chaos on the world, which I need to clean up."

"It's not that bad," I retorted, looking away from him.

"Yes, it is. You still haven't told me how you ended up so close to home, yet still needed a ride."

"We followed Devika through the Market to Sri Lanka," I explained. "There were some politics, I'm sure you and I will have a lot of fun going over, but we can do it later. We got this neat little portal chalk to get home. I picked here because I didn't want to leave my address on a cabin door in the middle of Sri Lanka."

"Well then." Cassius sighed. "You have had an exciting day. Did you find the answers you wanted?"

I ran my fingers over the box in my hand.

No, there's still one more I need.

"Yeah. My mother named me after who I was in my past life. I now have all his memories and know what's going on with that. All I need now is a couple of days to process it, then I'll start writing it all down." I turned back to Raphael. "The cambions he knew, they had time to work out what they were and how certain things worked for them, like mating. I just need some time to go through all of it. There's so much, and I don't want to haphazardly tell people things until I know what's fact and what's not."

"We can wait," Raphael promised. "As far as I'm concerned, the cambions and I are in a good place. We still have questions about how we work, but that's nothing we can't keep figuring out on our own. Don't carry that burden on your shoulders."

I nodded.

"So….you are Kaliya, the serpent-demon," Cassius said softly. "You realize you would have gotten that nickname on your own with the way you've been going, don't you? Demonic magics now being something you can do…"

"Yeah," I whispered. "I think that was my mother's intention. She knew my memories were blocked, so she named me Kaliya. Big writing on the wall. I won't know until…" I ran a hand over the top of the box again. "I have all the answers I went looking for. This is just…closure, at this point."

"Well, it's not complete closure. We still need to figure out who was working with Mehar and Devika. Obviously, someone powerful is out there, and they want you dead, Kaliya, and not dead by their minions. They want to be the one who kills you."

"We'll find whoever it is. I'll need to talk to Adhar, but

I think we need to go to India and search through the old legends. There has to be an answer there somewhere."

"Then we'll go to India," Raphael promised.

"You will both go to India and leave Sorcha and me to babysit the even more unruly children. Wonderful." Cassius laughed as I reached out and swatted his arm. "We're happy to do it."

"We didn't even ask!"

"No, but you were going to."

Yes, I would have asked Cassius to keep an eye on everything while we were gone. There was no one else I trusted with it.

When he parked in front of my home, he left the car running. I didn't jump out, wondering what he wanted to say.

"You two should spend an evening winding down and figuring out what you want from here on. I'll stay the night with the cambions, Raphael. Sorcha is already back, so she's with them now."

"You're a good man, Cassius. Thanks for looking out for us." I reached out and gave him a one-armed hug he was nice enough to return instead of making me feel awkward.

"Yeah, thank you."

"I'll send Leith and Terry to get your car if you haven't lost the key."

I shuffled around in my pockets. I didn't keep big keychains, so my car key was snug in my front pocket and hadn't been lost in the adventures at the Market. I handed it to him, and he shooed me out of the car.

Raphael and I jumped out, and Cassius drove off.

Walking in, we dropped everything haphazardly. We were covered in dirt and blood. I chuckled as I thought about how Cassius had been unsurprised by that. He had just wondered how we ended up in the desert.

He knew us too well.

"Kaliya—"

"I'm going to shower, then call Adhar," I said, looking over the bed at Raphael. "Then I'm going to open this... gift my mother left me. We'll talk after. Is that okay?"

There was still so much to talk about. There were apologies neither of us had accepted yet. We had an eternity together, and we had started it off on the wrong foot. We needed to set it right.

"I'll be waiting," he said, nodding as he headed out of the room. He didn't seem upset I had put him last.

But I sure as hell felt guilty.

At least we were home to figure it out.

34

CHAPTER THIRTY-FOUR

"Kaliya, are you telling me Devika is dead?" Adhar asked, his arms crossed.

"Yeah. I wish I could say I killed her, but her apprentice got the final blow. Apparently, Devika was casting a death spell. Since the apprentice didn't know who Devika was targeting..." I shrugged. It wasn't the first time I had shrugged as I told him what happened during my endlessly long weekend. Friday, three days ago, when I left the cambions after training, I didn't have a mate, hadn't known what my future held or the secrets of my past. Now, it was Monday afternoon, and my entire life was different.

"It's for the best," he said softly, sitting down. Adhar had taken my call immediately. He'd known I was out and about and had been waiting to hear from me. "I was always wary of having outsiders as help. They could be bought or swayed."

"She wanted immortality, power, the normal stuff." It

was surprising from Devika at the moment of her betrayal, but in the grand scheme of things, there was a reason I didn't like most witches. They were the cause of so many problems. They wanted what everyone else had. They were intelligent problem-solvers, yet they were trapped in a human life span.

Devika wasn't the first witch who wanted immortality and was willing to kill for it. She won't be the last. Hopefully, she'll be the last one I have to deal with for a very long time.

"Yes. She had extended her life beyond what many humans could, but she couldn't unlock the secrets of the most powerful witches who lived for a thousand years or more. She would be greedy for that information."

"Taking on a young, pretty apprentice was her finally admitting she would never get the answer. Unless I mated." I tried my best to put it all in order, but coming out of my mouth, it sounded like a jumbled mess.

"You haven't told me if you found the secrets of your memories," Adhar pointed out. "With Devika dead, what do you plan to do now? I assume she didn't help you."

"Oh, she did," I replied casually. "She accidentally said some things that gave me the clues I needed to figure it out. This is where the story gets more complicated."

"I'm not sure I like the sound of that."

I couldn't resist laughing in dismay.

"Oh yeah. You shouldn't. Devika and my mother, they figured it out. When I was a baby, they tried to reveal who I had been in my past life. They succeeded but were left with a baby who had a...life. I was no longer a clean slate, as was promised to me on being reincarnated." I looked away from him, trying to imagine what was going through my mother's mind at that moment. There were still memories I couldn't find or get to. I had been too young to store them to be remembered later.

"Devika sealed my memories and added a twist, a simple mental manipulation. Denial. Whenever I brushed too close to the truth, I would be shoved away because I would refuse to believe it. I don't think my mother wanted that part of the spell to hide my memories from me."

"And..."

"With both of them dead, how they did it is lost," I said at his amazed and horrified expression. "And we will never try to recreate it."

"I agree," he said, nodding slowly as I watched him try to come to terms with what was done to me. "And... will you go to someone to remove the block?"

"I broke it on my own. I finally put the pieces of the puzzle together in a way that was undeniable. It couldn't be denied, so the spell was broken. Then I had to survive the rush of...an entire life pouring through my mind." I thought about what had changed since then.

Something was still a little different about me. I could feel it, deep inside, a shift in who I was. Merging two lives, it was a process. I wasn't fighting the feelings of the original Kaliya. He was no longer real, just a fragment of myself. He had brimming confidence and surety that matched my own. He had been powerful, graceful, and well respected. The differences in his personality and my own were actually very small. While people called me crazy and paranoid, people called him a mastermind, a genius. So, he didn't have the crippling self-confidence issues I had thought I had buried.

"Kaliya? You don't have to tell me, but I would like to know," Adhar said softly.

"My mother gave us the biggest hint," I said with a smirk. "It's really not all that complicated."

His eyes went wide.

"You are *Kaliya*."

"I am Kaliya. I have always been Kaliya. I'm still the Kaliya you know, yet I'm also the Kaliya from the legend. Yes. My mother kept it simple." I looked back at the box. "I think she had Devika write in a failsafe to the blocking spell—something that would unlock my memories. If she didn't, then mating was the trigger. My mating to a cambion was a reflection of the mating he...I...we'll go with *he,* had in the past. I don't love Rama. She was a wife from a different time. I have a new life."

"You must feel so strange, trying to reconcile two lives," he said, sympathy and empathy dripping from him. "I'm so sorry this has happened to you."

"I'm going to step up," I said softly. "I'm going to be a ruler you can be proud of. I'm too powerful to keep being the disaster I have been for a century, but things are going to change. We're not going to hold ceremonies where we figure out who is whose mate anymore. If we do, we're moving the age."

"What age would you like?"

"Twenty-five. They'll be adults, either immortal or on the verge of immortality. They'll have a better understanding of the concept and what they're looking for in a mate."

"Done, but if they meet their mate beforehand—"

It was a problem. There was a reason why the nagas of old had done immediate introductions as I had gone through to try to discover the mate young. Teenagers, which is what we all had been, were not good at control. They could rush into it without the guidance of parents to temper the heady emotional torment of knowing your soulmate was right there. Parents who could put up boundaries of respectability and protection between the couple, allowing them to get to know each other in a protected space. That way, accidents never happened.

Thanks to the memories of my past life, I had more understanding of the necessity. I didn't need to imagine what disaster led to the way nagas did things now. I could remember it. My past life heard the gossip of the situation and the new rules his brothers had placed for their children.

"Then the older of the two must talk to the parents. Arrangements will be made for them to safely get to know each other, just as we've always done when one or both parties is just too young for that commitment. We're not going to keep pressuring them. We need to change with the times. The hurt feelings of the males as they hope and pray a female naga will be their mate is hard on a woman, much less a teenage girl. We're no longer in the age where it's likely any nagas will mate together."

"Then we shall change," he agreed, looking away from me. "Your mother said similar, but I was too stubborn to listen. This was the way our people had worked for thousands of years. If you feel it would be better for little Roshni, then I believe you. You know more about growing up as a nagini than I ever will."

"You're only listening to me now because I'm the great Kaliya, serpent-demon and warrior, only felled by Krishna," I smirked. It was both a teasing jab and a real concern. I still wanted Adhar to look at me as *me*.

"No...I'm listening to you because you have finally grown wise enough to plead your case with understanding and without screaming at me like a teenage girl," he retorted with a small smile. "And because I have finally stepped back and seen all the ways I went wrong in our relationship."

"I went wrong, too," I reminded him.

"So, great Kaliya, serpent-demon and warrior of renown, what's next for you?"

I chuckled, unable to contain it.

"I was thinking Raphael and I might visit India. We're still hunting for who worked with Mehar and Devika and will have trouble with the rakshasas. Mehar was the king, and I killed off the rest of the royal family. I want to come to India to try to figure that out as well. We won't be moving there, but I think a visit is necessary. I know some fae who might make portals between here and there, but that's too much of a security risk. So, Raphael and I are just going to fly private."

"Let me know the dates, and we shall make an event out of it. There are naga here who haven't seen you since you were a child. I'm sure they would like to know their ruler who is out there fighting for them every single day. And her mate. I would like to meet him once again as well, talk to him finally."

"He's not ever going to follow your rules," I warned.

"I wouldn't ask it of him. He and I are equals, and you have educated him about the supernatural world. He is also not human. The human mates are very fragile."

"They are," I agreed. "I'll let you know what Raphael and I decide. It might be a few months. We have a lot we need to work out, but this is a top priority."

"Take your time."

We said quick goodbyes and hung up. I went out to the gym and found Raphael. He was weightlifting, sweat creating a sheen on his skin.

"I just got off the call with Adhar. I'm going to go see what's in this box, then we'll talk, okay?"

"I'll be waiting," he said, continuing with what he was doing, only throwing me a glance.

I sighed and left him there. Maybe he was upset I didn't put him first. Going back into my office, I sat down behind the desk, my eyes on the box in the center of it. The backdrop? The Board.

My entire life could be summed up in these two objects.

Obsessions and secrets.

I played with the little latch, then got the courage to open it. Inside, I found a small journal and opened it to see my mother's handwriting. It wasn't really addressed to me. The first page indicated it was the beginning of a pregnancy, and she was going to record her thoughts as she did every pregnancy, thoughts about and for her future child. In one line, she even said how she couldn't believe she was being blessed to get a third chance to do this.

That probably means she had these set aside for my brothers, too, for when they mated. I wonder what happened to them.

I found a handful of jewelry pieces carefully wrapped in silk and an ornate dagger, a beautiful gift parents often got their children when they mated. The symbology was simple. It was something to help defend the home.

At the bottom, I found a letter addressed to me. I picked it up and sighed. The paper was preserved well, but it was still aged. I used a small letter opener, so I didn't risk tearing the letter inside. It was a single piece of paper, not a very long letter.

But it was her last words to me.

Kaliya,

Congratulations on mating, my beautiful girl. If you have this letter, that means I didn't survive to give you this box. I would have removed it if I had the chance to give you these gifts in person.

Since I'm gone, you probably have so many questions and no one who can answer them. I'm not even sure I can answer them, and I'm the one who changed the course of your life in my own foolhardiness. I was arrogant and didn't understand how my deed would hurt my children. I do now. I hear our enemies scratching at the door, trying to find a weakness in our defenses. They grow bolder every day. Hence the reason for this.

Now, onto the things I should be telling you, things a mother should tell her daughter.

Your mate is the other half of your soul. In every life, your soul will have different needs and find someone who is perfect for it. Trust that. I had two options, but in the end, I knew there was only one answer, and that was your father. No matter what you do, trust in the bond you have with your mate. It will take you further than anything else in this world.

Knowing you, you'll probably fight it. You're too stubbornly independent, thinking you can run at the world full speed and defeat whatever evils come your way. Give your mate my condolences on getting such a hardheaded woman as his mate. I have a feeling that much has not changed since you were a child.

I LOVE YOU.

Savitri

I CRIED as the letter fell from my hands onto the table.

Raphael wrapped his arms around me. He must have come in, knowing I was going to talk to him soon.

"Did it help answer any of your questions?" he asked softly, holding my head to his chest.

"Only one," I admitted. "She loved me. She made mistakes, and she tried to fix them, but she never got the chance."

My mother hadn't explicitly said anything, but I could read between the lines and catch the meaning in her words she hadn't written.

"But she loved you," he whispered, kissing the top of my head.

"Yes," I said, taking a deep breath. "She did." I looked up at him. "I guess that's all that matters, isn't it?"

"Is it?" he asked.

"Yes. Just like the only thing that matters is that I love you," I said softly, reaching up to touch his cheek, forcing him to keep his eyes on me. "She wanted me to pass along her condolences to you for getting stuck with me."

We both laughed as he lifted me out of my chair, leaving behind the last piece of my mother sitting in the office.

"I don't need her pity," he said softly as he carried me to the living room. "Now, we need to talk. I've been thinking about what I was going to say since we walked through that door. We both hurt each other."

"We did," I agreed.

"Let's start over. A fresh slate, as you will. Our entire relationship has been built on secrets and dismissals of each other's needs."

"A fresh slate sounds good." If there was anyone who understood how important that was, it was certainly me, with my past life bouncing around my head. "We're going to let go of the past and look to the future. The two of us."

"I would like to," he said softly. "It's what I think we both deserve."

"I would, too." Grabbing his shirt, I pulled him in for a kiss. When it was over, I leaned back. "We need to make plans to go to India. I told Adhar—"

"Tomorrow," he growled, leaning in and taking over, his kiss holding a lot more passion than mine had. I fell back and let him crawl over me. "Tomorrow, we'll start hunting legends," he said again.

I could do it tomorrow.

Tomorrow sounded nice.

Keep reading for more information about the next release, special news, and more.

DEAR READER,

Thank you for reading!

Raphael was never going to convince Kaliya to give up her convictions (and look at that, she was right!), and Kaliya was never going to see the light at the end of the tunnel.

Thank goodness there was a bad guy that needed to prove there were mates. Just imagine me giving you a very evil smile right now because this has been all apart of my master plan.

Well, if it's not totally apparent Kaliya and Raphael are now fully mated, with some quirks they need to deal with thanks to the clash of their two species. Kaliya must also continue to deal with the memories of a past life.

And oh, yeah... they're going to India. Kaliya hasn't been there for a hundred years, when she ran away as a teenager. I wonder what they're going to find....

LEGENDS

KALIYA SAHNI BOOK FIVE

Dear Reader,

NOVEMBER 16, 2021

If I still have you, head over to my website to get the latest updates on the next book in the series. Head over to my website and sign up for my mailing list! There are exclusive teasers for those who are signed up: Knbanet.com/newsletter

Also, I have a Patreon, where I write a monthly short story or novella. You can check that out here: Patreon.com/knbanet

And remember,

Reviews are always welcome, whether you loved or hated the book. Please consider taking a few moments to leave one and know I appreciate every second of your time and I'm thankful.

THE TRIBUNAL ARCHIVES

The Kaliya Sahni series is set in the world of The Tribunal. Every series and standalone novel is written so it can be read alone.

For more information about The Tribunal Archives and the different series in it, you can go here:

tribunalarchives.com

ACKNOWLEDGMENTS

I'm very bad at giving really public praise. I shower people in praise in private. But that's not everyone's love language and that's okay.

So this little page shall now be dedicated to everyone who helps me get these books from the concept to the release and beyond. From my PA, to my editor and my proofreader, to my wonderful friends helping me through the hardest moments. To my husband, who doesn't read my books, but loves that I write them and is willing to listen to me talk about them for hours.

And to you, the reader, for without you, I wouldn't have anyone to share these stories with. I'm a storyteller at heart and you have given me the greatest gift of listening.

I love all of you. Thank you for continuing to go on this journey with me.

ABOUT THE AUTHOR

KNBanet.com

Living in Arizona with her husband and 5 pets (2 dogs and 3 cats), K.N. Banet is a voracious... video game player. Actually, she spends most of her time writing, and when she's not writing she's either gaming or reading.

She enjoys writing about the complexities of relationships, no matter the type. Familial, romantic, or even political. The connections between characters is what draws her into writing all of her work. The ideas of responsibility, passion, and forging one's own path all make appearances.

facebook.com/KNBanet
instagram.com/Knbanetauthor
bookbub.com/authors/k-n-banet
amazon.com/K.N.-Banet/e/B08412L9VV
patreon.com/knbanet

ALSO BY K.N. BANET

The Jacky Leon Series

Oath Sworn

Family and Honor

Broken Loyalty

Echoed Defiance

Shades of Hate

Royal Pawn

Rogue Alpha

Bitter Discord

Volume One: Books 1-3

The Kaliya Sahni Series

Bounty

Snared

Monsters

Reborn

Legends

Destiny

Volume One: Books 1-3

The Everly Abbott Series

Servant of the Blood

Blood of the Wicked

Tribunal Archives Stories

Ancient and Immortal (Call of Magic Anthology)

Hearts at War

Full Moon Magic (Rituals and Runes Anthology)

Made in the USA
Columbia, SC
21 April 2025

56898877R00224